The Case of the

Three Dead Horses

Bedside Books
An imprint of American Book Publishing
American Book Publishing
P.O. Box 65624
Salt Lake City, UT 84165
www.american-book.com
Printed in the United States of America on acid-free paper.

The Case of the Three Dead Horses

Designed by Chris Krupinski, design@american-book.com

Publisher's Note: *This is a work of fiction. Names, characters, places, and incidents either are the product of the author's imagination, or are used fictitiously, and any resemblance to actual persons, living or dead, events, or locales is entirely coincidental.*

ISBN 1-58982-221-8

Fisher, Marilyn M., The Case of the Three Dead Horses

Special Sales

These books are available at special discounts for bulk purchases. Special editions, including personalized covers, excerpts of existing books, and corporate imprints, can be created in large quantities for special needs. For more information e-mail orders@american-book.com, 801-486-8639.

The Case of the

Three Dead Horses

by

Marilyn M. Fisher

This book is dedicated to Sally Roseveare and Jan Shaffer, for their steadfast support.

"Think when we talk of horses that you see them
Printing their proud hoofs i' the receiving earth."

Henry V
—William Shakespeare

Prologue

The drive tonight had been difficult in more ways than one. Cursing nervously, the intruder continued to maneuver the car over the steep, twisting, frozen roads that led ever closer to Rod Payson's breeding farm, where Woolwine, soon to be dead, probably stood drowsing in his stall.

I have to do it. The thought echoed, as though trying to push out the doubts. *I have to do it.*

Black clothing, drenched with sweat, chafed a tired and tense body. The dangerous trip had taken its toll. An ice storm had hit Central Virginia with such force that by midnight, when the desperate decision to get it over with had been made, trees had toppled onto power lines, plunging the region into darkness and cold. *Why tonight, why did I have to pick tonight?* Carefully inching the creeping car up US 29 toward Amherst County had been frustrating. Half a dozen wrecks, surrounded by troopers' cruisers and tow trucks made progress infuriatingly slow. It was 1:30 AM when the car finally entered Payson's road and started the ascent.

Approaching the large open space between the house on the left and the show barn on the right, the intruder turned off the lights, parked the car facing down the hill, and walked quietly to the barn.

It was not a surprise to find the doors unlocked. It was a known fact that Rod was not paying proper attention to his horses. Easing the big doors open, starting down the center aisle, and pointing a flashlight at the floor to guide the way, the intruder spoke calmly to the horses that began to stir at the interruption of their routine.

"Hey there, please don't spook on me. Don't make it any harder."

The words were not important, only the soft, calm voice. The horses remained quiet.

The intruder paused before Woolwine's stall, fumbled with the instrument of death, and then opened the door carefully, aiming the flashlight at the horse. The powerful beam shifted to the horse's eyes, making him blind and confused. After waiting a few moments to make sure the horse would remain still, and then whispering "Good boy, good boy," the intruder moved in and put an end to the great stallion's life.

Immediately after the fatal act, Woolwine panicked. He reared and plunged, reared and plunged, screaming with fright.

Barely escaping the flailing hooves, the intruder stumbled down the aisle, ran to the car, jerked the door open, turned the key in the ignition, heard the engine come to life, and started the perilous descent to the main road, all the while straining to breathe normally to ease the heart's frenzied pumping.

The first one down. Maybe next time it'll be easier.

Chapter One

The champion quarter horse lay on his side with staring and sightless eyes. His bay coat shone. It looked as if, in the last throes, he'd rammed into a side wall of his stall, slid down it, and died.

His head was tilted up at an odd angle.

For a moment, Connie Holt contemplated the still body. She remembered the last time she'd seen Woolwine. He was running joyously in the summer pasture, first in one direction, and then veering off to run even faster in the opposite direction, his black tail streaming behind him. This loss of freedom, innocence and beauty caused her throat to throb— the prelude to tears. Connie had seen many dead horses in her work and always had this reaction. She'd learned to swallow hard and get on with the job at hand. But this death was especially poignant, for it was clear that Woolwine had been terrified by what was happening to him.

In the midst of his panic, he'd kicked a hole in the back wall.

When the phone on her bedside table rang, waking her out of a deep, dreamless sleep, insurance agent Connie Holt groaned. She'd spent the day visiting three farms to discuss complicated insurance claims the owners had submitted to the McCutcheon Equine Insurance Agency. Since the farms were widely separated from each other in Bedford, Amherst and Nelson counties, she'd been in her truck too many hours. She'd gone to bed around eight o'clock that night, her back and head aching. Now she remembered that it was her turn to be on night duty. The caller was probably her boss, Cary McCutcheon. A horse must be injured, sick or dead somewhere. It would be her job to examine the horse at the site and write a detailed report. Sighing, she put on her glasses and pressed "Talk."

"That you, Cary?"

"Sorry, Connie."

She mouthed a silent "Hell!" into the darkness of her warm, cozy bedroom.

"It's Rod Payson's horse Woolwine," Cary continued. Dead."

"That marvelous stallion? Poor Rod. First Donna's death and now this."

"And to make it worse," said Cary, "there's a dead man in the stall. Rod said he knew him. Police are on their way. Rod called them first, then his veterinarian, Jase Tyree, then us. Be careful driving up there, the roads are terrible. Ice storm. "

Both of them knew it would be a hard trip to Payson's isolated horse farm in Amherst County. The hilly roads would be slippery and treacherous.

"See you later."

Connie dressed quickly in her working gear. First, she put on warm thermal underwear, and then an oversize dark blue turtleneck, followed by a baggy wool sweater. She pulled jeans over her long legs. Next came comfortable boots permanently stained with stable muck. When she took a perfunctory glance in the mirror, she saw that her thick red hair had mutinied again. Marge at the Clip n' Curl knew just what to do with it, but Connie hated the bother of getting her hair cut. No time to brush the snarls out tonight. Her favorite working hat would take care of the problem. She jammed on the old Stetson she'd picked up in Dallas visiting her son, then grabbed her fleece-lined coat, which had seldom failed to keep her warm in many a dank stall. The wind stung her face as she opened the door of her truck.

The weather was unseasonably cold for November in Central Virginia. People who lived in the James River valley were usually protected from rugged weather by the bulwark of the Blue Ridge Mountains. If a little snow fell, it generally melted on contact. The biggest danger was an ice storm and the inevitable slick roads.

It took a long time to get to Rod's farm. She drove warily up US 29, passing wrecks of cars and trucks and frantic people trying to clear the road and get the injured to the hospital. Connie remembered it was the day after Thanksgiving. *It's time to mail the Christmas presents to the kids,* she thought. Danny lived in Texas, Ellen in New Hampshire.

Her thoughts turned to Rod Payson and his problems. At one time, Payson had as many as ten stallions for breeding purposes. He trained and boarded as well, so his operation at Payson Stud was extensive: indoor and outdoor rings, two hundred acres of hilly pasturage.

Since Donna's death, Connie had been told, Rod had downsized his operation. But he had hung on to Woolwine, his most valuable horse. Everyone knew about Rod's prize stallion and how much he was worth. Jase Tyree had documented the horse's superb condition. Cary had approved coverage for a quarter of a million, based on Woolwine's show record as a three-time prize winner of the Grand National Quarter Horse Competition, and his projected stud honors. Connie's mind was full of questions. *How could such a healthy horse die? Who is the dead man? How does he fit in?*

Connie turned onto the series of steep and winding roads that led toward the mountains and Rod's farm. In summer, the mountain ridges were covered with lush, blue-green vegetation. Driving within their confines made her feel serene and protected. But she didn't like the blue mountains in November. In winter's icy sterility, they inspired only melancholy.

A police car with flashing lights and idling motor was parked in front of the show barn where Rod kept Woolwine. Someone had turned on all the lights in the barn, and the unaccustomed blaze of light when it should have been quiet and dark was confusing the animals. They moved restlessly and poked wondering heads over the half doors of their stalls.

Connie walked down the central aisle to Woolwine's large stall. Two policemen were whispering to one another over the body of a dead man huddled in one corner. Rod was kneeling beside Woolwine, his hand still caressing the animal's soft coat.

"Excuse me," she said to the policemen from the door of the stall, "I'm Connie Holt from McCutcheon Equine Insurance. I've come to look at Woolwine." One of the men waved her in.

She caught a glimpse of the dead man's shattered head, red and pulpy, before she knelt beside Rod. The familiar odor of hay, manure, and horseflesh hung over the stall, but to it had been added the smell of blood from the man's body and the cigarette-permeated coats of the police. *Must be about forty degrees in here,* Connie thought.

She glanced at the side of Rod's face. The twisting scars with hypertrophic tissue were plainly visible. He'd taken a terrible pounding from a stallion a few years earlier. Surgeons at the University of Virginia Health Sciences Center had managed to put that side of his face back together again, but hadn't predicted Rod's tendency to scar badly. With Donna's care, he'd endured the surgery, the pain, and even the mirror's reflection. In lucid moments away from the Demerol, he'd told Donna how to keep their business together. When he was finally able to give up the painkiller, he went right back to his office and the stables.

Last spring, Donna had died from a quick-growing cancer. Rod still couldn't adjust to her absence. At the McCutcheon office, people heard he'd become silent, apathetic, and easily distracted.

Before Donna's death, Rod looked after every detail of his successful breeding farm. Tall and powerfully muscled, he often delighted in breaking his colts himself. He'd loved Donna without reservation. His pride in his wife and in his farm extended to his cultural heritage. He was descended from the Monacans, the first people in Albemarle and Amherst counties. The ancient Monacans had hunted, fished, and mined copper. Modern-day Monacans still lived close to the sacred Bear Mountain near the town of Amherst.

Rod straightened and moved away. His shoulders drooped with the terrible weariness of depression.

"Go ahead, Connie," he said.

After a moment's contemplation of the body, she swallowed hard and began the careful visual scan that always started her investigation. She wanted to examine the horse and his stall as thoroughly as possible before Jase Tyree came.

The policemen finished their discussion, and waited for her to tell them what she found.

"His femur appears to be broken," she said. Rod nodded. "Looks like something happened to him and he panicked. He kicked that hole in the wall, breaking his femur, and then slid down into the straw. The postmortem might show more."

"I did rounds at seven last night," Rod said. "He was fine then. I walked through the stables again around two thirty."

"Why did you make another inspection?" asked the older policeman. "Did you expect any trouble? Have you had a problem with intruders?"

"I haven't been sleeping well so I often get up and walk through the barns. There haven't been any prowlers, no, nothing like that.

"I found Woolwine and Job, there." He nodded toward the man's body. "Called the police, my insurance company, and Jase Tyree, my vet."

The younger policeman now asked, "So you know who the dead man is, Mr. Payson?"

"Yes. It's Job. Job Hoskins."

"How do you know? His face is pretty bad."

"By his size, that old barn coat he always wore, and oh yes, that earring," said Rod. His face was sad. "I always meant to ask him where he got that earring."

"What would he be doing in the stall? Does he work here?"

"Yes, but he's only temporary. He's a," Rod paused, swallowed and said, "*was* a wanderer. Came through here every winter, must be ten or eleven years now. I gave him odd jobs; come spring, he moved on. He told me once he had no kin. Never left an address or telephone number, so I couldn't contact him."

"Where was he sleeping?"

"In the bunkhouse. My hands only come during the day, so he had it all to himself."

"Mr. Payson, could this man have tried to hurt the horse?"

"Oh no, he loved horses. My guess is he heard Wooley in trouble, went in to calm him down, and was killed. Poor old man."

The officer nodded. "Without anyone to claim him, he'll have to go to potter's field in Lynchburg."

"I'll see to it he's taken care of, funeral and burial," said Rod. "After all, he worked for me a long time. I'll sign any papers you need."

"All right. An investigator and medical examiner are on the way, but it seems pretty clear what happened to Mr. Hoskins."

"If the medical examiner and everyone else agree, I'll call a funeral home in Amherst to come and get Job."

"The horse is another matter. We'll wait around for Dr. Tyree to tell us what he finds out."

Connie heard Jase's lumbering old pickup in the drive and straightened her aching back. She had withdrawn to an empty corner by the time Jase entered the stall and, after a startled look at the man's body, knelt by Woolwine.

Throwing back the hood of his down jacket, he brushed the hair from his forehead. He looked briefly at the horse, betraying no emotion at the trauma of the horse's final moments. Rod, Connie, and the two cops stood awkwardly, watching Jase's thin-fingered clever hands move slowly over the animal's body.

The hopelessness of her love for Jase washed over her, and she thought again, as she had many times in his presence, *Why can't I just stop loving him?*

Over six feet tall and rail-thin, the vet worked too many hours a day, wrestling with obstinate horses all over Central Virginia and operating his clinic in Monroe, an unincorporated area between the City of Lynchburg and the Town of Amherst. With broad shoulders, small waist, and long legs, a high energy level, and irreverent sense of humor, he had retained everything attractive about young men, even though he was almost forty-five. Now, watching him work, she noticed his taut facial muscles, compressed lips, strained face. His hands had a slight tremor.

It must be Les, she thought.

Jase had married Leslie Scott Wingfield two years ago after a courtship of six months. Before he'd become infatuated with Les, Connie had met him many times in her work. They had even dated for a while.

His energy always seemed inexhaustible. While he had always expressed his sadness over an animal's problem in private, he was highly professional at the scene, staying in an uncomfortable stall as long as it took to form a working hypothesis.

She wanted to take him back to her house and hold him in her arms until he slept away whatever it was transforming him into the tight-lipped, strung-out man she saw.

After a few minutes, Rod admitted to the police, "I'm wiped out. All right if I go back to the house?"

They nodded.

"You know where I'll be if you need me again," said Rod. "Jase, come up to the house when you're done." Jase, examining Woolwine's neck, nodded. "Let's get some coffee, Connie."

"Glad to," she said. She was tired of her love for Jase.

With careful steps, they walked up the icy brick path to the long, low fieldstone and timber house. The Payson Labs came running, barking with excited yelps over the unaccustomed activity.

"Quiet, boys," Rod said.

In his office, Rod excused himself to get the coffee. The dogs threw themselves down. Connie found a leather wing chair. She noticed that the stained Oriental rug was dusty, as were the shelves on either side of the stone fireplace and the trophies that graced them.

Rod returned with steaming mugs on an antique black metal toleware tray. His large hands almost obscured the painted pattern of purple violets and pink ribbons.

It was clear he didn't want to talk. The two sat quietly, sipping coffee, until they heard the front door slam.

Jase came in, white with fatigue, and without sitting down, said abruptly, "I don't know what to tell you. Wooley was obviously frightened by something and panicked. I wonder what could have scared him. You know, Rod, Wooley was sometimes spooked by small animals. I remember a couple of times when a feral cat got into his stall. Could you have left the doors to the barn open so something could get in?"

Rod looked uncertain, ran a hand over his stubbled chin. "I can't remember whether they were open or not. Ever since Donna…oh, God, I just can't remember. Hard to believe an outside animal could cause him to do that much damage to himself, Jase, even though he was pretty high-strung."

"I'll do the post later today. But I don't think it will show anything wrong with the way he died."

"I hope you're right about that. If not, I'm in for a hell of a time. Wooley was insured for a lot of money. I don't know what I'll do if Cary doesn't pay."

"By the way, the medical examiner and detective showed up. I told them the same thing I told you about Wooley."

"Are they still out there?"

"Yes," said Jase.

"I'll just sit here and wait for them to ring the bell," said Rod. "Thanks for coming, Connie, Jase."

"Try and get some sleep, Rod," said Connie. "I'll talk to Cary later today."

"I'm so sorry, Rod," said Jase.

Jase and Connie walked to their trucks.

"Hell of a thing," said Jase.

"Yes. See you, Jase."

"You bet, Con."

They maneuvered their trucks slowly down the long, icy drive to US 29 and drove home, Jase to Monroe, Connie to Bedford County.

Neither man had asked Connie what she thought about the cause of Woolwine's death. Usually she was angry if people in a case she was investigating gave no credence to her informed opinion, and she made sure they listened to her before she left the scene.

This time, she was glad no one had asked.

Chapter Two

As she drove south toward Bedford County and home, Connie couldn't forget the death scene. What would she say when she wrote her loss report? And what would Jase find as the cause of death in his necropsy? Her usual anticipation of a whiskey, hot bath and warm bed was blunted by a bad feeling. There was something wrong with Woolwine's death.

She was so busy thinking about what could have possibly killed the horse that she completely missed Jack Wampler's police cruiser parked in a service area with its lights off.

He pulled out smoothly and came up behind her, shining his high beams into the back of her truck.

There he is, there's Wampler, she thought. She felt her heart start to pound, and tried to think calmly.

She decided to brazen it out. It was only a few miles before the cut-off that led to her home. Maybe he'd get sick of the game he played every time he saw her truck alone on the road in the early hours. She'd just keep driving.

She'd tried that ploy once before and he'd given up. Maybe it would work again. No good. Jack's cruiser had tailgated her for only a couple of miles, the bright headlights making it hard for her to see the road ahead clearly, when he suddenly twisted the wheel to the left and accelerated sharply into the oncoming lane. The cruiser was now next to her truck, keeping pace with her careful speed. She tried as hard as she could to control the truck on the slippery road, and was finally forced to stop.

To Connie's annoyance, her hands on the wheel were shaking. A finger of cold perspiration moved slowly down her back.

Wampler swaggered over to the driver's side window, which she barely rolled down.

Jack Wampler had been pursuing Connie for three months. He'd first stopped her to issue a citation for speeding, saying that since it had rained earlier, her truck was in danger of hydroplaning. She wasn't speeding and the road was dry. The burly trooper had hinted he would tear up the citation if she would meet him on his next night off at Bullocks, the favored night spot of the local good old boys.

Connie's smile had been pleasant, as she said, "Sorry, I have to work."

He said nothing as he scribbled the summons, but his face was red with rage. He gave her the information about her court appearance, turned on his heel, and walked back to his cruiser. In court, the judge admonished her and she had to pay a very large fine. She'd thought it wise to swallow her first impulse to argue her case, avoiding any trouble for herself and the Agency.

She'd decided the incident was ugly but isolated, and turned her mind to other things.

But since then, he'd stopped her on two more occasions, each time reminding her with a sneer that, "You won't be able to work, baby, if you don't have a license."

Connie had to admit to herself that he frightened her. The Commonwealth motor vehicle laws were tough. There was a good chance she would lose her license if he wrote another summons.

But there was more to worry about.

She was five feet, ten inches. She'd taken self-defense lessons, carried Mace, and planned what she would do if ever threatened with rape. But she knew she was no match for Wampler.

He stood about six feet, four inches, and had to be at least 250 pounds of muscle and blubber. Given the way he'd been stalking her, she had an even more serious problem than losing her job.

Now she looked through the window and noticed again that Wampler's oversize head was the shape of a bullet. His piggy eyes were vaguely gray. His nose was long and mottled with tiny veins, and his lips were so thin they looked like slashes in the pasty, stubbled skin.

He grinned, revealing small discolored teeth.

"What're you doin' out so late, honey? Got another sick horse?" After the first time he'd stopped her, he'd made it a point to find out what she did for a living.

She responded as good-naturedly as she could, hoping this would be a night when he'd let her go right away.

"How's business, Jack? Any speeders this morning?"

"Nah. Pretty soon my shift is over, and I can get me some breakfast at Ma Rooney's. Sausage biscuits, red-eye gravy, grits, lots o' coffee. Another half hour and I'm off. How about it, Red? Want to join me? I'll even buy."

His voice was high-pitched for such a big man. *Creepy*, she thought.

She forced herself to smile. "No thanks, I've got a meeting in a couple of hours. Have to get some sleep."

Now she'd done it. She'd said "sleep." That would trigger "bed" in his one-track mind.

Sure enough, he said, "What kind o' bed you got, baby? Why don't you tell me all about it so I can think o' you in it? Wear anything in bed, honey?"

"Now come on, Jack," she said. "Give me a break. I've got to get going."

Before he could reply, she hastily rolled up the window, gave him a cheery smile, and took off. To her great relief, he just stood there, staring at her departing truck.

As soon as she reached home, she made sure the deadbolts were fastened on both the back and front doors, and for good measure, propped chairs under the doorknobs of both.

Chapter Three

At eight o'clock, the radio woke Connie with the sound of singer and pianist Diana Krall, wowing a Paris audience with her up-tempo jazz treatment of an old classic. Connie laughed with delight, and lay in the warm bed, swinging with the music, completely absorbed and happy. But the mood only lasted until the radio went off. Then she remembered the dark problems of Woolwine's death and Jake Wampler.

When she opened the blinds, she saw feathery snow falling onto the frozen ground. As always, she looked at the oval garden she'd put in last summer, now a desolate patch of dirt and decayed leaves. *I'll be glad when it gets warm so I can plant again,* she thought, remembering especially the brilliant yellows and golds of the old-fashioned zinnias she liked so much. She looked forward to working in the garden, even though it meant always putting on sun block and her straw hat, and slathering herself with insect repellent to fend off the gnats. And although it wasn't possible to work long when the temperature reached 95 degrees or higher in the hot, humid Central Virginia summer, she still looked forward to making things grow in the red soil.

Yawning, she microwaved a bowl of instant oatmeal, sliced a banana, and ate standing at the kitchen counter. Usually she liked to scan *The News & Advance*, but she couldn't concentrate this morning. The strange death of Woolwine coupled with yet another encounter with Wampler made her uneasy and fearful.

She decided to wear the comfortable midnight blue wool jacket and pants she'd recently bought in Charlottesville. Unlike many women with dark red hair, she wore only a small number of colors that complemented her hair. No oranges for her. *The alterations lady in Lynchburg did a good job,* she thought. *I wish I could just put something on from the rack. If I weren't so tall and thin...* As she fastened a pair of heavy gold earrings, she scrutinized her face in the mirror.

More lines, she thought. Shrugging, she finished her makeup, inserted her contact lenses, and moussed her unruly hair. As she waited for the truck to defrost, she went over the events at Payson Stud for her presentation at the Agency's weekly meeting.

Connie turned off US 221 and drove down the long entrance road that wound lazily through thick woods, passing the 1840 brick mansion on the left with its imposing portico and gracious front door, already adorned with a scarlet-ribboned spray of green branches for the holidays. Cary's wife, Pam, loved Christmas, and liked to start decorating early.

At one time Cary had rented office space in the city of Bedford, but his business prospered, and he built an addition to his home, Otter Hill. The office in the back was a brick and frame addition, harmonizing nicely with the stately old home.

She went through the heavy glass doors and smiled at the receptionist, Lonnie Flemmings, who was explaining some forms to a client. There were six private offices for agents, three on each side of a central space occupied by secretaries with their computers, green plants and colorful coffee mugs.

Bypassing her office, Connie went through a door in the back that accessed Cary's suite.

In the first office on the left, she saw Gypsy Black, Cary's private secretary, fingering her keyboard at a dizzying speed. "Hi, Gyp," she called and waved. She walked through the door directly opposite Gyp's office and took one of the chairs at the round cherrywood table where staff meetings were held.

If she had continued to the end of the hall, she would have entered Cary's large office, which he accessed from the house via the kitchen. Both Gyp's office and the conference room opened into Cary's office.

Almost everyone was there. Only Mac McDougal and Bob King were missing.

Cary started the meeting by saying that Mac was in Staunton with an injured runaway horse case, while Bob was conferring with an owner whose horse had died in the night. Looked like a routine death. He then gave a general rundown of the company's activities and settlements.

Connie's report was last. She told her story evenly and waited for reaction from the others. In the silence that followed, Cary finally said, "Are you satisfied with the intruding animal theory, Connie?"

She knew, as did everybody else at the table, that most horses are easily frightened. She had been in a group of trail riders once when she saw a peacefully grazing stallion suddenly spook over a plastic bag that had blown onto a fence post. The wind rattling it caused the Arabian to panic, rear, and then break into an all-out run. Leaping his owner's fence, he continued his breakneck flight through the neighbor's pasture, where he finally caught his hoof in a hole and broke his leg. He had to be put down.

She answered carefully, unsure of how Cary wanted this matter handled. Sometimes he preferred to discuss suspicious circumstances with only the agent involved.

"Right now, I can't prove it wasn't some kind of animal that caused him to panic," she said. "Rod has always been careful with his horses. I used to ride up there before his wife died. Everything was well run then, with good, tight stable security. But the doors might have been open, he says, when he found Woolwine. And Wooley was very high-strung. Remember, he was a "running" quarter horse. They tend to be more skittish than most. And he didn't like other animals in his stall, as Jase pointed out."

During the pause that followed, Connie glanced at the others. She noticed that several people were frowning, while others were shaking their heads. They were skeptical. *And so am I,* she thought.

"Are you sure you didn't see anything? Evidence of any kind of tampering?" asked Joe Mattox.

"No. Jase's report should turn up a needle mark or something else."

Cary nodded with finality and smiled.

"Thanks, everybody. I guess that's all. Randy, don't forget to give the voucher for your trip to Roanoke last week to Gyp. And you're all welcome here on Sunday afternoon. Pam and I are having an open house to show off our new colt, coming in from Kentucky on Saturday. You're welcome to come any time between two and five." Joe looked at Connie and grinned in anticipation of the delicious food Cary always provided at his parties.

As everyone left, Cary said, "Step into my office, Connie. Make yourself comfortable. I've got to see Gyp a minute."

Connie seated herself in front of Cary's antique mahogany desk. In the wall behind it, French doors were flanked by floor-to-ceiling windows. Built-in mahogany bookshelves on the side walls held business-related reference books and some of Cary's private collection on the American and British navies of the nineteenth century. His computer was humming, his desktop crowded with applications, contracts, printouts.

Connie looked out the windows and smiled broadly. Gazing back at her was a seventeen-hand brown Thoroughbred with a star on his forehead. Beyond him was pasture land and in the far distance, mountains. The three Peaks of Otter—Flat Top, Harkening Hill, and Sharp Top—were clearly defined against the bluish-gray sky. Three years ago, Connie remembered, she and Jase had hiked to the summit of Sharp Top. Once there, they had sat quietly, companionably, absorbing the panorama of the Blue Ridge Mountains. Later they had eaten dinner at the Peaks of Otter Lodge. She had looked around at the other dining couples, envying them for their obvious love. Many would stay overnight in the pleasant rooms. By ten o'clock she was back home, and Jase on his way to Monroe.

She pulled herself back to the present.

She knew why Old Sam, the horse, was hanging around. When Cary could spare the time from business, he liked to slip out and give his horses an apple or carrot, much to the disgust of his stable manager, who thought horses should have a rigorous, scientifically planned diet.

Sam was part of Cary's other business, training Thoroughbreds as jumpers. Cary had told her that his wife

Pam and he dreamed of seeing one of their horses win an international steeplechase event one day, maybe in the Pan American or Olympic games. Their biggest thrill had been several years ago when a horse of theirs had been entered in the International Gold Cup. Cary had invited Connie and several other guests to attend the event, always held at the height of fall foliage in Fauquier County.

The traditional tailgate party had featured a wide selection of foods, from caviar to black beans to smoked turkey. Then they had all watched the seven exciting steeplechase events, breathing in as the horses approached the jumps, breathing out with relief when they landed safely on the other side, glad that nothing had happened to the horses or their brightly dressed jockeys. Entered in the third event, the McCutcheon horse had come in last. Cary and Pam took it in stride, and didn't let it spoil their dream. The excitement and color of the steeplechase had remained with Connie all the way home.

Although Sam didn't look anything like the beautiful steeplechase horse he'd been long ago, he still played a part in the training at Otter Hill. Pam, whose ribbons and trophies for excellence in jumping, were displayed in their library, specialized in training jumpers and also taught young people how to jump horses. Sam was just right for training the youngest of her students.

Cary came in, sat down behind his desk.

"About the Payson case, Connie." The smile was gone, replaced by a guarded expression.

He suspects something, she thought. Outwardly, she only raised her eyebrows.

"All right, I'm skeptical about the intruding animal theory. And I have heard things about Rod and the financial condition of his farm. But until we establish there's some foundation for the rumors, I'd rather not repeat them. I want you to go back up there now. You know what to do.

"Rake the stall, examine every inch of it. If Rod wonders, tell him your further investigation is standard procedure when a horse dies mysteriously. And Connie, I know you won't like what I'm going to ask you to do, but I have my reasons. If you can manage it, take a look around the place, the barns, everything. See if there's anything there that looks unusual. You used to go up there when Donna was alive, so you're in a position to know if anything is different. I dislike stuff like this, you know that. But he's a client as well as a friend, and we're insuring other horses at Payson Stud. Handle it as tactfully as you can.

"By the way, Jase called during the meeting. He had another emergency this morning. Horse sick in Rustburg. He's trying to save the horse, he'll have to stay there indefinitely. So his post on Woolwine will be delayed. That's a break for us."

Connie nodded, and hesitated for a moment before she left, wondering if she should talk to him about the Wampler mess.

People who didn't know Cary well saw a genial Virginia gentleman who at almost seventy could still charm every horsewoman he met into insuring her horses with him. He was known throughout the Commonwealth for his loyalty to friends and his never-failing hospitality.

But the man behind the genial façade was complicated. Stubborn, sometimes unfathomable, tough, loving, smart, and occasionally too hot-tempered for his own good. When he witnessed cruelty to another person or an animal, he sometimes exploded. Connie could never forget an incident she had seen. Cary knocked a man unconscious who had broken a golden palomino's leg with a two-by-four.

Afterwards, he said the satisfaction was well worth the hefty fine and the broken hand, which had caused him months of pain and impairment.

Cary might barge into State Police headquarters and demand Wampler be brought up on charges. She wasn't sure that Wampler would be punished. She had learned through discreet inquiries that his record was unspotted, even exemplary. There would be only her testimony that he'd stalked her. The trooper always harassed her in the early morning hours when she was driving alone. With no witnesses, he could claim that Connie was just a disgruntled, habitual speeder. Better avoid bad publicity for Cary and the company at all costs.

"Something else, Connie?"

"No. See you later."

On her way down the hall, she looked in on her friend, Gypsy Black.

"Hey, kiddo," she said. "Can you have dinner with me after work? I want to talk to you about something."

Gyp paused. "Sure. Where do you want to go?"

"How about The Gardens at seven? I feel like eating something besides canned corned beef hash for once."

Gyp smiled and signaled "thumbs up."

Connie left the office and drove home, feeling bad about her role as a spy. It wasn't as if she hadn't been asked to be sharply observant of a client's place before. But this was different. Rod and Donna had been friends.

At home once more, she donned clean old clothes, her boots, and a warm coat, and retrieved the Stetson from the newel post where she'd hastily hung it in the dark hours of the morning.

Chapter Three

In the truck, she slid in a Getz and Gilberto CD. Their classic collaboration on the languorous and melodic bossa nova always cheered her up.

At Payson Stud, she found Rod looking at a mare that had cut herself on a barbed wire fence. After he "threw" antiseptic powder in the wide gash on her chest and had asked Beau Taylor, one of the hands, to be on the watch for infection, he turned to Connie.

"I hope you're bringing me good news. Did the report come in? Did Cary decide to pay?" Under the scars, his dark skin had a gray cast.

"Jase is with a very sick horse right now, and between that and his clinic, he won't be able to write the report for a couple of days. I'm here to do a little more investigation, standard procedure when a horse dies without apparent cause."

"Sure," he said, his face a mask. He left for the house. From the barn doors, Connie watched him walk slowly away, the powerful body stooped, his vital energy gone. She reflected for a moment on what he had lost with Donna's death and then turned back into the barn to start her job.

Two hours later, she was finished. Despite her thorough examination of Woolwine's stall, she found nothing suspicious. She walked slowly down the length of the show barn, and then into the other barns, peering into the stalls and noting the condition of each horse and its little universe of barred window, straw bedding, food, and water. Before Donna's death, Rod had made sure that each stall was as pristine as possible with a 1200 pound animal in it, but today, at two o'clock in the afternoon, the stalls had not been cleaned. And the animals needed grooming. *He's cut his staff so much that he can't get the work done,* she thought.

When she saw Beau mending a paddock rail, she walked over to ask a few careful questions. He gave her a shy smile, a few words, and no answers. He was a secretive young man who was devoted to Rod and kept his own counsel; he trusted very few. His dyslexia had caused problems in school, and he quit at fifteen when he got sick of brawling with students who mocked his slowness. Rod had been glad to hire the boy who'd been coming over to help him with his horses since he was small. Rod had told Connie he remembered the taunting of his own high school years because he was a Monacan.

Rod came to the door when she knocked to say thank you. He nodded and shut the door, his face bleak.

Chapter Four

Bundled up against the cold, Cary stood by a paddock petting the wide brow of a chestnut mare. Soon it would be time to put Proud Mary in the barn. Her foal was due in about six weeks. At nineteen, she was old to be giving birth, but she was hardy and had produced four champions. Still, he was worried. *This is the last time for you,* he thought. *Once you have this foal, I'll keep you happy until the end of your days.*

Connie came out of the office and strode across the snowy ground.

"Find anything?" he asked.

"Nothing. I noticed, though, that the horses and barns, as well as the house and grounds are neglected."

"That tallies with what I know," admitted Cary.

Both were silent, probably thinking the same thing. Rod had a good motive for murder. A quarter of a million would go a long way: enough to recharge his ailing business or start over some other place.

"I can't believe Rod would kill his own horse," Cary continued.

"I can't either. But Cary, I saw him in the stall the night of the murder and again today. I'm no expert, but he appears to be clinically depressed. And I think he might be a victim of Tony Stephens and his empire."

Cary's face was bleak. "Stephens's operation at Fayence is so big that he's forced some smaller breeders to shut down. The thing is, Connie, Woolwine's death is damn suspicious. I don't accept Jase's theory. An animal coming into the barn and scaring Woolwine so much he dies? There have been some strange cases where a sensitive horse died from fear, I know. But it would take more to kill a horse than, say, a feral cat creeping in for a bit of warmth."

Mary butted her head into Cary's chest, causing him to smile for a minute. Then his face grew dark again.

"I can delay making a decision for a few days yet. By the way, the big muckety-muck himself up at Fayence called earlier. Sick horse. Demanded I send someone right away and asked for a man. He told me Pres Carter had been out. Carter said it wasn't anything risky, gave the horse an injection. But Stephens wanted someone from the firm anyway. Since he's one of our biggest clients, hell, the biggest one, you'll have to demonstrate our concern and make an appearance. Tomorrow's time enough.

"You know," he went on, "Stephens has lived here for three years, but he still doesn't understand or tolerate our southern courtesy. He's arrogant and crude, demands attention immediately. Never asks politely, just demands. Oh, yes, he'll be mad if someone doesn't come right away, but I refuse to put up with his arrogance."

"Which horse is it?"

Cary snorted. "Pride of the Yankees." He considered the name insulting to the Central Virginia community.

"Remember the first time I went up there?" Connie asked. "He accepted my services that once but said he would never let me step foot on his property again." Mimicking Stephen's hoarse, flat voice, she growled his last words to her as she had gotten into her truck: "'You have no business trying to do the same things men do.'"

Cary shook his head in disgust.

"Now how am I supposed to 'demonstrate our concern' if he won't deal with me?" she asked, grinning.

"Come on, Connie," he said. "Quit fooling around. We both know you want to go back to Fayence and put that loudmouthed bully in his place. I know you'll find a way."

* * *

At The Gardens restaurant, Connie sipped a whiskey sour while she waited for Gyp. She was too tired to fend off thoughts about Jase. Her mind echoed the dreary mantra she'd taken to repeating, the one she always hoped would bring release: *He's married to Les. It's none of my business if his marriage is troubled. Even if they divorced, nothing would change. I'm just a good friend to him.*

Before his marriage, they'd enjoyed each other's company. Jase had taken her to horse shows, a Hunt Ball in Charlottesville, a concert at the University of Virginia to celebrate his birthday. There was plenty of good-natured teasing, laughter, and nonstop talk about books they were reading and movies they liked, but above all, they spoke of horses.

Once he'd surprised her when he mentioned he loved some Shakespearean lines about horses. "I've always remembered them, Con. We had to read *Henry V* in college." Slowly, he repeated them: "'Think when we talk of horses that you see them/Printing their proud hoofs i' the receiving earth.'"

Connie had later paid a calligrapher to write the lines on fine white paper for Jase. She'd had it framed in walnut by an art store in Lynchburg, and Jase had hung it with great delight on his office wall. She had word-processed the lines for herself, bought a frame at Wal-Mart, and placed the humble copy on her bedside table. Besides being a perfect expression of how she regarded horses, it gave Jase and her something in common.

"Hey, Connie. You look grim." Gyp was smiling sweetly.

Connie relaxed. "What shall we have?"

Over mocha torte, Connie told her friend the whole story about Jack Wampler, including the real facts about the citation he'd given her.

"I realize now I should have fought the summons."

"Have you told Cary? I'm sure he wouldn't let you be treated this way."

"I can't, Gyp. You know his temper. He's pretty powerful in the business community but with the state police? He'd go to headquarters and demand angrily that Wampler be prosecuted. It would get into the papers and be bad publicity for the company.

"When I asked my trooper friend, Eula Jones, about Jack," Connie continued, "I found out that he's considered a good cop. He got a commendation from the governor for catching a man who'd raped and killed a woman in Roanoke. You see, Gyp, even if I went to the state or even local police by myself, I don't know if they'd believe me. It would be the word of a hero cop against mine."

"Has he a wife?"

"Yes. Married when they were sixteen. He's one of those men who think women were made to be dominated. In that respect, he's like Tony Stephens. But Stephens is all bluff, all bully. Jack scares me. There's something in his eyes when he looks at me."

Gyp thought for a moment. "I feel terrible about this, Con. I just can't think of any good advice right now. What will you do?"

"I guess it will have to come to a head some time, when he gets tired of baiting me and I get tired of putting up with it. But since he only works at night and doesn't dare harass me unless the road is deserted, it will be a while before I see him again, I hope."

Gyp still had lines of worry in her face as they went to the parking lot. Even though nothing was solved, and Connie was dreading the next encounter with Jack, she felt better for having told her friend.

Once behind the wheel, fatigue overtook her. It was now nine thirty and she'd had only a few hours of sleep the night before. Nor had she eaten wisely. No breakfast. A burger on the way to Rod's. And too much rich food for dinner. Her eyelids drooped as she cautiously drove home on icy roads. It wouldn't be long before she could crawl under the comforter and get a good night's sleep.

But at two thirty in the morning, she was driving up US 29 to Dick and Laura Latham's Redbud Farm in Albemarle County. Another horse was dead.

As Connie drove to Redbud Farm, she thought about the Lathams and what she knew about them. They had both been professors at local colleges. Dick had taught history at Sweet Briar while Laura was an English teacher at Randolph-Macon Woman's College.

The childless couple had shared a passion for horses, owning a string of beloved Thoroughbreds over the years and demonstrating their considerable equestrian abilities in competitions. Their aching joints and Laura's broken shoulder finally put an end to their riding.

They had always dreamed of owning a very fine horse and after they retired, started their search.

Dick Latham had told Connie at a party how they finally found their cherished horse, Finn. One day, Laura had heard about a Thoroughbred for sale named Finn Maccumhail. His original owner, a book-loving teenager who named him after the great Irish mythological warrior, had been forced to sell him when she went away to college. But she and her parents had sold him to Al Simms, who was shiftless and stupid, and one of those people who buy an animal and then neglect it. Simms had coveted Finn when he learned about the horse's pedigree, but he soon lost interest when he became a partner in a horse-racing venture in Northern Virginia.

When the Lathams went to the Simms farm, they saw with horror that Finn looked so bad that they might not be able to save him. He had a virulent case of mange. Raw, inflamed, bald patches covered his tailhead, legs, and base of his mane. As the couple watched, the miserable black horse repeatedly bit the sore, itching parts on his body, and rubbed against the stall walls in a futile attempt to get relief. Simms had tried halfheartedly to help Finn by smearing salve on the bad areas, but when it didn't work, he advertised the horse for sale.

Dick and Laura entered the stall and spoke softly to the agonized animal, who wouldn't let himself be touched. He didn't react violently, but simply backed away from them. The couple stepped back into the aisle, looked at one another without words, and nodded. Both saw the two-year-old's promise.

Simms had wanted five thousand dollars, saying he could supply Finn's papers documenting a glorious breeding line and a negative Coggins Test, which assured the Lathams that the horse didn't have EIA—equine infectious anemia. The couple gladly paid and made arrangements for Finn to be taken to Preston Carter's clinic. It was several days before he told the anxious couple that mange mites were indeed in Finn's body, and prescribed a dressing of 0.6 percent lindane and 0.5 percent toxaphene solution, which had to be brushed into the afflicted areas regularly.

Finn continued to back away from Dick and Laura, but they were patient, and took turns simply stroking his temple or neck. Slowly they gained his confidence. One spring day, Finn let Laura brush a little of the solution into one of the sores. It took a long time for the mange to clear, but as he started to get better, Finn's true nature emerged. At heart, he was gentle and malleable.

The couple decided that with his superb Thoroughbred conformation and love of running, Finn was ideal for a hunter. Training started. Connie remembered that given Finn's bloodlines, excellent physical condition, and sunny future, Cary had insured the horse for $125,000.

As Connie drove up the steep driveway to the Latham barn, she saw the couple standing outside in the damp cold, arms around one another. *They must be waiting for me,* she thought.

The she noticed their white faces and staring eyes. *They're in shock,* she thought. *What happened here?*

Chapter Five

Connie took Laura's outstretched hand in hers. The older woman could say nothing.

"He's dead, Connie. Finn is gone," said Dick.

"I'm very sorry."

"We had brought him so far. Why, only last month Pres said he was in perfect health."

"We'll try to find some answers." She paused, and said, "I'd better go into the barn now, before Pres's assistant comes."

"Of course. And I should take Laurie back to the house. She's shivering. Coffee will be waiting when you're both finished."

Connie was almost inside the barn when she heard the Carter Clinic truck pulling up the steep hill, and soon lights stabbed the darkness where she stood and waited. She was surprised to see Pres Carter. He usually preferred to leave night calls to his assistants. He got out of his truck, acknowledging her presence with a curt nod.

Connie despised Carter's chauvinism, and he both hated and derided her competence. "She doesn't belong in that job," the drunken vet had complained at a party within her hearing. "Pretty woman like that should be someone's secretary."

She had always wished the Lathams used another vet, but Dick was related to Carter, and the couple honored family ties. The fleshy, handsome man was descended from a far less glamorous branch of the famous Virginia Carters, who had lived in Central Virginia. Before the Civil War, the family's highly successful tobacco enterprise and large house on the James River had made Preston's ancestors a power to reckon with. Like many families, they lost everything during the war and never recovered. The mansion was now ramshackle. Marauding cows had tromped through it for years. Carter bragged that he was restoring it to its former glory.

In Finn's stall, Connie and Carter stood silently contemplating the body. It appeared that the horse had just fallen and died. The fidgeting vet dropped to his knees and started a cursory examination. *Why is he in such a hurry?* Connie wondered.

Trying to maintain civility, she said, "Pres, Dick and Laura asked me to invite you to the house for coffee when you're done."

He didn't answer.

Jerk. Then she reproached herself. Pres would always be a jerk and her attitude wasn't helping Dick and Laura.

She left the barn and walked up the flagstone path to the couple's restored farmhouse. When she entered the low-ceilinged parlor, Dick and Laura were sitting at a gateleg table. Accepting a cup of coffee, Connie sat down in a rocking chair by the fireplace, and took a few sips.

"Did you see anything, Connie?" asked Dick.

"I only had a quick look, but no. Pres is looking him over right now. He may find something. I decided to wait until he's done before I look around."

"Finn was fine earlier this evening," said Laura. Her face had regained a little color. "We looked in on him about nine, and he nuzzled my hand. I told him he was a good boy and he…" She shut her eyes.

Connie waited, and then asked, "Was the barn door open?"

"It was barred, but I suppose anyone could have lifted the bar and gone in," Dick answered. "It's kind of deserted up here, you know, and we were watching television until quite late. We might not have heard a truck. But surely, no one would harm Finn. He must have been sick."

The Lathams had restored the old stone barn but had thought the nineteenth-century latch on the double doors sufficient in their deeply wooded hideaway.

There was nothing more to say. The three waited for Carter to come. Dick gazed steadily at a photograph of Finn on the piano, eyes wet with tears. Laura's face was desolate. An old grandfather clock ticked away in one corner.

Pres Carter came in the front door about fifteen minutes later, tracking snow and stable muck onto the yellow carpet. Refusing coffee with a wave of his hand, he said, "Well, Dick and Laura, I don't have anything to tell you right now. It's possible his heart failed him, much as humans sometimes drop dead from a cardiac arrest. Was he out in the pasture today, running hard?"

"Yes," Dick replied. "We didn't see any harm in letting him out for a little while since it wasn't snowing this morning and the sun was shining."

"There you are. I'll do some tests but he probably just keeled over when his heart gave out. A congenital problem no one suspected. I'll send a man to pick him up later today."

At the last words, the couple's faces twisted in pain.

Before anyone could respond, Carter turned abruptly and dashed back outside. In a few moments, they heard his truck pull away.

He could have at least said some comforting words, thought Connie.

She said, "I'll leave you alone now. I just want to say again how sorry I am about Finn. He was such a love. I'll report my findings to Cary later today and see what he says. He may send me up here again to do another examination of the stall and barn. Either way, I'll call this afternoon."

She excused herself and went out to the barn. But her careful examination revealed nothing—as she had expected. Finn lay as if asleep.

When she was finally back in her truck, Connie looked at the dashboard clock. Close to six o'clock. She drove toward Bedford County, thinking about the dead horse she had just seen, and Woolwine, and what she would say to Cary.

Slowly she came to the horrifying conclusion that both horses could have been murdered. *Woolwine and Finn had no marks on their bodies, at least none I could see. And there was no blood, no mucous, no excrement. Nothing. How were the death scenes alike? Both horses were lying in the straw. Woolwine's head tilted up at that odd angle, Finn just lying there. Didn't seem to be any sign Finn panicked, but I think Woolwine knew something wrong was happening to him and kicked the hole in the wall. What about opportunity? Both Payson Stud and Redbud Farm are isolated, easy for the murderer to get to the horses. Rod could have left the barn door open, the Latham door was easily opened. But why would anyone kill these two horses? Could*

Rod and the Lathams have done this or hired it done for the insurance settlement?

Connie knew about drifters who kill for pay. She had read about a short, skinny, nondescript man in another state known as Dr. Death by insiders. Whenever he appeared, horse people knew why he had come to town.

She looked for Wampler's cruiser all the way home and resolutely tried to put her anxieties about Jase aside. When her small cottage came into view, she sighed with relief.

As she got ready for bed, she remembered the trip she had to make to Albemarle County, but right now she was too tired to devise a strategy by which to outwit Tony Stephens.

Just before she sank into sleep, she wondered, *If there have been two horses murdered, will there be more?*

Chapter Six

It had snowed and then frozen during the night, and the slippery hill glimmered with ice-enclosed stems of dead grass. His heavy boots made a crunching sound as he struggled to his usual vantage point, the place where the woods began. Then he turned and looked down. His dark eyes ranged over the luxurious estate spread out below, and he smiled.

Fayence. His.

Smart all his life, he mused. Smart enough to realize he didn't belong in the dingy city in western New York, where all his parents ever thought of was eking out a living in their small-time bakery and going to church.

Against his will, thoughts of his early life with his parents once again assailed his mind. He didn't understand why he seemed compelled to keep remembering the childhood he was desperate to forget.

From the time he was old enough to reason, he knew he didn't belong to the parents with whom he lived. He wondered often if he had been adopted, but when he questioned his mother, she would always say, "You are our little Tony, you belong to us," and then kiss him.

Looking down at his estate, spread like some legendary necklace owned by a queen and displayed upon white velvet, he thought, *I wasn't the kind of son they wanted. But I didn't want them either.*

He had refused to go to Greek school, where Father Theodore taught the ancient language and Greek orthodox theology. Why would he want to learn to speak Greek? So what if his father spoke it to his mother in their home. His father should have used English all the time. They were Americans. And why would he want to listen to all that boring religion stuff when his parents made him sit in church at least once a week and on every holy day? Stephens remembered the deadly boredom of those hallowed days, countless in number to the boy. Even the modest apartment where the family lived was given over to a stifling obsession with religion, or so the child thought. He cared nothing about the icons with their flat, sad, yellow faces that his mother had hung everywhere, or the little shrine she had set up in the parlor. He had thought his mother odd for doing so.

In high school, an unhappy young man, he barely passed anything but math. There he excelled. He found his mind thrived on figuring out solutions to math problems, and he would keep at it, for hours sometimes, until he succeeded. He decided that success in life, as well as in his beloved numbers, lay in never giving up until the problem was solved. When he had taken all the math courses offered, he convinced the principal to let him go to a school in the richest section of the city—where most of the students were destined for universities—just for calculus. Tony knew that Mr. Sutton had never liked him. Few did because of his unsmiling face, his silence, and the implied threat his large muscular body represented. But the principal was a kind man, still idealistic enough to try to help all the students in his rundown school. So he pulled strings and got Tony into the advanced course.

His eventual mastery of calculus started a lifelong pattern; if he cared about something, he'd learn it.

Tony started to make figures work for him. He needed money to escape from the city when he graduated. If he stayed, the only future for him would be working at an auto plant or steel mill—if the failing factories even managed to stay open. So he took on two part-time jobs in addition to his work at the bakery. He could have refused to get up every morning at two AM to mix the sweet dough for the kourabiedes and other Greek specialties, but for some reason he could not even explain to himself, he continued to help his father. He also drove the truck when John, the wizened little deliveryman, was laid up with what he said was arthritis but was really too much ouzo.

One day Tony heard from a good customer of the bakery that his employer, a wealthy man who lived on Bidwell Parkway, needed a part-time driver. The customer didn't like Tony but had formed a fast friendship with his father over the years, and knew how hard Tony's parents had to work to earn a skimpy living.

Tony thought hard and then allowed the man to arrange an interview.

When Tony presented himself to Mr. Angeli, he knew the old Sicilian was impressed by what he saw. A huge young man who almost never smiled and answered questions with very few words was just what he was looking for. He told Tony he didn't want to talk to his chauffeur. He just wanted to be transported back and forth between his home and his office on Eagle Street.

Tony came to respect the secretive Angeli for his business ability. He admired the fruits of Angeli's hard work, an imposing home in one of the oldest and still beautiful parts of the city, filled with exquisite art. Sometimes he was allowed to look at his employer's collection of drawings and paintings for a few minutes as he waited for Angeli to come downstairs. *This is for me,* the boy would think. *I want all this.* And Angeli, against his own misanthropic principles, became fond of Tony. Perhaps he saw something of himself in the youth.

Eventually, Tony confided in him, as he never could with his parents, stumbling over the words but clearly conveying his great ambition to leave the wretched city and use his talent with numbers to have a house like Mr. Angeli's some day. Mr. Angeli seemed to lose his reticence about talking to his young driver and began to expand his education. Tony knew it amused Angeli to teach him many things as he carefully drove his employer in his black Cadillac from his home to the busy downtown street where he conducted the mysterious business that made him rich. Gesturing with his La Corona from the back seat, Angeli would talk about how to conduct canny business practices, what wines were worth investing in, how to acquire valuable art. "Always buy the best, kid. The best men to work for you, the best of everything." Tony would then go to school and return to Eagle Street later to pick up the old man and to receive yet another lesson.

Tony graduated from high school at eighteen, through sheer stubbornness. He had wanted to quit school many times after he had taken all the math courses he could, but Angeli had told Tony he intended to employ him and didn't want any ignorant men working for him. Angeli bought him a new suit as a

Chapter Six

graduation present and arranged a job for Tony in Chicago where he had "business interests." When Tony told him hesitantly he didn't even know exactly what his patron did for a living, the old man grinned in his vulpine way.

"Don't worry about it. My man out there will help you. And you're a fast learner." He chuckled. "Look how much you've picked up from me already! With your talent for numbers, you'll be a real asset to my Chicago office."

After graduation, Tony left the dying city for good.

His parents never saw him again.

To this day, the smell of sweet things nauseated him. His chef had orders never to prepare desserts, not even for guests.

He'd told himself there was no need to feel guilty about his parents. Occasionally he'd make a short call or write a noncommittal postcard from the glamorous cities where his work took him. His mother and father were always pathetically glad to hear from him. When they had their last illnesses, he'd sent money to help with expenses but didn't go home.

Eventually he did learn how Angeli earned his fortune. He worried at first about the things he was asked to do with his numbers. Some of his parents' rigid honesty had rubbed off on him, but he came to realize that he would never prosper if he let scruples stand in his way. Jobs were, after all, just exercises in finding answers by considering all possible solutions. Gradually, he dismissed from his mind that his artful manipulation of money was often illegal.

Along the way, Tony learned he could use his powerful body and intimidating presence, as well as his sharp mind for figures, to get what he wanted. He moved upward fast in Mr. Angeli's companies, living in New York, Los Angeles, and Denver, and acquiring a thin facade of respectability and culture along the way.

His wealth increased when the old man died and left him half a million dollars. Angeli had smirked, exposing his yellow dentures, when his lawyer protested Tony as a beneficiary. But Angeli was happy to go to his grave knowing his greedy relatives, who had always feared and despised him, weren't going to get everything.

Tony's parents would be sad if they knew he had changed his surname by lopping off a bunch of syllables. Stephens. Easier to say, to remember. And the name fit here in Albemarle County, where he had taken it into his head to start a horse breeding business and become part of what he considered an aristocratic culture. The name "Tony" was all right, he had decided. It could be English as well as Greek or Italian. So he kept it.

Abruptly, he started down the hill, dismissing the past from his mind as having no practical value. *Only the present matters,* he thought.

Once at the bottom, he strode toward the centerpiece of his estate, the French manor house the previous owners had built. He was thinking with pleasure of the bottle of Mavrodaphne waiting for him, when he saw her. Someone had buzzed her through the gate and she was just getting out of that stupid truck she drove.

Wait till I find out who let her in.

He felt the anger flame within him as he walked steadily onward. She hadn't seen him yet.

Why the hell did McCutcheon send her out when he could have easily sent one of his men? He thought he'd gotten rid of her the last time.

Chapter Seven

Connie turned and saw him coming toward her with determined step.

She stared at his tightened lips, his tense body, and braced herself for what was coming. *Keep calm,* she told herself. *He's only a bully with a loud mouth. He wouldn't dare do anything. He needs us too much. Remember the plan.*

By the time she had reached the roller coaster section of US 29 north that marked the beginning of Albemarle County, Connie had prepared a plan for the encounter with Tony Stephens. She knew if she gave in to his bullying again and let herself be thrown off the property for a second time, her fine professional reputation with the firm's clients—so painstakingly acquired—would suffer. At their first meeting, she made a grievous mistake by losing her temper at his crude words of dismissal. *Men seem to be able to do that and get away with it,* she thought sourly as the truck covered mile after mile of cold landscape. *If women do it, they're called abrasive, arrogant. I have to handle him differently this time.*

She had decided on a plan, a galling one to be sure. But she had to maintain her credibility.

After the first humiliating experience, she learned as much about Stephens as she could, talking to people who had dealt with him and reading the very few newspaper articles about his renovation of the old Cameron place. It was generally agreed among tradespeople that he was hard to deal with, peremptory, demanding, patronizing. Those who had met him socially said that he wasn't much for polite conversation, but very willing to talk about his breeding farm. He entertained lavishly but rarely, and only, it seemed, for business purposes. When he asked people to come to Fayence for dinner, there was always such an abundance and variety of foods that the guests could never manage to eat it all. But strangely, there was never any dessert. People laughed uneasily when they told Connie about this quirk of Stephens, and invariably wondered if he were watching his weight. But if so, why didn't he provide dessert for those who wanted it?

No one called him friend. His background was mysterious. The longest article Connie could find was an interview published in the feature section of Charlottesville's *Daily Progress*. His answers to the reporter's questions revealed a man swollen with pride.

Now she would depend on that pride.

The slippery roads were almost empty today as she drove carefully toward the Stephens estate. She had turned the heater up to its highest setting, and warm, smothering blasts of air blew in her face. Her feet were icy, though, even in the lined boots she reserved for the coldest days in winter. *Something's wrong with the heater,* she thought absently. *Better get it fixed.* Her stomach ached with hunger. *When I get this over with, I'm going to drop in at Rooney's and have a big hot ham and cheese sandwich.* She'd only been able to sleep a few hours after getting back from Redbud Farm. A shower and several mugs of strong black tea hadn't helped much.

Yawning, she wondered again what he had done before he came to Virginia, how he had managed to amass the wealth it took to buy the Cameron property and transform it into one of the finest breeding and training farms in the state.

At the time of the article several years ago, the huge farm on the Hardware River housed fifteen select stallions to service clients' mares. Other horses were being trained for their owners as jumpers, hunters, and racers. He said to the reporter, "I hope to make Fayence the biggest horse farm in the United States. While I only have fifteen stallions right now, I intend to buy more, but only the best. I'm just getting started."

The equestrian complex on the estate clearly showed the scope of his ambition. It included a manager's house, trainer's cottage, training barn with fifty stalls and four apartments, yearling barn with thirty stalls, indoor and outdoor arenas, paddocks, pastures, and a pool in which the horses could exercise. It was rumored that he was planning a six furlong training track with starting gates.

The centerpiece of Fayence was the manor house.

Connie had learned about the sale of the property and its subsequent renovation from Frank Faulconer, the owner of a prosperous real estate agency in Charlottesville. "I have to know more about him," she had said after Tony had ordered her off the property. "It will help me deal with him next time I have to go to Fayence." Cary had thought it was a good idea, and arranged for Connie to talk to the very discreet Faulconer, who only agreed because Cary was a trusted friend.

Faulconer told Connie that Fayence was one of five properties his company had located in Albemarle, Nelson, and Bedford counties in response to Stephens's twenty-page fax of requirements from Colorado. Tony and his expert had flown in from Denver to stay for a week and inspect the properties. Tony had hired the best man he could find, the renowned William L. Wright, who was a connoisseur of fine houses. Wright also had a comprehensive knowledge of the horse business since he owned a large breeding farm outside Denver.

The real estate agent for Fayence was Florence Carrington, but upon finding this out, Tony had insisted he would only deal with a man. To save the possible very large commission, Frank Faulconer had taken over. He silenced Florence's shrill and ongoing protests by giving her two city houses that would surely sell fast. After one look at Stephens's glowering face when he came to the office on the first day of the tours, she shivered and protested no more. Faulconer, on the other hand, felt sure of himself. He had researched the five estates rigorously and could recite the history of each in minute detail. He had provided copies of the plats. And he had arranged his schedule to devote day and evening for the whole week, if necessary, to sell Stephens a property. He felt satisfied that he had done everything possible to get a sale. And he would have another reward. He would meet William Wright, whose books on Southern architecture were Faulconer's bible.

The Denver fax had stressed privacy of location as all-important. Even though Stephens planned to admit the public to his estate for business purposes, he wanted a place to seclude himself. On the day the three men—Faulconer, Stephens, and Wright—turned off the road and entered the lush but overgrown grounds of Fayence, Faulconer thought, *This is the best of them all.*

After driving several miles through the woods, the men saw the manor house come into view. Faulconer was honest about the condition of the house. "I hope you'll understand that the Camerons got old and neglected the place. It needs a lot of work," he said as he pulled into the circular drive.

Faulconer was thrilled to see Wright's eyes widen with pleasure as he surveyed the huge foyer. The expert listened intently as Faulconer recited the house's architectural glories: twelve-foot coffered ceilings, museum-quality woodwork including fine wainscoting, heart-pine floors, even the original hardware. "The landmark portion dates back to 1825." The expert nodded. Stephens looked bored. He shrugged his massive shoulders in the cashmere coat and started up the curving staircase with its walnut balustrade.

It took a long time to see the rest of the house and the extensive grounds.

Faulconer never forgot dinner that night in the Omni Hotel. Stephens and Wright told him they wanted Fayence and Stephens agreed to the price without haggling. Faulconer didn't dare think about his huge commission but concentrated on making the evening pleasant. He had given up trying to carry on a conversation with Stephens, who communicated as little as possible, but he and Wright talked shop long after Stephens had gone upstairs to his room, Wright telling stories of the fantastic commissions he had earned in the United States and abroad. With the final glass of Beaujolais, they agreed to meet at the office the next day to complete the transaction.

Faulconer told Connie that Stephens had infinite resources, it seemed, to transform Fayence. Tony ordered his decorators to gut all the rooms in the house. Everything had to be changed. But when they asked him how he wanted his mansion to look, he could only describe a house he had seen and admired as a boy. "Newport," whispered one decorator behind his hand to another. And indeed, Angeli's home had been a small imitation of one of the great mansions of Newport, built by an oil-rich lord of conspicuous consumption who had furnished his home with the finest Europe could supply.

"At Fayence," Faulconer told Connie, "the walls in the downstairs rooms were covered with imported fabric, complementing exquisite Aubusson rugs. Scouts from all over the world were kept busy locating new finds of antique furniture for Stephens's experts to examine."

"You've probably talked to people who've been invited there," said Connie. "What do they have to say?"

"Quite a few of the guests noticed that while the styles of the antique furniture in the downstairs rooms varied, all of it was massive and dark. One woman told me that it cast depressing shadows on the floor. Another guest particularly disliked a huge Renaissance chest that resembled a sarcophagus."

Faulconer went on to describe the collection of paintings and drawings decorating the walls.

"To say Stephens is a strange man is an understatement," Faulconer said. "He's made Fayence a museum, a wonderful place to entertain guests, but only a select few are invited to visit, mostly influential people in society and business. From what I can tell, he prefers to be alone most of the time."

Connie remembered Faulconer's parting words.

"If you ever get into that house, take a look at his bedroom."

On the day Stephens let the reporter and photographer from the *Daily Progress* into his home for the interview, he unintentionally revealed something of himself. Puffed up with pride and egotism, Stephens had let his guard down with the man and woman who accompanied him on the tour of the house.

He allowed his bedroom to be described and photographed. Connie had puzzled over the color photographs in the newspaper.

The oddness of his bedroom lay in its sharp contrast with the lavish décor of the rest of the house. The room, for one thing, was almost empty. The article said that the huge oak bed had been made to Stephens's own design. Its plain headboard and footboard were made of finely finished wood, stained a pale hue. There was a large, simple clothes cupboard matching the bed. The bed itself, covered with a handmade, imported spread in white, beige and black and featuring the ancient Greek key design, faced a wall of uncovered floor-to-ceiling windows, framing the Blue Ridge Mountains. Highly polished oak floors were bare but for area carpets, which repeated the color scheme and added touches of rust and orange. Stephens had chosen only one work of art for his bedroom, a somber painting by a famous minimalist to hang over the Spartan bed. There were no personal photographs or mementos. In the newspaper photo, Stephens's face looked dark and grim.

To Connie, studying the picture intently, the room looked like the quarters of a general in the field who is not interested in luxury, but needs only a utilitarian bed in which to get the necessary rest to enable him to fight again the next day—a general to whom the war is his whole life.

Now, as Connie pulled her truck up to the ornate entry gates that stretched between the pillars of Fayence, she thought, *and he's a general with no past.*

Chapter Eight

Before Stephens could open his mouth, she said loudly and quickly, "Mr. Stephens, I apologize!" She smiled as winsomely as she could manage. *I hate to have to do this,* she thought savagely.

He was caught unawares. She hurried on. "The last time I was here, I lost my temper with you. The only thing I can blame it on was that I had been working a lot of hours with not enough sleep. I hope you'll forgive me and let me look at your horse. I promise to make my exam quickly and then leave."

She saw the massive shoulders relax a bit, but his face still scowled with suspicion.

"I thought I made it clear to McCutcheon he was not to send you again."

"I asked Cary if I could come back next time you needed an agent."

The heavy black eyebrows rose in disbelief.

"Well, I'll confess something. I wanted to come back because I might get a chance to see a little of your equestrian complex. I read about it in the *Daily Progress*, and I believe that nothing can touch it for top-of-the-line equipment, efficiency, or layout, here or in Kentucky." The last was sheer embroidery. She really didn't know if it was the best or not.

"Or in Texas," he growled.

"Right."

There was a long silence while he stared at Connie, clearly trying to make up his mind whether to order her off the place.

Finally, he said, "Okay. I've been worried about Pride. I'll take you to his stall."

"Thank you, Mr. Stephens," she said in her best humble voice.

Frowning, he turned and walked briskly toward the show barn where Pride of the Yankees lived. She followed in his steps, feeling like a fool. *Hold on, hold on. You've gotten at least this far.*

Once in the barn, she saw a perfectly healthy horse with bright eyes and swishing tail, noisily chewing his special compound of food. Anyone could see there was nothing wrong with him. But she entered the stall anyway, and made a show of her usual examination while Stephens stood outside looking in. He had declined to enter the stall, muttering that he didn't know anything about horses' bodies and didn't care to know.

"He's fine, Mr. Stephens. I can't see anything wrong with him. He's doing fine."

Stephens turned to leave the barn, and she risked the question to which every proud horse owner responds. "If you wouldn't mind, would you tell me how you acquired Pride of the Yankees?"

His flat voice gained a little color and enthusiasm as he described the negotiations he had carried on over a matter of months with a stubborn woman in Kentucky, finally wearing her down until she agreed to a price about 70 percent of what she had originally asked. His voice turned contemptuous as he described the woman's capitulation.

"And now," he finished, "I've got things to do. You'll tell McCutcheon about Pride." It was not a question, but a command.

"Yes." As they emerged into the thin winter sunshine, she took another risk.

"Mr. Stephens."

He said nothing.

She rushed on. "I've heard so much about your setup here. Would you mind if I walked around a bit? I won't interfere with anything." She struggled to keep her voice deferential.

He stared at her again, hesitating.

"Okay. But I'll have a guy go with you. I don't allow anyone to walk around here alone."

He motioned to an old man who was taking a brown and white mare into another barn. "Show her the place, right? After that, escort her to her truck."

"Hello, Buck," Connie said.

Stephens looked from one to the other as the man grinned. Burned by years of exposure to the blazing Virginia sun, his blotchy skin of brown and white patches resembled the dappled hide of the horse he led.

Turning to Stephens, Connie said, "Buck used to work at Payson Stud. Rod Payson is a client of ours." Shrugging, Tony strode away without another word.

"Show me everything, Buck," she said.

Two hours later, Connie had not seen a tenth of the estate, but felt compelled to leave because Buck was so nervous. As time passed, he looked over his shoulder more and more, as if he were afraid Stephens would come back and take it out on him because Connie was still there. It was easy to understand the old man's fear.

During that short time, Buck showed her some of the horse breeding facilities, and now Connie fully understood that Stephens had made Fayence the foremost horse farm of the area. She had never seen any breeding farm in Virginia that came close to its layout and accommodations. A lame Morgan paddled in the horse pool to strengthen his sore shoulder. Glossy pregnant mares and spirited stallions looked like textbook pictures of healthy horses. Breeding sheds held the latest equipment and small but compact, well-equipped labs.

The greatest thrill was when Buck took her to see the rest of the horses in the show barn. "Looks like he's cornered the market on every perfect horse there is, Buck," said Connie. She noticed a variety of breeds, horses who would be trained for racing, steeple chasing, fox hunting, or pleasure. Some came readily to the stall doors as Connie made a clucking sound; others shied away abruptly at the presence of strangers.

"Only special hands can work in here," remarked Buck. Connie saw that he was embarrassed. Obviously, Stephens didn't consider Buck "special," even with his years of experience. She pointed to a gray Arabian. "What's he worth, Buck?"

"He's new. Went for $90,000, someone said. Came from North Carolina."

The barn was immaculate. "Oh, yes," said Buck. "He doesn't want nothing to do with the horses—like touching them or even talking to them—but he makes sure it's clean in all the barns. If it ain't, well——." In a low voice, he said, "He often takes a walk through the farm after dinner. Last night he found something wrong. Nobody seems to know what it was, but this morning, he told one of the hands to get out. Just like that. Didn't even bother to say what was wrong and give the guy a chance to defend himself or do better the next time."

Back outside, Buck said loudly, "Did you notice how everything's painted up slick and there's flowers all over? And we have a lot of famous people visiting. Why, last week, there was some movie stars here. They live somewhere in Albemarle County. Forget their names, though."

When they walked back to her truck, Buck was obviously relieved. Connie asked why he had left Rod Payson's place.

"Why, he let me go, Connie. Said he didn't want to but had to do it. Trouble keeping his farm going. I told him he was cutting back too much, but all he said was he'd write me a good letter. I used that to get on here.

"He's been awful bad since Miz Payson's death—guess you heard about it. He wanders around that place, does a little here, a little there. Worry about him. I liked it a lot there. He was always good to me, liked everything I done. Made me want to do more, you know? Here, well." Then he said, "I'd go back in a minute. If you see him, tell him hello from Buck."

Connie promised she would and drove down the winding road to US 29, turned left and started home. She pondered all she had seen and felt discomfited by Fayence. If Stephens continued to be successful here, he'd put people like Rod and Earlene Collins, her breeder friend in Nelson County, out of business in a matter of months.

Chapter Nine

It was Sunday and the day of Cary's party to show his new colt. He was combining events this time, celebrating the approach of Christmas as well. The weather had cleared but was still cold. The sun shone thinly through bluish-black clouds.

There was nothing Cary liked better when he acquired a fine horse than to share his joy with clients, special friends, and employees. But Cary knew also that his lavish parties were powerful reminders that his company was flourishing. He had made the shrewd decision long ago that the expense was well worth the business it generated.

As Cary and Pam McCutcheon came into the dining room, Daisy Ryan, the caterer, leaned over the table to adjust a red gauze ribbon tied around the top of an extravagant silver candlestick. Pam said, "You've done it again, Daisy. This table should be in *Southern Living!*"

Daisy barely smiled in response to the compliment and went into the kitchen.

Pam and Cary watched as the swinging door to the kitchen closed, and smiled at each other. "Daisy is Daisy," said Cary. Then he took Pam's hands, stepped back to arms' length, and looked at her. He loved her quiet face and wide-set eyes. Her long brown hair—he noticed with private amusement a little gray showing—was pulled back, held by a gold clip at the nape of her neck. As usual, she was dressed simply. But Cary knew that her clothes were expensive and elegant. Unlike many men, he was aware of such things

Today her dress was dark brown, setting off his gift—a topaz necklace and earrings. It pleased him to add a piece to her antique jewelry collection now and then. He shook his head in mock dismay. "You look too good, today, honey. I'll have to fight a couple of duels. Can't you go back upstairs and uglify yourself?"

She giggled. "'Uglify' can't be a word. You're a silly man, Cary McCutcheon."

He caught her to him, held her close for a moment. Then he looked at his watch. "Show time, honey." After a kiss, they parted, he for the stable where he would hold court until everyone possible had seen and admired the horse, and she for the foyer to greet the guests.

* * *

As Connie dressed for the party, she resolved she would try to avoid thinking about the deaths of Woolwine and Finn, at least during the afternoon. She had read the reports from Jase Tyree and Pres Carter. Both vets blamed heart failure as the cause for the deaths of the two horses. But Cary was dissatisfied, and was still considering the Payson and Latham settlements.

She put on an emerald velvet suit with a floor-length skirt she had bought in November, anticipating Cary's annual holiday party, and fastened a delicate gold filigree pin—a Christmas wreath ornamented with tiny pearls—on the jacket. It had been a gift from Mike at a time when they had been temporarily in the black. She inserted plain gold studs in her ears and took a last look in the full-length mirror in the bedroom. *Not bad. My hair looks good too. I should get it cut more often.* She put on a long, black wool coat and headed out to begin the drive to Otter Hill.

Wearing Mike's pin had started a chain of memories, as it always did. Connie and her husband Mike had come to Lynchburg to make yet another in a series of new starts in their fortunes and their marriage. Mike had begun a consulting business that hadn't taken off, despite his hard work. It was another failure in his ill-conceived plan to make a fortune by assisting businesses with their computer problems. His previous ventures in Alexandria and Charlottesville had also failed.

Mike Holt had become impatient with the low pay and hazards of teaching history in an underfunded northern high school. To make matters worse, the "rust bucket" city where the Holts had spent all their lives was dying a slow death. Impetuous by nature, he quit his job one day and told Connie that night that they were moving south where the opportunities were greater and the weather gentler.

"It's making me sick walking in that door every morning," he'd said. "The students don't care, the administration doesn't support its teachers, I don't make any money. I have to get out of here."

Connie had argued that they were just getting on their feet financially. But he wouldn't listen and gave her an ultimatum: "You can either come with me or not, but I'm going."

It had been a struggle getting their two children through college. Connie had long ago taken over the budgeting, for her husband had no financial sense. She had saved everything she could toward college expenses from his paycheck and from the salary she earned as a science teacher at an honors high school. She managed to stitch together a patchwork of scholarships, grants, and student loans. The children had part-time jobs. Hampering Connie's efforts to pay the college expenses was Mike's interest in computers. He insisted on taking classes, and Connie had to find a way to pay for them.

When both children finally graduated and got good jobs—Danny in Texas, Ellen in New Hampshire—Connie thought maybe she and Mike could work toward financial stability. Maybe their marriage would improve. Through a combination of frustration, anger and despair over his career, the ongoing money problems, and the way his life had turned out, Connie's husband had become a cold, insensitive stranger.

And then came Mike's ultimatum.

She had resigned her job with regret, not wanting to leave the city. Both sets of parents died when the two were teens; neither had siblings or other relatives. Their loneliness had been a major reason for their marriage. While there would be no family to miss once they moved, Connie mourned the loss of old friends. To Mike, unable to relate to people easily, her sorrow was inexplicable. "I don't see why you're so upset," he said. "You'll meet new people."

When the Lynchburg business failed, Mike decided to go elsewhere and try again, but Connie dug in her heels, refusing to go west for what she sensed would be another chapter of struggle and failure in their tired marriage. They divided up their meager savings and Mike left on a Greyhound, letting Connie have their old truck—which promptly died. It was imperative that Connie find a job right away. She had been trying to be a waitress for about a week after Mike left when one day, Cary McCutcheon and his guests came to his favorite restaurant.

She had noticed the handsome older man who seemed to be amused at her clumsy attempt to serve huge plates of hot beef sandwiches and fries to the hungry horse trainers and owners at his big table. He had watched her carefully as she slowly maneuvered her way around the table. Then it was his turn.

Embarrassed by the intensity of his gaze, she hesitated before lowering his plate, afraid she would dump the contents all over his tweed jacket and jeans. He shot his hand out, helping her position the plate. Then he laughed outright, a consoling laugh that said, "Take it easy, no big deal." Red-faced and tense, Connie had tried to apologize for her lack of skill, explaining that she had just gotten the job and was learning, but really wasn't very good at it. Seeing his sympathetic expression, she went on more bravely: "I have to have this job."

"Do you know how to use a computer?" he'd asked, and when she said yes, invited her to drive down the road and try being a receptionist at his company. (Much later, she'd asked him why he had taken a chance with her. "Just liked your honesty," was all he'd say.)

Soon she was promoted to secretary, entering information on sick, injured, and dead horses into her computer. The agents' reports were fascinating, and when one day, she asked Cary to train her as an agent, he was skeptical.

"This is Virginia," he said. "Men don't want a woman in this job."

But Connie persisted. "Maybe it's time for a change."

"Well, yes," he admitted, for Cary was a fair man, above all. And because he admired her spirit, he said, "Tell you what. We'll give you a chance. You'll work with Joe."

Connie proved to be a quick study. But Cary made Joe Mattox go out with her on every case for a year until Joe grumbled, "Hell, Cary, she doesn't need me any more."

By that time, she and Mike were divorced.

Connie knew Cary took a big chance in making her his representative. When she started working alone, many horsemen didn't want to deal with her. But Cary could be stubborn, especially when his judgment was questioned.

"I've known you for thirty years, but you work with Connie Holt or we part company," he'd say to the reluctant clients.

All this was said in his low, Jim Beam voice and accompanied by a big grin, but the men knew he was serious. Reluctantly, most accepted her services, for they had depended on Cary for a long time and couldn't see going with anyone else. But once in a while, even with Cary's backing, she'd have a hard time with one of them.

It was different with the women horse breeders. As soon as they discovered she could do the job, they welcomed her. Earlene Collins, a weather-beaten breeder of expensive Arabians, summed it up: "You're good, Connie. Doesn't make any difference if you're a woman."

Thank heavens for Cary, Connie thought to herself, not for the first time, as she pulled into Otter Hill. Cars and trucks lined the long drive.

Connie first visited the barn to admire the awkward colt with beautiful conformation and congratulate Cary. He was retelling the story of how he had acquired the Thoroughbred to yet another visitor when she left for the house.

Inside the foyer, the cheerful sound of people having a good time raised her spirits.

She made her way toward the dining room through the crowd of guests and the loud babble of their multiple conversations, pausing now and then to greet someone she knew. Once through the doorway of her favorite room in Cary's home, she paused to look around.

At the far end of the long rectangular room, the deep windowsills of two tall and narrow windows held glowing candles. An ornate sideboard sat between the windows. The wall to the right held mahogany bookshelves with glass doors, which Cary had added several years ago. (His book collection had outgrown his library.) Her eyes moved to the fine, early nineteenth-century fireplace dominating the left wall. Its wood, stained a rich walnut color, had a glossy patina. A speckled brown marble surround framed the leaping fire. The mantel held gaily wrapped packages, their brilliant ribbons reflected in the gold-framed mirror above. And to the left of the fireplace stood a twelve-foot blue spruce whose top touched the ceiling. The tree was bejeweled with all manner of gold Christmas ornaments, some very old, that Pam McCutcheon had collected.

Taking a red china plate from the sideboard, Connie moved to the massive table in the center of the room and stood looking with great pleasure at the food displayed there. The mingled aromas of the rich and tempting Virginia cuisine set her mouth to watering. She saw brown, flaky sausage biscuits, and platters of hot Virginia ham and sliced turkey. Salmon-pink, crescent-shaped shrimp were arranged on a bed of ice, and succulent crab cakes were piled in a silver chafing dish. An oval china dish held golden fried apples, and a silver bowl, fragile raspberries. Two pedestal cake dishes held a plain-looking pound cake made with Kentucky bourbon and brown sugar, and a glamorous three-layer Lane Cake with fluffy white icing, which Connie knew (she had asked Daisy) contained eight eggs, coconut, pecans, raisins, and brandy. Gold wire baskets held breads, rolls, and muffins: thin breadsticks made with rosemary, streusel-topped muffins with raisins popping out, orange-cranberry bread, and yellow corn bread. And there were rounds of yellow, white, and orange cheeses and bowls of the famous salty peanuts from southeast Virginia.

Something attracted her attention, and she looked up to see Jase entering the dining room, followed by Leslie, his wife. He paused for a moment in the doorway when he saw her, a smile lighting up his face. Connie thought she saw something else in his expression, admiration perhaps. Or maybe it was just a brief flare-up of the old comfortable companionship they had once had.

I miss just talking to him, she thought.

She saw Les push on his back with one strong, long-fingered hand. He moved forward, giving Connie a sad little salute as he made his way to the sideboard. She raised her hand in quiet greeting, acknowledged Les with a nod. She noticed Jase was haggard, his skin sallow.

Chapter Ten

Les was vibrant tonight. Her large brown eyes sparkled as she greeted Pres Carter and started an intense discussion with him. Connie guessed they were talking about the old homes both were restoring. Les had finally convinced Jase to buy a derelict Federal-style home in Lynchburg. Built in the 1820s, it could become the most famous house in the city—if enough money were poured into its restoration.

Now Connie chose her food fast, the pleasure of contemplating the festive table gone. She wanted to leave the dining room as soon as possible and sit with the other guests in the foyer or parlor, where tables had been set up. In a covert glance, she saw Les laughing at something Pres had said, her hand on his arm.

Les had obviously been brought up in the Scarlet O'Hara school of getting what she wanted from a man. Opening her eyes very wide and giving rapt attention to her farrier or councilman or current restoration expert, Les would give the impression she was saying to him, "Please help me, I'm just a woman." Flirting and touching the man frequently were part of her arsenal. Connie thought this disgusting and wondered why Jase, who hated all phoniness, had succumbed to it. Probably it was because their relationship had been so passionate at its outset. She had seen, with anguish, the looks and caresses that passed between them when Jase was courting Leslie. For a moment she felt a renewal of the sorrow that never quite left her. How could Jase have come to the disastrous decision to marry Leslie, who, to judge from Jase's appearance and manner, was destroying everything vital in him?

As she filled her plate, Connie tried to be fair. *She can be genuinely warm and kind to some women*, she thought. *But be honest, only to those who can't compete with her in beauty or intelligence.* Presenting no threat, these women were qualified to receive Les's friendship. But Connie knew that she made Les uneasy. Les had made it clear from the outset that she resented Jase's affection for Connie. She failed to understand how a man and woman could be friends. Even now, Connie knew that Les undercut her whenever she had the chance. When someone mentioned Connie's job, Les would laugh with amused condescension. "What a bizarre job for a woman," she would say. But Connie knew that Les had been known to stay in a stall all night to help her mare in the throes of labor.

Now Les walked toward the table, lovely face alight with anticipation. Her flame-colored dress flared around her. She smiled sweetly at Connie, who returned the smile and left the room.

After she finished eating, Connie circulated among the guests to renew friendships and catch up on news of the horse world.

Chapter Ten

In one corner of the parlor, she noticed Beau Taylor talking to Cary, who had finally come in from the barn to join the festivities. The young man seemed to be describing a horse problem, for at one point, he limped back and forth on the Oriental rug, Cary giving the movement his whole attention and then, with a nod of his head, commenting.

Connie was not surprised Beau was talking freely to Cary, who, with little effort, could get almost anyone to talk. Rod Payson stood quietly by with a drink in his hand, adding a word now and then. *Rod looks a little better,* she thought. *I'm so glad he came tonight.* He looked at Connie and gave her a ghost of a smile. Like every other man there, he was wearing his best suit, but with his high cheekbones and dark eyes and skin, he looked nothing like any other guest. Accustomed to his scarred face, Connie thought, *He's really handsome, and the nice thing is, he doesn't know it.*

Rod touched Cary's arm and asked something. Cary nodded and the two men moved into a side room and closed the door. *Rod must be terribly anxious about the settlement,* Connie thought. Connie noticed that Beau hesitated for a moment and then walked toward the dining room. She gave him her biggest smile as he passed by and he gave a careful nod.

By the time Cary and Rod came back, Connie had joined Dick and Laura Latham in a large group. The couple wasn't talking much but listened with polite attention. Connie sympathized with them. Finn must be much on their minds. A woman was telling a story about a horse she once had, that couldn't stand being mounted. His previous owner never put a blanket on his back before placing the saddle. The constant friction had resulted in a large sore. Even after the woman bought him and cleared up the abscess, she had to be careful not to pull on the saddle when mounting, for the horse always remembered his tormented back.

Everyone nodded; the long memory of a horse is common knowledge. Someone else had started a story about a roan mare when Connie saw movement at the entrance to the parlor and turned to see who had come in.

It was Tony Stephens.

Cary and Pam moved to meet him. His dark eyes ranged over the crowd. A superbly tailored dark suit and a glaringly white shirt set off by a Sulka tie did nothing to hide his weightlifter's body. His thick, black hair with its extravagant waves was perfectly cut. He wore a diamond ring.

Connie's skin crawled.

Now Tony saw Connie. He started toward her but was waylaid by a fawning feed store owner who did a lucrative business with the master of Fayence. Dismissing him with a few curt words, Tony forced his way through the crowd and came to Connie's side.

"I want to talk to you," he said.

She stepped apart from the group, dreading what he would say. Had he found out from Buck that she had stayed two hours? Worse still, had he fired Buck?

"I talked to the old man," he started.

"You mean Buck, don't you?"

Staring into her eyes, he said, "Yes. He told me how much you know, how good you are at your job." With an effort, almost stammering, he said, "I guess, uh, I was wrong. You can come out to the place any time I need you."

Connie felt a rush of anger. *Patronizing. Allowing me to do my work.*

"All right, Mr. Stephens. Let's hope there isn't any occasion soon when I have to look at your horses," she said lightly, and moved away before he could answer.

She joined Gyp and her husband who were looking at an excellent copy of a Stubbs painting over the divan. "I really need to join you two." Gyp glanced over to where Stephens stood motionless, staring at Connie with closed face. "What did you say to him, Connie?"

"Nothing. I just replied gracefully when he told me he guessed I know something after all and he would let me come to Fayence next time he has a problem. You remember how he threw me off his place. The other day I went back up there to look at his horse. I had to flatter him to do my job. I just don't feel like stroking him today. I hate that stuff. I guess he doesn't know what to make of me."

The conversation turned elsewhere and after a half hour, Connie decided to leave for home. She thanked Cary and Pam and as she retrieved her coat she noticed Jase, Pres, and Stephens talking. Oddly, Stephens had no resident veterinarian at his farm, but summoned vets whenever one was needed. She knew Stephens employed Jase and Pres most often, but also used others. Everyone was disgusted with this practice. It seemed he was playing them off against one another for his own profit. Yet he paid his bills in full and on time. And he created a lot of work for vets and farriers.

She opened the front door and went out, shivering as she got into her cold truck.

* * *

By seven o'clock, the guests had all gone. Daisy and her crew were busy, so to find a quiet space, Cary and Pam took a pot of tea to the office. They sat close to one another on the sofa, talking of their successful party and the new colt.

At the first pause in the conversation, Pam took his hand and asked, "What's the matter, dear? There's been something wrong for the past couple of weeks."

Cary looked at her calm face for a moment, thinking as he always did how lucky he was to have Pam as his wife.

"I want to tell you about two horses," he began.

* * *

Rod drove the truck up the side road that led to Beau's house. Neither had talked much on the way home.

"Did you have a good time, Beau?" he asked.

The boy shrugged. "I guess so. The food was good." And then, remembering his manners, he gave Rod a shy smile and said, "Thanks for taking me."

At the outset, Rod had intended to skip Cary's gala affair, afraid he couldn't bear the noise and festivity. But at the last minute, thinking of his self-imposed seclusion, which he was slowly coming to realize wasn't healthy, and Beau's stunted social skills, he had decided they might benefit from the party. Whenever his mind could pull itself away from Donna's death and his failing farm, worry about the boy took over. Although Beau wasn't his son—he and Donna had been childless—he had come to love him. He looked over at the silent boy. *Coming to the farm seems to be the only life he has. I'll have to talk to Ed and Marta about Beau. Maybe we can all come up with something to help him.* One thing he did know, Beau would do anything for him.

* * *

As Tony Stephens drove back up US 29 toward Fayence, he thought about the way he had acted at the party. As usual, he was unhappy about it.

He thought about how he had tried to find out what was the matter with him. Ten years ago—torn between his obsessive memories of his former life and the inarticulate, solitary man he was—he had consulted a noted Denver doctor. He needed answers. He had never dreamed he would ever consult a psychiatrist; he could solve his own problems. But he knew he couldn't explain the mystery that was himself. Why did he seem doomed to go over and over his life in the dying city in the north? Why couldn't he interact in a normal way with other people?

After a few months' therapy, he had stopped going. Dr. Rains had implored him to continue, but Tony was convinced that the sessions of what he considered aimless talking with no immediate results were useless. Tony solved problems quickly, efficiently, ruthlessly, and when the doctor told him it might take years to discover the truth, Tony quit in frustration. He had learned one important thing about himself, though. The anger that always lay just under the surface was deep, and it had a lot to do with his isolation from others. He realized he would have to spend the rest of his life trying to control that rage. He wished he had McCutcheon's easy ways.

He put aside the ever-present dissatisfaction with himself and thought about Connie Holt. He'd found it hard to look away from her at the party. He had stared at her hair flaming around her face, and the way the emerald suit complemented her dark blue eyes. He thought back to the first time he'd seen her. She'd worn an ugly old Stetson, a shapeless coat and stained boots. When he told her not to come back the next time he needed an agent, she'd lost her temper and stormed off. His overwhelming impression of Connie had been that she was a hot-tempered woman trying to do a man's job. The next time she came to Fayence, he'd seen only a tall, rather thin woman who didn't flare up this time but flattered him into accepting her services. When he realized later that her flattery was a ploy to regain her footing as a professional person he'd accept at his farm, he'd respected her for it. He'd thought it best to have a private investigator look into her background, a habit of his when someone managed to get the best of him. The investigator's report was short, but Tony learned about the decaying northern city where she'd been born and lived with her husband, her job as a high school science teacher, and her two grown children. Her driver's license revealed she was 5' 10" tall and weighed 135 pounds. Out of curiosity, he'd had Mike Holt traced as well. After reading that report, which told him that Holt was out west trying to be a computer consultant and failing, he'd concluded that Holt was a loser and Connie was well rid of him.

When he'd approached her at the party, he'd intended to let her know he'd been wrong about her, to apologize— something that was almost impossible for him to do. Connie was wearing high heels, and their eyes were almost level. When he started to speak, her beautiful face—for he had discovered that Connie was beautiful—had unnerved him. The words had come out wrong. She had made it very clear what she thought of him when she said she hoped she wouldn't have to look at his horses soon. He'd seen the barely suppressed anger in her face. He shook his head at the memory and drove on.

He had never met anyone like her. *All the women I've ever been with had dollar signs in their eyes*, he thought. *She's smart too. But she doesn't like me.*

* * *

"Les, I have to talk to you about the house," said Jase, interrupting her excited comments about the party. They were driving home to Monroe.

"Oh, not again, Jase. If you're going to complain, I don't want to listen."

"Well, you're trapped in the car until we get home, honey, so you're going to have to be patient."

She didn't smile.

"Please hear me, Les. What I'm telling you is the truth and you're going to have to face it. The house is costing too much. I'm almost tapped out. The man from the Lynchburg Historical Foundation analyzed the whole project carefully, and we made up our minds that it would take many years before the house was done. We also agreed—if you remember—that we would take it very slowly, one step at a time, so we could afford it. Do you remember, Les?"

"You agreed, you mean," she replied. "But Jase, it's coming along so well. I finally found someone who can recreate the fanlight. You don't know how hard it is to find craftsmen to do that kind of work."

"I ought to. You've talked about it enough. But we've got other responsibilities. Your horses, for one. Their feed, the upkeep of the pasture. And you're always buying clothes you don't need. I don't make enough for everything you want. I've had to start seeing small animals at the clinic for added income, and I'm worn out what with all the work."

"Well, I work too."

"Your salary at the museum is too small to help very much, Les."

He softened his tone. He knew from her sulky mouth that he was coming on too strong.

"Please, darling, please help me on this. Make up your mind that the house will have to be improved by very small stages. And another thing. Don't ask your parents for any more money. That embarrasses me. They're not flush either."

He forestalled her reply. "I know what you're going to talk about. The glorious Wingfield history. Your family used to be rich two hundred years ago. Like that ass, Pres Carter."

Her mouth tightened. She kept her eyes on the light snow dusting the windshield.

He tried once more.

"I need you to do something about your spending, Les," he said.

There was no answer. Her silence was full of unsaid, ugly things.

* * *

Pres Carter drove toward home. His wife was gushing about the party but he was only listening enough to make appropriate noises when needed. Between the woman he'd been seeing and the satisfaction of restoring his old house on the James, life was good except for one thing. He was short of money for completing the house. He had a trust fund but that was for sending the kids to good universities. He frowned and lost track of what his wife was saying.

Mame Carter prattled on.

Chapter Eleven

Two nights later, Bud Hurdle called Cary around midnight to say that his best horse was dangerously sick with colic. Quicksilver Magical Pete was an expensive three-year-old Arabian stallion Hurdle had barely managed to buy.

Pooling their money, Bud and a pal had driven Bud's truck and horse trailer to Fort Worth to look at a stallion the friend had seen advertised in a horseman's magazine. The two drove day and night, not even stopping at a motel. An impoverished rancher sold Pete to the two sweat-stained, bad-breathed Virginians for $10,000. Pete was spectacular to look at and his papers were impressive.

The two men drove back to Campbell County, talking all the way home about how they would train Pete and make a killing from renting him out to service mares. Pete hadn't proven himself yet, so Cary insured him for only $30,000. The horse was well-known in Central Virginia for his beauty and potential.

"Mary Evans has been out," Bud said when he called Cary. "Injected Pete. Seems like he's got less pain. She put a tube in. No results yet."

The other agents were sick, out of town, or otherwise tied up, and Connie caught the call.

She had been feeling out of sorts—chills and joint pains—and she groaned as she put on her warm clothes, hoping she didn't have the flu that was making its rounds at the office.

In the driveway, another problem awaited her. It had rained earlier and now a glaze of ice covered every inch of her truck. It took almost half an hour to clear the encrusted windows as the defroster circulated feeble gusts of tepid air. *Something wrong with the whole heating system,* she thought. *I better get it checked.* She felt guilty. She never took the truck in unless it was an emergency. She ought to follow the prescribed maintenance schedule but she was always too busy. Besides, she hated the dealership, where customers were consigned to the torture of a tiny waiting room with bitter coffee, blaring television, and a magazine rack filled with nothing but publications for auto salesmen.

When the handle of her plastic scraper broke, she did too. "Oh, hell, hell, hell!" she yelled into the night. She was immediately ashamed of herself. Then she smiled. Her reaction had to be a holdover from her beloved puritanical mother who had made her children say "heck" instead of the forbidden term.

Finally, the truck was ready, but as she drove toward Hurdle Farm in Campbell County, it started to snow. She strained her eyes to see the road as the window wipers sang their inane tune.

She inserted a CD of Christmas songs by Mel Torme′ and turned up the volume to its highest. The perfectly pitched, melodic, sweet voice filled the truck, and for a while she let herself be charmed.

Her mind drifted to Christmas morning, when she'd ceremoniously set up her cup of tea and a couple of Gyp's famous sticky buns, open the Texas and New Hampshire boxes, and call the kids to say thank you. She'd tell them she was planning to visit in the spring.

But tonight, not even the "Christmas Song" could divert her mind very long from the problem of the horse she was soon to see.

Connie had first learned about colic when a favorite horse she had ridden as a teenager died of it. She knew the word "colic" is an all-purpose term that covers a number of stomach problems a horse can have because of his tricky digestive system. His stomach is small compared to his overall size. He's unable to vomit. And to make matters worse, his cecum, where fermentation takes place, is located after the small intestine, making the whole digestive process inefficient. If a horse overeats or ingests spoiled hay, there's a good chance he'll get sick.

And I bet that explains Pete's colic, she thought, as she traveled through the snow and ice.

Hurdle was tight with a dollar. He didn't worm his horses often enough even though he knew full well worms can cause aneurysms in the intestines, slowing down an already cumbersome digestive process. Sometimes he fed his horses moldy hay. Worming medicine and good quality hay cost money he didn't want to spend. Everyone knew Bud Hurdle would sacrifice the well-being of his horses to save a buck.

His tightfistedness extended everywhere. His horses lived out their lives in barely maintained barns with inadequate lighting, both inside and outside. *Bud's going to lose that great horse some day through neglect,* thought Connie. His neighbors and vet and Cary had tried to point out the danger. Bud always reacted the same way: confused embarrassment. Then he would go back to his slipshod ways.

From what Hurdle had said, the vet had inserted a tube in the horse's stomach and pumped in oil to help the impacted matter make its way through Pete's digestive system. If it had been a twisted intestine, an often-deadly complication of colic, Evans probably would have operated by now. Connie didn't like to think of any horse dying the painful death that an intestine twisted around itself will cause. Even with surgery, gangrene may result since the blood supply to the area has been choked off.

Finally she reached Hurdle Farm and turned into the entrance road.

Immediately, she was in trouble.

A car coming the other way rushed toward her, wheels sliding on the icy surface. For a moment, the driver, startled by the truck's unexpected appearance, lost control of the wheel, and the car lurched toward her. Dazzled by the glare of the car's high-beam headlights, Connie fought to keep her truck on the road. If she swerved to the right, she'd plunge into a deep ditch. Expecting the worst, she braced herself for the crash. But miraculously, there was none. The driver made a desperate attempt to regain control of the car—and succeeded. It made its way to the main road, turned left, and disappeared.

She had no idea who had almost killed her, only a vague impression of a large, dark car.

Teeth clenched, she forced herself to drive slowly until she pulled into the open space outside Hurdle's barn and came to a stop. Her hands were gripping the wheel so tightly that she had to steel herself to disengage them. Finally she was able to get out of the truck. But as she looked at the barn, her breath caught. The doors were gaping open.

Hurdle came running from the house.

"Glad you're here. Pete's really sick."

"Bud! Who just pulled down the driveway?"

"What? What are you talking about?"

In the dim light, the farmer's face was white and strained.

"I just saw someone in a dark car, nearly ran me down. And the barn doors are open!"

For a moment, he just looked at Connie, as if he couldn't take in what she was shouting.

Then he turned to stare, open-mouthed, at the yawning doors.

"I thought I closed them," he said.

Both ran into the barn, the fear that she would find Pete dead closing up Connie's throat.

The door to Pete's stall was ajar.

Pete lay in the hay and muck. But he was still breathing, his heavy wheezing clearly audible. The fact that the horse was down didn't bother Connie. Horses with colic often get up and lie down repeatedly. And it looked as if the oil had worked.

"Mind if I go into the stall, Bud?"

"Go ahead."

"When's the last time you saw Pete?"

"About three hours ago, when Mary Evans was here."

She looked closer at the miserable horse lying in the inadequate, foul stall and tried to contain her anger at Bud. *He doesn't deserve this horse, let alone the other horses he owns*, she thought. Ignoring Bud, she decided after a few minutes that colic was the horse's only problem. She couldn't find anything that indicated an attempt on his life.

Just then, Mary Evans of Carter's Large Animal Service entered the barn.

Connie waited as the vet examined Pete.

"He's no worse than he was when I saw him earlier," Evans said. "I know he sounds bad, but he looks a little better. Got rid of the fecal mass, too."

Beside her, Hurdle's breath expelled in relief.

"I'll call you later, Bud," said Connie, not wanting to wait until the vet left. She was feeling very sick now. Hurdle nodded.

As Connie walked out of the barn, she heard the vet scolding Hurdle for his carelessness with his horses. "You probably caused this yourself. What was it? Bad hay again like the last time?"

Good for you, Mary, thought Connie.

* * *

He was sitting in his hiding place in Campbell County. The entire shift had been a waste of time. Only one hapless motorist had passed him by, going an unexciting 57 miles an hour. He'd debated whether to stop him and issue a citation. But hell, it was snowing and guys were having a hard time. He'd give the motorist in the gray Honda a break this time. He felt virtuous.

Hell, it was so cramped in the cruiser. He shifted his bulk and looked at his watch. Only half an hour before he could leave what he thought of as his "duck blind." He wondered if there was anything left in the takeout he'd gotten earlier. His big hand ranged the dashboard, grabbed the greasy bag. Still a few chips in the bottom. A little coffee. In defiance of the police doc who'd told him at his recent checkup he was too fat, he'd stopped at Kroger's and bought cheesecake to go with his dinner. He'd eaten that first, even before the bacon cheeseburger. He took a sip of the coffee. His thin lips twisted with the acrid sludge in the bottom of the polystyrene cup. Like battery acid. Why wouldn't Emily make him a lunch and thermos of good coffee like she used to? She just didn't want to bother any more, but he was her husband. She could do that much for him.

Emily. The quarrel before leaving for work. Just one of many. She used to be so happy when they were first married. He remembered her on their wedding day at the old country church in Buchanan County. Tiny waist, delicate wrists. And her hair. There was so much of it, pale and thick and long. She used to laugh when he'd touch it with his ham-fisted hands. Her dress that day, he could still remember it. She'd been only sixteen years old, no experience of men, and so her dress was white. Her mother had made it since the family was poor and couldn't afford anything store-bought. Their parents had been proud of them both, Jack already a member of the Lynchburg police and ambitious to be a trooper some day, Emily devoted only to being a wife and having children.

Abruptly then, in the middle of the lovely memory, he scowled.

How much did she weigh now, he wondered?

225? 250?

When they went to Kroger's, she waddled through the aisles slowly, her dress working its way up in the back, exposing her unlovely legs with the flesh from her huge thighs hanging down. She took so long to choose each food he could scream. She had to check the file of coupons in the gray plastic box she always carried with her, shaking with excitement when she found a delicious bargain. He regretted now he'd forbidden her to take driving lessons. He'd suggested recently that she learn, but she wasn't having any. "You drive me wherever I want to go," she'd said.

Their five kids gone, with kids of their own. Never invited their parents to visit them.

Today he'd tried to interest her in Weight Watchers. Because he still loved her, he tried not to say she was ugly to him because of her weight, although he couldn't stand to touch her any more. But she'd known what he meant and turned on him, told him he was just as repulsive to her. Screamed at him that having all those kids had done it to her and that weight ran in her family. She couldn't help it. She'd gone on making the cookies for the coffee hour at church all through the argument, forming the dough into round shapes. When she wasn't eating it.

My life is pretty bad, he thought. *No home life, no sex, nowhere to go in this job.*

Ah, forget it.

He stared out the windshield, hoping now for someone to nail, his good feeling of benevolence gone. Suddenly, he stiffened. There it was, her truck. He'd have some fun tonight after all.

* * *

When Wampler's cruiser emerged from its hiding place and slid into the road behind her, it was almost an anticlimax after the events at Hurdle Farm, Connie thought grimly. Only a few miles more and she would have been home.

The siren wailed, the blue lights flashed.

He wasn't smiling as he walked to the truck. She let the window down a little.

"I'm pretty tired, I might have that flu going around," she said. "No time to talk." She couldn't act the role of friendly motorist tonight. She felt too wretched. She knew she was sick and the near-accident at Hurdle's had shaken her.

With growing dismay, she saw his lips tighten at the coldness in her voice.

"Look, Red, I've shown I like you, and you're not showing no interest in me. You ain't got no one, I checked you out."

She hesitated. The fear of how he might react to the truth struck her in the pit of her stomach like the blow of a massive fist.

I'm so tired of this, she thought.

Her bones ached and she had a sudden chill.

"I'm sorry, Jack, but I'm just not interested in getting to know you better. And besides, aren't you a married man?"

At once, she knew she had gone too far.

His face darkened with rage.

"What the hell business is that of yours? It don't matter if I'm married or not. Come on now, meet me for a drink. I'm almost off shift."

"No," she said.

"I'm goin' to keep after you and after you until you give in, Red. You can't get away from me. And if you got any idea of turning me in, I'll say you're making it up. And you'll look like a fool."

With that, he strode back to his cruiser, gunned the motor, and pulled past her, coming so close to her truck there was almost a collision.

Connie started driving again, maintaining a fierce concentration on the road. Finally home, she made a mug of hot lemon juice and whiskey, wrapped herself in a shabby but comfortable old robe she saved for times like these, and got into bed. One down comforter wasn't enough—she piled on another. Her eyes felt as if there were sand under her eyelids. Her temples pulsed with pain, and her stomach churned with nausea. Alternate waves of heat and cold rolled over her.

Desperate for sleep, she closed her eyes, but her anxious mind wouldn't allow her to drop off. She went over and over what had happened tonight and the evidence in the deaths of Woolwine and Finn. She was certain in her mind now that the two horses had been murdered. And Job Hoskins had died too. Since his death occurred as the result of a crime, it might very well be considered a homicide. If that was so, the murderer had killed a human being as well as the horses. Further, she was convinced that the driver of the dark car, who had almost run her down, had been at Hurdle Farm to kill Quicksilver Magical Pete. But Pete was still alive.

Cary hadn't said openly that they were dealing with murder yet, but she knew the way his mind worked in a matter as serious as this one. Occasionally, the McCutcheon Agency had to deal with mistreatment of horses; one case Connie couldn't forget involved torture. In this case, as in the earlier ones, he would be reluctant to conclude too hastily that someone he might know could have committed terrible crimes against horses. But this time, a man had died too. Cary had to think the whole thing through carefully before he reached a decision. He had to be sure he was right. Once he finally made up his mind that murder had been committed, he would act swiftly to find the truth. She knew, too, that he would work only with the agent who had discovered the crime. He believed in keeping an investigation of this enormity as confidential as possible, even within the Agency. She would just have to wait until he acknowledged the crimes to her. Then they would work on the investigation together.

And there was Wampler. What was she going to do about him?

She turned on her side, straightened out her aching legs, and thought about going to see her children when the weather was nicer. They were always glad when she could come.

Finally, she drifted off into a troubled sleep.

Chapter Twelve

When she awoke the next morning, her head was still reeling, stomach still churning. She sat on the side of the bed and called Gyp at the office to tell her she was sick.

"Is there anything I can do, Connie? Want me to come by and make you some soup?"

"No thanks, Gyp. My stomach is so queasy I couldn't hold a thing down. I'll just get back in bed and try to get some more sleep. But I do have to have a word with Cary before I collapse."

"Sure, Connie, he's right here."

Hurry up, hurry up, Cary, she thought.

Cary's voice boomed over the telephone. "Gyp tells me you're sick. Take all the time you need, Connie. We'll survive here. Do you want any help? Do you need anything? Pam and I will drop over…"

"Not necessary, Cary. But I need to talk to you about the Hurdle case."

Cary listened quietly without interrupting.

"Mary Evans thinks Pete is better, but was yelling at Bud about bad hay as I left," she finished.

Quick, hard, sharp words crackled over the wire as Cary told her what he thought of the closefisted farmer.

"I agree. And something else. Obviously the person in the dark car wasn't a friend of Bud's. Bud didn't even know he'd been there. Why else could that person have been there but to harm Bud's horse? I know Bud went in with one of his cronies to buy that horse. Pete is worth a lot of money. Like Woolwine and Finn."

"I told Bud he was a fool when he did that. He isn't in any financial shape to go into the breeding business. And of course he's put Janey and the kids in danger with his half-assed schemes. I had to insure Pete, because Bud's a long-time client. But I hate the way he treats his horses and his family."

His voice became flat and hard.

"If the killer had succeeded, Bud would have lost everything. Connie, when you get better, I want to talk to you about the three horses, Woolwine, Finn, and Pete."

When Connie heard the word "killer," she knew Cary was now convinced that the two horses had been murdered, and an attempt made on the third. That's why he was withholding settlement payments to Rod Payson and the Lathams.

She wanted to keep talking about the murders, but a wave of nausea hit her stomach again. "I'll call you as soon as I can, Cary," she said.

Connie had been struck with the flu before and preferred to suffer through it alone, although appreciating friends' desire to help. Knowing she'd be in and out of bed for a while, she was glad she'd visited a used book store in Lynchburg around Thanksgiving and stocked up on paperbacks to tide her over the Christmas season.

Like many other single people, she had a hard time on holidays. Her world seemed to be entirely populated by married couples, and even though she was invited to a lot of holiday parties, and attended out of duty, she always seemed to be the odd woman out. She'd formed the habit of coming late and leaving early.

Connie had given up on remarrying. *No one would be interested in me*, she often thought. *My job is demanding. I'm on the road all the time. Never was very skilled at cooking, hate vacuuming and scrubbing, although I'll do it because I like my house clean. I don't fit into the "wife" niche.* All the same, she wished Cary had an unmarried brother.

After three days she felt sufficiently better to eat chicken soup and crackers, and was spending less time in bed. But the horses' deaths never left her mind. Even at her sickest, fragments of the mystery, like sharp, odd-shaped pieces of glass that wouldn't fit together, pierced her mind. She had no doubt the motive for the deaths must have been financial profit from an insurance settlement.

But how had the murders been done?

When she'd been new on the job, she came across a short article in an equine magazine about killing horses. She remembered the horror she felt as she read about the electrocution of a tired old animal whose owner no longer had any use for him. Learning about how horses could be killed was part of her job, so she found out as much as she could. When she finished compiling the information, she realized that there still wasn't much on the subject. Not a lot of people wrote about murdering horses. She had only been able to read through the grisly collection of articles once. Then she had put the file away, hoping she would never have to use it.

However, the methods she read about stayed in her mind and she looked for certain indications on a dead horse's body every time she did her examination in the stall or in the field. To her relief, she had never found any of the tell-tale marks on any horse, including Woolwine, Finn, or Pete.

After breakfast on the fourth morning, she took the file into her bedroom. A few rays of cheerless sun shone through the window. She got into bed, pulled the comforter over her, and began to read.

Later, unable to continue reading, Connie went to the kitchen and prepared a mug of strong black tea. She took it and the file to the big round table she used as a desk; she was tired of lying in bed. She could hardly bear the stories of equine murder, but knew she had to finish reading them to see if any of the methods could have been used in the deaths of Woolwine and Finn.

As Connie read the cases, she found that although the circumstances might differ, two details were always the same. The motive was the insurance payoff that followed the death of a high-dollar horse. Maybe a jumper grew too old to leap over a hurdle. Or a racehorse showed promise as a three-year-old but fizzled on the track. With no return on an investment, animals like these were too expensive to maintain. Owners then sought to recoup their fortunes by killing their "inconvenient" horses. The tragic stories were linked by another fact: the horses always suffered as they were killed.

The killing methods varied, but all were merciless and amoral, Connie decided. No amount of insurance money justified such cruelty.

There was a clipping about Sandy, for instance, who contracted life-threatening colic. His owner withheld care, a sure-fire way to collect a payout since the policy on the horse didn't stipulate that no payment would be made in colic cases. If the policy had mentioned colic, the owner could have killed Sandy the same way Sunshine City died—by electrocution, a method that mimics a colic death. Sunny's killer knew the method had the twin advantages of being both quick and hard to detect. He cut a common extension cord down the middle, producing two lengths of wire. Then he fastened alligator clips to the wires and attached them to the horse's ear and rectum. He then plugged the cord into a socket. Sunny dropped to the floor, suffering a moment of agony. Another horse, Kevin M., was wired to a 110-volt fuse box and put in a pool of water, where he died of electrocution.

Vets examining the bodies of both horses should have suspected electrocution had occurred when they found singe marks from the clips on Sunny and marks inside Kevin's nose. If they were suspicious, they could have performed a rigorous examination of the horses' brains, which would have validated a finding of murder by electrocution. Both vets were deceived, and both insurance companies paid up.

Joshua Jericho was murdered in a risky way, but a post mortem detected it and the murderer and instigator were punished. Josh's dorsal aorta was cut and he bled to death. This could have only been done by a person intimately acquainted with the horse's physiology, who knew the location of the artery—high up in back of the abdomen, about two feet—and had the skill to reach it internally.

After heavily sedating the horse, the killer cut the artery. Josh died slowly. An equine insurance agent was suspicious when he saw a trickle of blood issuing from the horse's rectum, and voiced his doubts to his agency, resulting in a post mortem performed by a doctor not connected with the case.

Subsequent investigation discovered that the horse's vet, in collusion with the owner, had cut the aorta.

Several stories concerned racehorses killed by infection. A murderer who knew horse anatomy punctured the bladder of a worn-out race horse named Henry with a coat hangar. Henry died, after long suffering, from a massive infection. The killer was never found and there was a large insurance payout. Injections of toxic material were also used. Another settlement came when it was thought but not proved that an injection of parasitic bloodworms caused a racehorse to die from thromboembolic colic.

Two other racehorses Connie read about suffered infection and death after fecal matter, in the first instance, and turpentine in the second, were injected into their knees; in those cases, the killers were both stable hands, identified by witnesses of the incidents.

In another case, a trainer, impatient to get rid of a disappointing horse, pierced the animal's leg with a rusty nail. Fortunately, the vet found the piercing tool in the stall. The trainer confessed. The horse just barely pulled through. The insurance agency escaped paying settlements.

Asphyxiation was suspected in the case of Martha Sue, a broodmare, but the evidence was gone. Ping pong balls could have been stuffed up her nose or a plastic bag put over her head. A vet who did the post mortem had no choice but to determine that the animal died of pulmonary distress. The insurance company had to pay.

Two other cases described bizarre methods of killing horses. A stable hand confessed to putting two Alka-Seltzers in Rudy's oats, and his stomach exploded. Rudy's owner had paid the hand to "get rid of that nag." The perpetrators were punished. No payment was made. Another horse died from ingesting something in a salt lick. Bismuth was suspected but couldn't be substantiated. Green Racer's owner rejoiced in the payout.

Another method involved a crippled racehorse who was given a massive insulin injection that caused his blood sugar to drop. He died. An astute pathologist picked it up and the owner was punished. No settlement.

Connie went on to several more articles in which the owners, anxious to get their hands on the insurance money, chose other ways to kill their horses. Everyone knows that a horse's leg is vulnerable. When a horse breaks his leg in an accident—real or feigned by a killer—there is a good chance he might have to be euthanized. Swinging a crowbar or a sledgehammer like a bat, it didn't take much for a killer to break Rag Time Blues' leg in a remote pasture. The leg dangled helplessly, and the horse, screaming with pain, reared and then somehow struggled to his feet and tried to run away. He ran and fell, ran and fell, until he collapsed. He was found six hours later, but by that time, it was too late. He had to be euthanized. The suspicious insurance company stood its ground and refused to pay, saying there was no evidence that the horse had an accident that could have caused his injury. The owner sued, but the company was upheld in court. However, it could not be proved that the owner was guilty because the hired killer was never found.

Another horse named William was hit in the head with a hammer by its trainer and succumbed. Fortunately the owner's daughter came upon the scene, saw everything, and ran screaming to the house. The trainer was arrested and confessed. But there was no settlement. Payment for murder was not in the insurance policy.

The last group of articles detailed a number of suspicious horse deaths by fire in which the murderers were never caught. In one crime, a horse was killed in a stable fire. An equine insurance agent found cigarette butts in the ruins. In another case, a horse named Duffy Jones burned to death in his trailer. A strong smell of lighter fluid hung over the death scene. The two owners were investigated, for it was suspected that they may have wanted to substitute a worthless corpse for a valuable one. But the burned carcasses couldn't be identified as the original insured horses; nothing could be proved. The owner of the first horse never filed for payment. But Duffy's owner said the corpse in the trailer was not Duffy but his champion steeplechaser, and he received a large insurance payment.

Connie closed the file. She had learned that horses can be murdered by anyone in their small world, owners, trainers, vets, riders, even professional horse killers. In their greed for insurance settlements, people would go to any length to kill a horse. The insurance companies often paid when the deaths were doubtful, because there was no proof of exactly how the horse had been killed or who the murderer was.

Reflecting on the methods used, Connie combed her memory. No, she hadn't seen any tell-tale marks on the bodies of Woolwine, Finn, or Pete. There hadn't been any evidence in the stalls like needles or other foreign material. The matter-of-fact reports written by Pres Carter and Jase Tyree suggested unsuspected heart problems in the two dead horses. There was no mention of anything questionable.

But Connie thought she knew how the horses were killed. She just didn't have the specifics.

Now she decided she would go to a movie. She'd try to put all the tragic deaths out of her mind—at least for a couple of hours. While she dressed, her eyes fell on the framed lines from *Henry V*:

> "Think when we talk of horses that you see them
> Printing their proud hoofs i' the receiving earth."

She thought of Jase, his love and respect for horses, his dedication to helping them survive in the world of men.

But someone had murdered Woolwine and Finn, the identity of the killer and the details of the deaths yet to be discovered.

Who was it?

She could not believe that anyone in her circle of friends or clients could be capable of such savagery.

Chapter Thirteen

On this same cold December morning, Tony Stephens entered one of the barns, a duty he hated. If Stephens had his way, he'd sit in his opulent house and never set foot in the stable. Through the years, he had managed to develop a superficial aesthetic sense of what was considered beautiful in houses and art. But it didn't extend to the horse. He saw nothing pleasing about the horse's body, nothing of beauty in the large, liquid eyes or the elegant curve of the back. And the sights, the activities, and especially the smells in the barn disgusted him. He particularly despised the sight of the men raking manure and piling it into a malodorous mound for spreading in the gardens later.

To Stephens the horse was a means to make money and to gain entrée into a prestigious world where he might achieve wealth and power, but above all, status. He would belong. Out of necessity, much of his adult life had been spent in the shadows. Now he wanted to be respectable, to count for something. He felt he had earned the right. That, above all, was what had induced him to leave Denver and start over again in Albemarle County.

Today, he had to be here in the barn. Jase Tyree was coming to Fayence to examine a valuable pregnant mare named Dogwood Dancer of the Blue Ridge. It was important that Tony follow her progress, for she was one of many mares who had been bred by the man-made system he had installed at the farm. His future depended on the successful production of foals by mares like this little one in the stall. After a cursory look at the horse through the bars, Stephens stood in the aisle, waiting for Jase to come. *Why the hell can't these guys be on time?* Irritated, he folded his arms around his body.

It was cold like this, he remembered, when he had watched the mating of his prize stallion with this small gray mare all those months before.

Stephens had prepared for the difficulties of bringing mares to successful births by consulting experts. He had finally decided to use a man-made system of breeding, convinced by a Kentucky master who endorsed the method. Stephens would breed the finest horses by the most complicated of processes. Tony knew that all breeding is a gamble, with any number of threatening variables. But it was the risk that interested him; he had always liked a business venture with an element of danger.

When he started the farm, the first thing Tony learned was that the gestation period for a mare is almost one year, and he had to decide which method he would use for breeding—natural or man-made. In the first method, broodmares are bred in their natural periods of heat. That meant that Stephens could only breed from April through October. But Tony's mentor said if the man-made system were used, it would be possible to breed mares beginning in February and ending in

July, more advantageous than the traditional breeding period, which many people like Rod Payson preferred. Rod liked foaling to occur in spring, when weather and forage would be most profitable for the foals.

Most breed registries and Thoroughbred racing associations designate January 1 as the universal birth date. Foals born during the year become yearlings on the following January 1.

Hence early foals—born early in the year—are more valuable than those born later. More mature physically, early foals have a better chance to be champions at competition. It was to Stephens's economic advantage, then, to breed as many early foals as possible. Owners of expensive broodmares who chose to do business with Stephens were told that at Fayence, their mares' natural physiologic breeding patterns would be "adjusted" in order to produce the finest foals.

In Stephens's system, a mare's adjusted breeding time was brought about by manipulating the amount of light she received. Dogwood Dancer was exposed to a longer photoperiod by using a combination of natural and artificial light. This shortened her winter anestrus, or period of infertility, and advanced her follicle growth by about two months. The follicle was the structure within her ovary that would hold an egg. Because artificial light only advances the date of the follicle development and not of ovulation itself, Dogwood Dancer was given human chorionic gonadotropin to improve the chances of successful ovulation.

She lived in sixteen hours of continuous light per day, both natural and artificial, until natural daylight reached about sixteen hours. The lighting program had started between November 15 and December 1 the year before. Fortunately, Dogwood Dancer ovulated, and was ready to be impregnated. She would be hand bred—a complicated and dangerous procedure. Guided by his mentor's advice, Stephens had chosen hand breeding rather than letting Doggie stand in the pasture and take her chances with one of the stallions. He could have also chosen artificial insemination, where the stallion would mount what looked like a gym horse and ejaculate. His sperm would then be injected into the mare. From a business aspect, a big benefit of hand breeding, Stephens learned, is that the method uses the stallion's time efficiently, since he can be booked for servicing many mares. And Stephens had taken this to heart, instructing his manager to schedule his most valuable stallion, Darley Bulwer-Lytton, for as many trysts as he could.

Stephens had been tutored in the art of hand breeding—mating between a stallion and mare, assisted by farm personnel—by the Kentucky master. One thing he had insisted on was that the procedure must be sanitary. Doggie, the name by which the little mare had inevitably become known among her handlers, would stand a better chance of avoiding a venereal infection, unlike her humbler counterpart, May, now standing in Rod Payson's pasture. And the handlers, he cautioned, must be experienced enough to keep the animals from injuring one another. Stephens understood what was involved in hand breeding but that didn't mean he wanted to witness it.

On the day of Doggie's mating, Stephens went to the breeding shed and stood waiting for the process to begin, gritting his teeth. He smelled the mingled odors and felt sick: pungent manure, musty sweat of the hands' oddly assorted but highly practical clothing, and urine-soaked shavings in the stalls. He clenched his hands in their pigskin gloves and forced himself to watch the coupling that would soon begin.

He was here, he reminded himself again, because he should be, as master of Fayence, and because he knew the men would do a better job in his intimidating presence.

He was right.

He liked his stallion's name, at least. Darley Bulwer-Lytton. It smacked of British aristocracy. The stud fee for BL, as the hands affectionately called the horse, was $5,000.00 every time he covered a mare. Today, hopefully, BL would impregnate Doggie.

Leila Masters, Doggie's owner and a seventy-five-year old widow who lived on Park Street in Charlottesville, still loved breeding her horses. If a foal resulted from today's mating, she would trumpet Fayence far and wide. And Stephens's reputation would be made.

The handlers were variously occupied, waiting for the event to start. Some spoke a few words to each other, and two leaned against the walls and stared at nothing. They were trying to control their tension so the horses wouldn't pick it up. Everybody knew what happened in a breeding shed could never be prophesied. The horses in the stalls nearby, their sensitive ears moving back and forth like soft, furry antennae, nickered nervously, aware something momentous was afoot.

Stephens thought, *What are they waiting for? Why don't they just get the whole thing over?*

Jase Tyree came in, medical bag in hand. He nodded, said nothing, but stationed himself close to the breeding area. His job would be to watch the procedure, and be ready to act quickly if anything happened to the two horses. It was possible the frightened mare might kick BL in the penis, destroying his ability at stud, and with it, part of Stephens's projected fortune. Or the stallion, even with several people trying to hold him every inch of the way, might injure the mare with his hoofs. If anything bad happened to Doggie, the rich and influential widow would savage Stephens, spreading the word he let his animals get hurt.

Tony had hired the best man he could get to supervise the breeding process, Pat Morris.

Now Morris hurried in with brisk steps. A man of few words, he dominated his crew with little effort because they were awed by his skills; the stable hands obeyed him implicitly. For this, Tony was grateful. Morris nodded to Jase, who tipped his head in response.

About eleven hours earlier, Doggie had been taken to be teased by a non-breeding stallion named Joe. Doggie had stood on one side of a metal fence, Joe on the other, each attended by a handler. Nose-to-nose, they had sniffed one another. Then the little mare had turned her hindquarters to Joe, raised her tail, urinated, and displayed her labia. But since teasing is not infallible in establishing heat, Jase, taking no chances, had screened Doggie by both rectal palpation and ultrasonography.

Doggie was now ready to be bred. But it was clear to everyone who looked at the struggling horse that she was not going to cooperate. Because she remembered being bred before, she knew approximately what was going to happen. Her back shoes had been removed and she wore special felt boots. Morris had ordered that she wear a lip twitch to convince her she should stand still because so much depended on the success of this breeding encounter. She was also wearing a leather shield on her neck and back to protect her from getting bitten. Her tail had been wrapped and her reproductive area washed with mild soap and dried carefully with paper towels. Everyone knew she kicked when she was to be bred, and now she thrashed furiously. So a couple of hands rapidly hobbled her. She was free only to walk forward.

Doggie struggled against the constraints. She was panicking, her eyes rolling. The handlers brought in BL.

Morris had rehearsed his handlers in the breeding procedure, in some cases correcting parts of the technique that he thought they had performed incorrectly in their previous jobs. He had drilled into them where not to stand: between, in front of, or behind the horses. Morris knew that even experienced hands sometimes take chances.

With one handler trying to control Doggie's frenzied struggling, another led BL to the broodmare. He was careful to let her see the stallion approaching her so she could get ready.

Having been through this countless time, BL performed his part well, whinnying and curling his upper lip. He dropped his penis. One of the hands quickly washed and dried it off.

Everyone, it seemed, was ready, except Doggie. Her agitation only increased.

The stallion was led away.

"Tranq, Jase," said Morris.

"Easy, easy, Doggie." Jase's gentle voice and hands momentarily calmed Doggie and he was able to inject the tranquilizer.

"That's a good girl, sweetheart," Jase murmured. The hands were able to relax while the drug worked. In a few minutes, Doggie looked uncoordinated.

Again, BL was led to Doggie. This time, BL, his tail slapping up and down, managed to cover the dazed mare and completed his part of the job within twenty seconds. As soon as the horse lowered himself from Doggie's back, Jase obtained a semen sample to check to make sure the stallion had ejaculated.

BL was washed again, taken out of the breeding shed, and released into a large paddock close by. Here he could run for a while warmed a little by the thin sun. People in the shed soon heard BL proclaim his content by signaling his colleagues in the other paddocks or pastures, who then responded with all the strength in their lungs.

Doggie joined other mares in a separate paddock.

Jase shook everybody's hand and smiled, then went to the lab adjoining the breeding shed. Testing the semen and finding sperm verified that BL had indeed ejaculated. He sent a man to tell Morris the good news and then left for his clinic in Monroe.

Stephens dark face was dour. He knew full well there was a long way to go until a champion foal was delivered. Doggie's pregnancy might not go well. He recalled Morris telling him that 40% to 50% of mares don't produce live foals. Uncharacteristically, he winced as he added up the number of mares in his stables who had been bred by the man-made method.

This was the biggest gamble he'd ever taken.

Now, Tony was standing outside Doggie's stall once again, waiting for Jase to finish his examination of the mare. Stephens's thoughts of the past were interrupted abruptly by Jase, who said, "She's fine, Mr. Stephens. Just fine." Tony nodded and left for the house. As he walked toward his sanctuary, he thought of everything that could still happen to the mare and her potential foal, and the other pregnant mares serviced by BL and other studs. All of this was becoming more than he had bargained for when he started the horse farm. For a moment, he let himself worry and then squared his shoulders. He'd play this hand out.

Chapter Fourteen

Rod Payson shivered, pulled his coat collar up and plunged his hands into the pockets. He was inspecting the remaining horses in the barns this morning. He felt better for the exercise, he thought, as he looked at the horses in the stalls and made sure they'd been fed. He'd already appraised the outside of his home and the general appearance of the property. *Rundown*, he thought. *I'm ashamed of it. How did I ever let it get this way?* It was all tied in with his lassitude after Donna's death.

When Donna was alive, he liked to work long hours at physical tasks. She used to laugh at him because he could never relax. There was always something else to be done on his extensive farm. But he'd slowly come to realize in the last few weeks that Donna's death had paralyzed him physically as well as emotionally. He had become a silent person whose main activity was sitting in the house, brooding. When he managed to rouse himself from his torpor, it was to work on his accounts.

He came in from the barns, went to his office, poured a cup of coffee, and once more, opened his account book. What most people didn't know, he thought, was that the farm wasn't doing well even before Donna died. There were mundane reasons—the price of feed, bad luck with foals—but mainly, some of his clients had left him, attracted by the glamour of Fayence. Rod had hidden the truth from his wife while she was enduring her last terrible pain. The constant worry about his failing business and the huge medical expenses incurred with Donna's illness intensified his torment at seeing his wife's wasted body in their bed.

Letting most of the hands go after Donna's death saved on overhead. But then depression and apathy set in. More clients went to Tony Stephens. The figures in the old green account book were dire. He became desperate for money. Then Woolwine died.

He wished Cary would make up his mind to pay the settlement. He needed it, needed it bad. *I might lose this place altogether,* he thought.

* * *

That afternoon, working on an ailing cat in his clinic in Lynchburg, Pres Carter couldn't stop thinking about what had happened that morning. He'd driven to a shabby Roanoke motel where the woman was waiting for him.

They had made love this time more wildly than ever, because they had never been able to meet in the morning before. Meeting at night was easiest. He could always make an excuse that he had to go out on business. Her husband was often away.

"I'm thirsty, darlin'," he had said. She said she was too, so they got up. After the hot sticky bed, the room was cold, so they had wrapped the wrinkled and sweaty sheets around their lower bodies. They sat on rickety aluminum chairs at the fifties-vintage Formica-covered table, sipping from cans of tepid diet cola.

Pres remembered how they didn't speak but were content just to stare at one another, satiated with each other's bodies. As he put the cat back in its carrier, Pres thought how lucky he was to have the woman.

Les understands that we don't love one another. It's all about sex. That's the way we both want it.

Chapter Fifteen

The weeks before Christmas were quiet ones for the McCutcheon Equine Insurance Agency. Only two cases needed investigation, both involving aged horses.

Cary had a long-time client, a dentist who was devoted to riding every morning, all year round, before he went to his office to dig around in root canals or get a wailing child to "Open wide, honey!" One frosty morning, George, his elderly quarter horse, was shambling along with the half-asleep dentist on his back when he suddenly decided to make a dash for freedom.

He broke into a spirited gallop that quickly changed to an all-out run. Since the horse was twenty-one and had not foisted any surprises on him for years, his rider was taken unawares.

"What the hell!" he yelled. A moment later, he lost the reins and fell off. George disappeared into the distance. Two hours after Cary got the call that the horse was missing, the owner, who was still laughing about the incident, called back. His horse had been found a couple of pastures away.

"He's okay, Cary, got a large cut across his nose. I'll take care of it. Looks like he ran up against my neighbor's barbed wire. By gosh, George has some life left in him yet!"

Dressed in an elegant robe, coffee cup in hand, Cary chuckled and said, "I'll send someone out later this morning, Walt."

The other case concerned a mare, almost twenty-seven years old, found dead in a pasture by her owner, a high school principal. The lady cried as she told Cary about it. She had bred Suzie, and the two had been loving companions all those years. When the horse's legs weakened, making riding dangerous for them both, the owner concentrated on keeping the horse happy and well-fed. "I'm so sorry, Helen," Cary said. "Someone will be out by noon."

Since the two animals had both lived in Campbell County, Cary sent only Bob King to visit the owners. He reported the incidents were routine, Suzy's death probably of natural causes due to her extreme age. Suzy's vet, Pres Carter, later confirmed Bob's conclusion. No more clients reported suspicious deaths to Cary.

At the monthly horse owners' luncheon the second week of December, a distracted Cary tried to appear interested in the usual complaints about the high price of feed and the lack of good farriers. Without vanity, Cary was sure that if anyone was privately worried about the suspicious death of a horse, he would have been consulted in private later. Cary knew he was highly respected in Central Virginia and was trusted by his colleagues.

He told no one at the restaurant of his suspicions about Woolwine and Finn. In line with standard procedure when a horse died and a settlement was pending, Rod Payson and the

Lathams had been asked not to discuss the deaths with anyone. They had kept their silence.

* * *

Connie made an effort to enjoy Christmas. She hung a Della Robbia wreath with its bright fruits on the front door and put a pale green poinsettia on the hall table.

On a Sunday afternoon, she went to Poplar Forest. One of the highlights of the Christmas season was the open house at Thomas Jefferson's second home in Bedford County. The house was designed by Jefferson himself, who was an amateur architect. He utilized the concept of the Roman villa, Andrea Palladio's rules of design, and the French use of the alcove bed, the skylight, and most modern of all, the indoor privy to create an exquisite brick hideaway of an octagonal design.

Jefferson, Connie learned, had needed a retreat. Monticello in Charlottesville had become too famous, and as a result, too uncomfortable as a residence. Many guests wanted to stay there, and the hospitable Jefferson couldn't refuse them. They often ate him out of house and home. He was in no position to entertain that lavishly. Just as bad, many local people had made nuisances of themselves, feeling perfectly free to walk up the hill on which Monticello was perched and look in the windows. In writing of Poplar Forest, Jefferson said that it might be the best dwelling in Virginia because it was the home of a private man. Connie always liked to go to the house deep in the woods and see the latest advances in its renovation.

She also dutifully wrapped the gifts for her children in silver and gold foil paper and saw them off in plenty of time to reach Texas and New Hampshire by the twenty-fourth. As usual, she worried about Cary and Pam's gift. Finally she settled on a holiday cake she saw advertised in a gourmet catalog. Her friend Gypsy was easy. She liked things from a fashionable boutique in Charlottesville, so Connie would go there.

Connie planned her trip to Charlottesville with great care. It was to be an escape from the Wampler mess, the horses' deaths, and her hopeless love for Jase. She needed to get away from the problems, if only for a little while, and hoped a change of scenery might give her a new perspective.

Since Gyp had a fondness for earrings and never seemed to wear the same pair twice, Connie would buy her a new pair at her friend's favorite store. She resolved to keep an eye out for something attractive for herself to wear too. She knew she had a tendency to maintain too small a wardrobe because she disliked clothes shopping. She would usually only buy something if there was a big event coming up, like one of Cary's parties. Connie also wanted to browse in the bookstores, hoping to find several good books for the holidays. Fond of biographies, she had heard of a highly touted new book about FDR. Perhaps she would look for that. She planned to eat lunch at a small old restaurant specializing in crepes that she had visited many times. Finally, depending on how the day had gone, she might visit some antique shops before she drove home. Once in a while she picked up something small and affordable that caught her eye.

The day of the trip started out well. For one thing, the weather wasn't as cold and there was blue sky and sunshine. And as she crossed the James to start the ninety-minute drive, she felt a welcome sense of release. She realized how strung-out she really was.

By the time Connie was ready for lunch, her big canvas shopping bag bulged. She had found an unusual pair of jasper earrings for Gyp, and the FDR biography and a murder mystery by her favorite British author for herself. She had tried on clothes at the big Barracks Hill shopping plaza and found a pair of black silk pants that fit perfectly. For once, the legs weren't too short. She even went to a local store that specialized in foods from all countries and bought some expensive chocolate bars. She would take some to the office for everyone to enjoy.

By one o'clock she was happy with what she had accomplished. But she was ravenous. She drove to the crepes restaurant and opened the familiar red door that always needed a coat of paint. Joining the end of a long line of patrons in the small foyer, she was barely able to close the door behind her. As she stood contemplating the large menu on the wall and deciding what she would order, she heard the squeak of the door's hinges as another customer entered. An instant later, someone barged into her, knocking Connie against the woman in front of her. Her heavy bag thudded to the floor.

"I'm so sorry," she said to the flustered woman.

"I'm sorry too, Connie," said a familiar masculine voice behind her.

She swung around.

It was Jase.

Connie's chest tightened for a moment.

She hesitated and then smiled. The old hurt surfaced.

The line moved forward a little. She looked to see if Les were with him. No.

She waited for him to speak.

"I live my whole life too fast, Connie. I'm always behind, always in a hurry. Did I hurt you? Here, let me pick up your bag." He groaned with mock pain. "What the heck do you have in here?" He handed it to her, looked at her with anxious eyes.

She was torn between wanting to be with him and wanting to run away.

Try to relax, she told herself. *This is Jase, after all. Why hurt his feelings? It isn't his fault you love him. Make the effort.*

Her laugh sounded forced to her own ears as she took the bag.

"By the time guys reach your age, Jase, they don't have a lot of strength left."

It was a weak joke but it worked. He relaxed, grinned.

"What are you doing here?" she continued. "Didn't know you ever got away from work these days."

"I was in Leesburg for a conference at the Equine Medical Center. Thought I'd get a good lunch in Charlottesville before starting home. Remember the last time we ate here?"

Oh, yes. She remembered every occasion they had been together. Anywhere.

The line moved now to the hostess, who seated them at a table in the back by a window overlooking a garden. Everything was dead now, but when they had been there before, the garden had been in full bloom. She remembered the purple and white lilacs.

After they had given their order, they were quiet for a moment. Jase looked around at the restaurant. She noticed his careworn appearance. One hand lying on the tablecloth trembled slightly.

Connie spoke first. "Cary did himself proud at the party, didn't he? Did you have a good time?"

"It was all right. By the way, you looked great. I noticed you cut your hair."

She said, "Well, I suppose it did look good to you, since you usually see me in a stall with my old hat jammed on my head."

"You really ought to have it cut like that more often, Con. You have beautiful hair. And I thought that thing you had on was great too." Jase never could describe women's clothes.

She changed the subject, for she couldn't bear his compliments. "Did you hear about Walt Gowers falling off his old horse last week? He was so proud of that horse for pulling that trick on him. Luckily, the horse only had a cut nose."

He laughed and said, "Yes, I did hear about it. You know, years ago, that horse could hardly be ridden. Walt had his hands full with him. I remember watching him try to train him. That horse bucked, danced, twisted sideways trying to throw him off. But Walt kept working with him until he thought the horse was through with all his shenanigans. Well, I guess that old guy has been biding his time."

They both smiled.

"You know," Jase continued, "I'm taking small animals now. I had a cat the other day who…"

That led to Connie's story about a multi-colored cat with one ear who hung around the office.

He asked about her children and whether she had seen a new movie; she told him about the FDR biography in the bag. He said that if he had time to read now, he would ask her to lend it to him. They had swapped books often.

The meal came. When they had finished their crepes, both ordered coffee.

The mood was definitely better now. Connie felt a little of the old companionship. Since he had mentioned it, she felt free to ask him why he had enlarged his practice to include small animals.

He paused, taking time to answer.

She sensed by his silence he was not eager to talk about it. Finally he said, "I guess you've heard Les and I bought that old house in Lynchburg. It takes a lot of money to pay for the renovations, and of course the estimates are never accurate. Something else always crops up that's unexpected. I thought we could swing it if we made it a long-term project, but Les…well, she's got it in her head the house could be ready by Christmas next year. Her receptionist job at the museum doesn't pay much, and she hasn't had any training of any kind to get a better one. And you already know that she shows several horses and that costs plenty. So it's a constant outgo of money.

"Hey, I'm really being a whiner. Let's talk about something else." He smiled without pleasure.

But Connie wouldn't be distracted.

"That's hard on you," said Connie. "Your practice was plenty large when you only worked with horses."

"You got that right," said Jase. "It's a wonder you saw me here today. I'm usually running all over Virginia or working at my clinic until the wee hours. Today, for instance, I'm stopping at Stephens's place on the way home, and then I'll have the clinic to deal with."

Seeing the sympathetic expression on her face, he blurted out, "I wouldn't have gone to the conference, but I felt trapped. I had to get away. Just had to."

"That's the way I felt too." *Oh, why did I say that*, Connie thought.

"Why? What's wrong?"

But Connie couldn't confide in Jase. She shook her head, indicating she didn't want to talk about it.

"If you need me, Con, all you have to do is pick up the phone."

She nodded and asked about his work with Stephens.

"I'm not the only one he calls, Con. But he does call quite often. The other vets are plenty mad about it. They want him to choose one person who does his work exclusively. They don't like it that he gives me most of his business."

"He should, Jase. You really are good at your job."

"Carter and the rest don't seem to hold it against me, though, I've known all of them so long."

He told her about Doggie and the other pregnant mares. "Stephens seems to have enough money to do whatever he wants with breeding, and it is enjoyable to work with his state-of-the-art equipment. To give him his due, he lets me have the run of the place. He trusts me now. But it took a while before he would believe I knew what I was talking about."

She told him a little of her experiences with Tony.

"Jase, don't you find it awful to work with him, to have anything to do with him at all? Is it worth it?"

His answer was careful.

"Bottom line? He pays very well, and I need that money."

He looked at his watch. "Speaking of Stephens, I have an appointment at Fayence at 3:30 and I better get going. Stephens wants me to look at Doggie. Probably nothing wrong. It's done me a lot of good seeing you again, Con."

He hesitated and added, "I've missed you."

From her chair, Connie watched as he retrieved his down jacket from the old maple coat rack and put it on. He turned toward her, lifted his hand, and looked at her for a minute. Then he came back to the table, bent his tired face over hers, placed his hand under her chin, and kissed her on the cheek.

"Bye, Con."

She watched him pay the check for both of them, then stride through the red door.

Her eyes prickled with tears as she drove home, the antique shopping now forgotten.

On Monday, the week before Christmas, Connie had an appointment with Cary to discuss the deaths of Woolwine and Finn. It would be a relief to share the problem with him. They could talk about it freely and decide what to do. He had already been working for a long time when she entered his office at ten o'clock. His desk was strewn with documents, his computer humming.

"How're you feeling, Connie? All over the flu?"

"Long gone, Cary. But it was a bear while it lasted."

"Got plans for the break?" Cary's employees didn't have to go to the office the week after Christmas. But since horses don't let holidays keep them from getting sick or dying, Cary's team drew straws every year for who would be on call during that week. Joe Mattox had drawn the short straw this year, much to his disgust. Cary was the backup.

"Not really. I thought I might drive down to Roanoke for a concert, maybe shop a bit."

There was a little silence.

"What I'm going to say is private, Connie. I've confided in no one but you and Pam about the horses' deaths and of course, about Job Hoskins. I know you think I've taken too long coming to the conclusion that the horses were murdered. You've probably been stressed out waiting for me to make up my mind."

"I know the way your mind works, Cary. Anyway, it hasn't been that long since Woolwine died. The day after Thanksgiving. I didn't want to think that he was murdered, but then when Finn died, I decided that it must have been murder in both cases. And then I got more suspicious at Hurdle Farm two weeks ago. Thank God there haven't been any more deaths."

"I had to be sure, you know," Cary continued. "It's not unusual to have two horses die close to one another. It could have been some strange illness that hit them both. I've seen that happen. But the post mortems didn't reveal anything. And then there was Bud Hurdle's horse. When you told me that you were nearly hit by that dark car and Hurdle didn't know anything about a visitor…well, that clinched it for me. My conclusion took longer because I guess I didn't want to admit to myself that we have a murderer in our midst."

"When you mentioned the word 'killer' on the telephone," said Connie, "the night I was sick, I knew you'd made the same conclusion I'd reached earlier."

"I wanted to discuss this whole mess with you then, but you were in no shape to talk about it.

"I know you feel the same way I do about this crime, and about anyone who would do such a vicious thing." His face hardened, and she saw again the hot-tempered man who had lashed out at the owner who broke his own horse's leg. "If I ever find out who did this…"

He swiveled around in his chair and gazed out of the window at the Peaks for a moment. When he turned around again, Connie saw that he had brought himself under control.

"I've stalled and stalled in settling these cases. It's only because Rod Payson and the Lathams trust me so much that they haven't demanded their money or called their lawyers. But here's why I haven't paid up. First, if I do, the murderer will keep killing, for whatever reason he or she has, whether it's financial gain or some kind of psychological hang-up. I'll never understand how anyone could feel pleasure from killing horses.

"The other reason is I just plain resent paying that money when some arrogant, cruel person murdered those horses. I don't want him or her to get away with it. Now I know some agencies pay up when the circumstances are mysterious. I have too, in several cases of what could have been colic. But not this time. At least, not yet.

"We have to figure this out, Connie, and discover the person who destroyed those horses and was responsible for Job Hoskins's death."

She nodded in agreement.

"Let's find out, first, how the murders were done," Cary continued. "You told me you went through your research but none of the methods specifically fit our crimes. Now we need an expert. I want you to go to Virginia Tech and see Jim Marmion, an old friend of mine. He's a surgery faculty member at the Veterinary Teaching Hospital. He's helped me out before. Lay the whole thing out for him, see what he comes up with.

"When's the earliest you think you could go, Connie? This holiday week is bad but if you can drive down to Tech during the break, I'd sure appreciate it. Hate to spoil your time off, though."

"If Dr. Marmion can see me the Monday after Christmas, I'll go then. I'm anxious to find out the truth and do something about it fast.

"I'll make an appointment for you. In the meantime, Merry Christmas!"

Chapter Sixteen

Christmas Day.

A bleak day of snow and ice.

Connie rose late, savoring her Christmas breakfast at the kitchen table: orange juice, scrambled eggs, two of Gypsy Black's sticky buns, and a pot of Earl Grey. She had filled an old china pitcher with red roses she bought at the supermarket. Now it served as a prop for yesterday's *The New York Times*.

Later, she took her gifts down from the mantel and opened each one with great care, spinning out the surprise as long as possible. Then she telephoned each of the kids, told them how much she liked their presents, listened to their news and gave a positive report of her own life. She was tempted to tell them what was really going on, but she couldn't talk about the murders for professional reasons. It would embarrass her son and daughter—and Connie too—to tell them about her problem with Jase. And they would worry too much about Wampler's stalking, so she ended the calls with "Love you, Danny," and "Love you Ellen," and then found things to fill up the day. She wrote thank-you cards and letters to friends who were far away, checked her e-mail, updated her Christmas card list, and vacuumed every room in the house.

Now the long Christmas evening faced her.

She always planned in advance for holidays and had decided she would eat a microwave dinner and watch an old video of *The Nutcracker* ballet, but when it came time to prepare the meal around eight, she thought, *I can't eat one more dinner like that. Cardboard turkey, paste potatoes.* Then she remembered Rooney's Restaurant was open on holidays. Ma Rooney (as everyone called her) had a restaurant on US 29 in Albemarle County that featured country cooking. Ma was a dour old woman who glared at her patrons and didn't talk much, but her food was so tasty that the customers ignored her sour disposition. Connie had been there often, but never on Christmas. Surely there'd be hot turkey and dressing and other good things to eat. She put on black wool pants and a turquoise sweater, fastened back her hair with a silver and turquoise clasp Ellen had given her two Christmases ago, and put on a long coat and warm high-heeled boots.

It would be a long drive, she thought, but well worth it.

In the truck, she slid in a Charlie Daniels CD. Playing un-Christmas music was an old trick of hers to get through the one day when she felt most alone. Sometimes she invited friends over for dinner and that helped, but this year, she just hadn't felt like having a party. And she'd turned down several invitations to clients' open houses.

As she drove down the icy road toward Rooney's, she sang along with Charlie at the top of her lungs. She'd have a good dinner and then it would be home to bed. Christmas Day would at last be over.

The lights of the restaurant spilled out onto the snow as she pulled up. Inside, the air was filled with the tantalizing aroma of roast turkey. She'd have dessert too, Connie decided. It was Christmas. Her spirits picked up a little, but then she saw who was there.

Ma had rearranged her tables into three rows. It looked as if a state trooper occupied every seat. Too late, Connie remembered what Eula Jones, her trooper friend, once told her: Rooney's was a favored hangout for the police on duty holidays like Christmas, when the restaurant stayed open especially for them. Connie had no doubt Ma's catering to the state police paid well. Most restaurants closed on Christmas night.

Surveying the crowded place, Connie wondered if anyone at all was out there on the roads protecting travelers. She saw nothing but rows of tightly packed, big, sweating men, shoulders almost touching. She had no doubt they were all sweating, the restaurant was so hot. The troopers were indistinguishable from one another in their uniforms. How did they accommodate their side arms, crammed in like that? She listened to them laughing and kidding one another as they devoured their dinner.

As she stood by the cash register trying to decide whether a good dinner was worth invading the troopers' space, Mrs. Rooney shuffled out of the kitchen bearing a huge pot of steaming coffee, lips pressed together in a tight line of determination to fill everyone's cup. "Only one seat," she muttered. "Second table, end."

The smell of the food was making Connie faint with longing. All she wanted to do was eat. Why should the fact that the customers were all men intimidate her? Thinking no further, she started to make her way down the narrow aisle between tables two and three, sometimes turning sideways as she squeezed past a particularly beefy trooper. Most of the men were helpful and pushed their chairs closer to the table as she inched her way toward the empty seat. "Sorry," she said, "Sorry."

It was all right until she reached the last man before the vacant chair. Mountainous shoulders, bullet-shaped head, huge hands.

It was Jack Wampler.

He leered, and tipped his chair back so she couldn't get past. His belly, made soft by years of jelly doughnuts and redeye gravy, bulged over his pants. One hand holding a fork laden with food rested on the table.

He said nothing, but continued to smirk with the lipless slash of a mouth. The restaurant was suddenly silent. The troopers watched.

All at once, everything was too much: Christmas, Jase, the murders, and now, Jack Wampler again.

Keeping her eyes on his face to hold his attention, praying she wouldn't break her foot, and hoping he was off-balance enough to make it work, Connie quietly hooked the toe of her boot under the rung of Jack's chair and yanked it toward her with all her pent-up rage. Wampler's mouth made an O. His heavy body and the chair crashed to the floor, taking his turkey, gravy, biscuits, hot applesauce, broccoli, and coy red heart-shaped beet slices (Ma's trademark) with him.

Connie went back to the head of the aisle to wait until Jack picked himself up. The other men roared with laughter as he tried to wipe off his uniform, spattered with the brilliant colors of his Christmas dinner. He gave up and stomped down the aisle, cursing at every step. Keeping his head down, he lurched to the door, wrenched it open and slammed it shut. They all heard him rev up his patrol car and roar away.

Mrs. Rooney appeared, said nothing, and cleaned up the mess. Connie sat down and ordered. When a trooper tried to start a conversation, Connie answered in monosyllables. Her heart was thumping but she willed herself to eat, keeping her face expressionless. The troopers had resumed their meals, still chuckling about what she had done.

For all she knew, Connie might have been eating straw. Inside, she was desperate. *Why did I do that? What was the matter with me? Stupid. Stupid. Now I've humiliated him in front of his peers. I should have given up trying to get dinner and gone home. What have I done? He'll never let up on me now. I'll have to go to Cary. No choice left at all. My dumb temper. It always gets me in trouble. Stupid. What is the matter with me?*

Still berating herself, Connie left Rooney's and stepped into the parking lot. She knew she had pushed the thing over the edge now, and Wampler would get even any way he could. Fear squatted just below her breastbone.

Jack wasn't in the parking lot. He wouldn't be, with the police just inside the restaurant. She got into the truck, started the motor. Turned on the defroster. Fastened the seat belt. Made sure the door was locked. Sat for a few moments, waiting for the motor to warm up, trying to figure out what to do.

She knew she could ask one of the troopers to follow her home. But then the whole story of the stalking would have to come out, because he would ask her why she was afraid of Wampler. She would be put into the position of having to accuse him. The police would want her to sign a complaint. No. She needed someone to help her. She would see Cary first thing in the morning and tell him the whole thing. No doubt he would consult the agency's attorney. She hoped he would trust the lawyer to take care of the situation and not approach the State Police himself.

All I have to do is get home, she thought. Sitting in the cold truck, she was so frightened of the ordeal she was facing that she wasn't sure her judgment was sound. But it was the best she could do.

Driving down US 29 was going to be like running the gauntlet, she thought. Then, an absurd memory: a movie she had seen where a captive on a pirate ship had to walk a tightly stretched rope, cruel sailors with bright bandanas and gold earrings beating him from left and right. She willed herself to pull her mind back to the immediate problem. She knew Jack could pop out anywhere along the way. At Lynchburg, she would get off this road and take an alternate route home. All she could do was try.

She didn't want to think what Jack would do if he found her. She would just concentrate on getting home.

The truck was ready now. She pulled out of the parking lot, turned right at the entrance, and drove south. She looked at the clock. After ten. Allowing for the ice on the road, she'd be home by eleven thirty at the latest, with any luck at all.

The moon shone thinly. She drove cautiously along the road—now hilly, now flat—looking for Wampler's patrol car. Her eyes soon started to ache with tension. What she would do if she spotted him, she didn't know.

Now she left Albemarle County and entered Nelson County. Still no sign of him. She passed by the familiar landmarks, places she had seen a thousand times: a country store on the right, famous for its homemade ice cream, the dark town of Lovingston sprawled out along the road on the left.

Entering Amherst County with no sign of him yet, she considered the possibility that perhaps he went somewhere to change. After all, his shift wouldn't be over yet. And his uniform was such a mess, a rainbow of colors running down his shirt. She felt hysteria creeping up inside her. *Don't think about that. Just concentrate, keep your eyes open, don't think about anything else but getting home.*

She passed the second exit to the town of Amherst. Soon she'd be passing the entrance into the grounds of Sweet Briar College. Soon she'd reach Lynchburg.

She hadn't seen another car or truck all the way from Rooney's. Anxiously, she peered ahead, the fear biting sharper now, her head throbbing. Maybe he had gone somewhere to change.

* * *

Tony Stephens was trying to sleep.

Christmas Day had been long and monotonous. Like Connie, he'd had a hard time trying to get through it. He had gifts to open but they were from tradespeople he dealt with. He'd received at least a dozen Virginia hams, but he hated the salty meat. And then there were the fruitcakes in their bright metal cans. Too sweet for him. He'd distributed the hams and cakes among the stable hands on duty that day. He did like the Virginia peanuts, though, and stashed those in his office.

After a session in his weight room and a late dinner prepared by the chef he'd hired away from someone in Charlottesville at exorbitant cost, he put on a warm coat and went for a walk on the estate. While he was passing Morris' cottage, Pat's watchdog came bounding out of his doghouse to greet him. For some reason, the Doberman liked Tony. Stephens didn't know that the workers at Fayence always got a good laugh out of the dog's affection for their boss. He allowed the dog to accompany him on his walk.

He talked to the men in the stables and was reassured that all the horses were fine and nothing else was wrong. He noted that the stables were clean. Then he took one of the paths that crisscrossed the property, the dog running off now and then to investigate something only he could smell in the brush. The path led to the lake Stephens had put in. He walked as far as the lake and looked at the desolate scene. Clumps of debris mixed with snow lay on the black surface of the water. The trees were encrusted in ice. It was very cold. *Time to start back,* he told himself.

Once in his bedroom, he found the usual decanter of wine on his bedside table. He drank a glass or two every night in a futile attempt to relax and ward off his insomnia. Of course the ploy didn't work, but he enjoyed the wine anyway. He hadn't been able to sleep a full eight hours in years, and every night was a trial. He supposed it was his pent-up rage again or maybe some other reason, but he was through trying to discover the cause. And barbiturates were out. He'd tried them in Chicago. They put him to sleep all right but he loathed the fuzziness of his mind the next day.

Other ways to overcome his sleeplessness had proved useless. Best to accept it, work with it. He knew he'd come awake abruptly if he managed to drop off, and then he'd get up, read reports, or draft more grandiose plans for Fayence. He seldom slept for more than four hours.

After a hot shower, he got into bed, sipped the wine, read a breeding report from Morris, turned out the light, and closed his eyes.

But tonight he tossed, turned, and couldn't drop off at all. He realized with resignation that his mind was fully awake and alert. What could he do to pass the time until morning?

Finally he rose and dressed again. He'd drive for a while. He did this often when he couldn't sleep. Not bothering to rouse anyone, he entered the five-bay garage from the kitchen, choosing a powerful car he knew would be reliable on the slippery roads. He drove down the considerable length of winding roadway that led to US 29. At the gates of Fayence, he made a decision and turned south toward Lynchburg. There was a little café in the city that served breakfast all night. Perhaps he'd stop in and have coffee and scrambled eggs, although he really wasn't very hungry. His dinner had been sumptuous. Nevertheless, it was something to do, a way to occupy the dark and empty hours until the morning activities could begin.

* * *

Connie spotted Wampler parked on a service road between the Town of Amherst exit and the Sweet Briar College entrance. As soon as Wampler saw Connie, he started his engine and pulled his cruiser into the road behind her. *I'll keep going for a little while, see if he gives up*, she thought. But she knew it was a futile hope.

When she didn't stop immediately, he rammed into her truck. She fought to keep control of her truck as it swung from side to side on the ice.

After the third time, she knew she couldn't keep going.

Hands slipping on the wheel, Connie pulled over to the side of the road. He stopped behind her, the cruiser's blue lights flashing, got out, and walked quickly to her truck, gesturing for her to open her window. His huge body in its stained uniform was rigid with anger. The big head with its scowling face loomed in her window, muddy gray eyes cold and purposeful.

"Get out," he yelled.

"Now look, Jack," she said, "I'm really sorry I did it. I'll pay the cleaning bill."

"Get out of that truck!" His face was red with rage.

"What are you going to do if I do get out?"

"You attacked an officer back there in Rooney's. For starters, I'm going to look at your driver's license and registration, radio back to headquarters to see if you're wanted anywhere and if you have any violations. Do what I always do when I catch someone who committed a crime."

"I can sit in the truck while you do all that, Jack."

"No. Get the hell out of there."

She knew there would be more. First he was going to punish her by making her stand outside in the cold. But then what would he do? She looked more closely at him. He was breathing hard and his stubbled face was marred with red splotches.

"I'll stay in here."

"You're hindering an officer in his duty," he bellowed. "You have to get out when I tell you to."

"Not if I think you're going to attack me."

"Get out!"

She shook her head.

He tried to pull her door open.

It was locked.

He paused a moment. Then he pulled his .357 Sig-Sauer semiautomatic from its holster and brought it up.

Instinctively, Connie snapped her seat belt open and ducked down. Then showers of glass cascaded over her. He had smashed the window with the pistol butt.

He reached in, unlocked the door, ripped it open.

"Get out of there," he said with clenched teeth.

Paralyzed with fear now, she couldn't move.

He reached into the driver's seat and grasped her arm.

Pulling her violently out of the truck, he threw her onto the road. She fell on her side, the abrasive road surface scraping her face. She tried to get back up on her feet but something had happened to her arm. It folded under her. She fell back on her side.

Wampler stood there, staring down at Connie. Then, before she fully realized what was happening, he was straddling her body. He pushed down on her shoulders —Connie resisting, screaming with agony—until the pressure and the excruciating pain compelled her to lie on her back. She looked up at the heavy body suspended above her and saw his stern, relentless face. Then he tore open her coat. Connie tried to thrust her knee upwards, but he was too strong. Now he forced up her sweater and jerked down her pants and underwear. She felt the cold air hit her exposed body. As he started to take off his coat, he smiled and muttered something thick and inarticulate.

* * *

Tony glanced idly out of the car window as he drove to Lynchburg. It was quiet as usual.

Then he spotted a patrol car stopped ahead, its blue lights flashing. Some poor sucker probably exceeding the speed limit of 55 a little. Tony had no sympathy with the police.

He stared at the truck the trooper had pulled over. The driver's side window was smashed. The vehicle looked familiar.

The cruiser's headlights picked out two struggling people on the side of the road. The cop was on all fours above the figure on the ground. The person was trying to fend him off.

A flash of red hair…it was Connie Holt!

Tony thought, *That trooper is trying to rape her!* He pulled his car over as quickly as he dared on the icy road, jumped out, and ran back to the trooper and Connie. The trooper froze, staring at Tony.

"Get off her," Tony ordered. His voice was steely, his body menacing. The high-beamed headlights of the cruiser emphasized the strong planes of his swarthy face, making him a terrifying sight.

The trooper, still in a red mist of lust and rage, did not move fast enough to suit Tony.

He drew back his booted foot and kicked him in the side so hard that he fell over and off of Connie, who groaned with anguish. She looked up at Tony mutely. He reached down to help her, and she said, "My left arm. There's something wrong with my arm. Don't touch it."

Looking down at Connie, he paused a moment, thinking what to do.

Then, out of the corner of his eye, he saw the trooper trying to get up.

First things first, he thought.

He took off his fleece-lined coat and put it over her. "Lie still," he said, and turned to face the trooper.

The trooper had pulled himself to his feet with difficulty, and now stood appraising Tony, who stared back at him. Tony could read the cop's expression. He'd seen it many times before. The other man was thinking maybe he could take him. But then he sagged a little, just enough to let Tony know he had decided he was too big, or maybe he didn't like the look in Tony's eyes.

When he saw that the trooper was intimidated, Tony said in his flat voice, "I'm a witness to your attempted rape of this woman. Get out of here. I'll deal with you later." He watched the trooper carefully put on his coat, and noted with grim satisfaction that the big man was in pain. *I hope I broke a couple of his ribs,* he thought. He saw the name "Wampler" on the coat. He would remember that.

Wampler recognized power when he saw it. Bent over, holding his side, he limped to his cruiser, got behind the wheel with much effort, and slowly drove away.

Tony crouched down by Connie, who was struggling to sit up by using her good arm. His face betrayed nothing as he looked at her but he saw a lot. Her lips were compressed in a thin, white line as she tried to bear the pain. *Her shoulder could be dislocated or broken,* he thought. *Hell, maybe both.* One side of her face was abraded and her clothes and body were blood-spattered. She was exposed to the cold air as well. And if she wasn't in shock now, she soon would be.

"Did he…?"

"No," she whispered.

"I'm going to take you to the hospital."

He threw his coat to the side of the road impatiently, and helped her rearrange her clothes. His hands were clumsy, for he was not used to doing such things. She protested a little, saying, "I know this is embarrassing, Mr. Stephens. I can manage," but she couldn't, he knew. When she was fully dressed again, he picked her up and cradled her in his arms. She moaned.

Carrying her slowly and carefully to his still-running car, he said, "You're going to have to stand, now."

He opened the passenger door, helped her in.

Stephens retrieved his coat and got into the car. He watched intently as Connie tried to move her left arm, bracing herself for the pain. It still wasn't working right. She held the arm with her good one. He could see that she was in pain. Her lacerated face must hurt and her whole body probably ached from Wampler's brutal handling. She was shaking.

"Could you please make it a little warmer, Mr. Stephens? This car is wonderful but I'm freezing."

"I could kill him for what he was trying to do to you," he growled. He bent toward her to adjust the heat.

Then he pulled back onto the road and carefully drove toward the hospital.

Tony didn't talk much on the trip to the hospital except to ask several times if Connie was doing all right. At the first stop light, he'd looked over at Connie. Her eyes were closed. The brilliant red hair framed a face that was pale as moonlight, and her lips had a bluish cast.

She seemed to feel him looking at her and tried to smile. "Before we go any further, thank you for saving me from Jack Wampler." Her voice grew fainter. "I'll never forget it."

"Don't you worry any more about Wampler," Tony said. "First thing this morning I'm going to nail him. He'll never be a cop again."

At Lynchburg General's emergency entrance, he carried her in his arms through the doors.

"Take care of my friend," he ordered the receptionist at the admitting desk. "She's been in an accident." She took one look at Connie and summoned help—fast. When she asked Stephens how Connie had been hurt, he wouldn't comment, except to say, "I didn't do this to her."

Two aides placed her on a stretcher. She looked up at Tony for a moment, and then reached for his hand. Startled, he let her take it. "Thanks again," she said.

Then she was taken away.

"Sir," the receptionist said. He looked so ominous she hated to ask him to do anything. But it was her job.

"Sir, someone has to go to the admitting office for your friend."

To her surprise, he didn't object. But he did say before he left the desk, "I want her taken care of right away. There's something wrong with her shoulder and arm. And she's bleeding."

The lady assured him that Connie would be seen immediately. "Would you like to stay with her? You can go into the room where she's been taken."

"No." After he had insisted that Ms. Holt have a private room and completed the arrangements to have her bills sent to him, he left the hospital and drove to the all-night restaurant. He would call Cary, and then have breakfast. While he ate his sausage and scrambled eggs, he thought about how he would destroy Wampler. He couldn't wait.

Chapter Seventeen

Hours later, Connie awoke in her hospital room, woozy and woolly-minded. She licked her dry, raw lips and tried to lift her head to look around. The faint rustle in her bed woke Cary, who had fallen asleep in the visitor's chair in the corner. He jumped up, and walked stiff-legged to the bed. He was uncharacteristically rumpled and unshaven

"You're awake, Connie!"

"Cary, what am I doing here?"

"Do you remember that cop attacking you?"

Wampler. Now the whole thing came back. Cary was looking at her, concern in his eyes.

"Stephens called me, told me what he saw. How did this all happen, Connie?"

As she unfolded the story, she watched his face change from worry about her injuries to fury at Wampler's treatment of her.

He shook his head and asked, "But why didn't you tell me? It's been going on so long and I never knew. Austin Fellowes in the State Police is a friend, I would have called him and complained. You wouldn't have had to go through all this."

"I was trying to handle it myself, Cary, so the agency wouldn't be involved. And you have a quick temper sometimes. I was afraid you'd get angry and yell and…well, I just didn't think it was fair or in the interests of the company to involve you. It was my problem, not yours. But I made a huge mistake when I lost my temper and tipped over his chair at Rooney's. My stupid temper."

With a grin, Cary said, "Oh, how I wish I'd seen that. He deserved it. But listen to what you're saying, Connie. 'My stupid temper.' You were afraid I'd blow up and you did instead. We're two of a kind, aren't we? No wonder I like you so much!"

Connie's answering smile was tempered with rue. When would she ever accept other people's help and not consider it weakness to do so? All this could have been avoided if she had just consulted Cary when Wampler stopped her the first time.

Cary looked serious again. "Will you tell me if anything else happens that is…hard to fix?" He phrased it carefully. He'd found out long ago about her streak of independence.

Uncomfortable, she said she would, and changed the subject.

"Cary, I signed something to let them work on me, but then I must have passed out. Do you know what's wrong with my shoulder and arm?"

"I asked the nurse on duty—I know her husband—what happened. When Stephens brought you into the emergency room, you were suffering so much the orthopedist on duty decided to anesthetize you for the x-rays. But I don't know anything else. The doctor should be in soon."

She looked at her bandaged arms and touched her bandaged face. "Looks like the cuts have all been taken care of."

Just then, the short, energetic young orthopedist and a nurse entered, and Cary stepped out.

Connie thanked the doctor for his good care. He smiled and after unwrapping some of the bandages and inspecting the damage from the glass and the road, said, "I'll give you some printed instructions on how to clean these abrasions and cuts at home. The bruises will take care of themselves. Your foot is swollen, too, probably sprained. Stay off it as much as you can." He hesitated while Connie nodded, then said, "I know that shoulder is hurting, Ms. Holt. But the good news is that your shoulder wasn't dislocated, just wrenched—violently, it seems. And you fell hard on it. The range of motion is limited right now, lots of bruising, pain, and swelling. It will take a few months to get back to normal."

She asked, in a small voice, "How many months?"

"I can't say. I'll prescribe an anti-inflammatory to bring the swelling down and a pill for the pain. And I'll start you on physical therapy as soon as possible. For a while, you should wear a sling to support your arm." Seeing Connie's face, he added, "It will help with the pain. Just letting your injured arm dangle will hurt like hell."

Connie said, her voice glum, "How long do I have to keep the thing on?"

"Two to three weeks. When the sling comes off, you can start therapy."

She nodded and smiled but thought, *I'll get rid of that thing as soon as I can.* When Cary came back, she told him what the doctor had said. "If everything is all right later, I can go home tonight."

"Gyp is going to take you to her house to stay for a while. She said to tell you she knows you like to suffer through stuff alone but this time she insists on taking care of you. She'll pick you up at five. Pam and I fought her for the privilege of having you for a guest but she won."

Connie knew she needed help. She could barely shift in bed without pain. "That sounds good to me. By the way, where's my truck?"

"Stephens wanted to take care of that problem but I told him we'd do it. I woke up Joe and Mac and they went up to 29 and looked at it. It was still drivable but the rear end was in bad shape from Wampler's ramming." His face tightened for a moment as he thought of how frightened Connie must have been. "Don't worry, we're getting your truck fixed."

By now, her nose had registered the sweet smell of flowers.

Cary saw her looking at the baskets.

"You've been busy on the phone," she said.

"Want me to read the names?"

There was one that Lonnie Flemmings had sent from the Agency, several from the other agents, and of course baskets from Cary and Pam and Gyp and her husband. Connie saw a small but exquisite porcelain bowl, obviously expensive, containing yellow roses. When Cary read the name, his tone was wry.

"Leave it to Stephens to get the most unusual gift. I looked at the tag when you were sleeping to find out where he ordered it. But more important, Connie, I'm extremely grateful to him for what he did."

"Yes, he was wonderful. He swore he'd take care of Wampler. What has he done, do you know?"

"No, he just told me in that flat voice of his that he'd take care of him. Now I'm going to leave and go home and take a shower. That chair made a terrible bed. By the way, I'll cancel the trip to Tech. You'll still be feeling rotten."

"Thanks for everything, Cary. I couldn't have a better boss—or friend."

He put on his coat and left, raising his hand in farewell.

Sinking down in the bed, she thought, *Now it's over, it's finally over with Wampler.* She felt certain he couldn't harm her any more because Stephens would see to it.

* * *

As soon as Tony had notified Cary and finished his breakfast, he called the State Police and identified himself as a resident of Albemarle County. He said he had interrupted a rape in the making, and the rapist was none other than one of their own. He'd taken great satisfaction in describing everything he had seen in complete and graphic detail at state police headquarters later. Late in the afternoon, a policeman interviewed Connie and took her statement, which she signed.

Gypsy Black was there at five o'clock to take Connie to her house. After the requirements for signing out were completed, a nurse pushed Connie's wheelchair to the emergency entrance where Dan Black waited in a big, comfortable car.

Gyp had prepared her guest room for Connie's stay. After a quiet meal of homemade soup with Gyp and Dan, Connie slowly climbed the stairs and went to bed.

* * *

On Monday morning, Cary called.

"How is she, Gyp?"

"Miserable, Cary. She's sleeping a lot—the medicine is causing that—and, of course, she hates the sling. A few minutes ago, I found her trying to take it off, but I put it back on. Good thing she's too weak to resist right now! She's awfully pale and doesn't have much of an appetite. And, oh, is she tetchy. Definitely not the long-suffering, angelic type of patient."

"That's our Connie. If she's awake now, put her on, will you?"

She came to the phone, thanked him for expressing his commiseration, and told him that she would go to Virginia Tech on Wednesday. He wanted to make it later in the week but Connie said, "Cary, I'm determined to see Dr. Marmion on Wednesday. This investigation is too important to put off again because of me. I'm going!" Cary made the new appointment, telling his old friend only that Connie had sustained some injuries due to an accident and she would look battered.

* * *

Tuesday afternoon, Connie called Cary, underplaying the pain, and reassuring him that she felt much better.

"Sorry I was such an ogre when we last talked, Cary."

"You've been hurt so badly, Connie. Are you sure you want to go all the way to Tech tomorrow? I can drive there."

She paused. For a moment, she was tempted. She admitted to herself that everything still hurt a lot. And that wretched sling was getting on her nerves. A few more days in bed reading or watching television or just dozing sounded so good. But she knew she had to go as soon as possible. She kept remembering the two horses dead in their stalls. "I'll be all right, Cary. I'm going."

"All right. Now look, Connie. I don't want you to argue with me about this. With your arm in a sling, you can't drive. So I'm sending Gyp down with you."

"But I don't know how long I'll be. Seems unfair to Gyp."

"No problem. She's got people there she'll be glad to visit with while you're talking to Jim. You'll simply call her when you're ready to go home."

She slept most of the day, and by that evening, felt strong enough to ask Gyp if she could drive her home.

At Connie's door, she told Gyp how grateful she was for her friend's loving care.

"I think you should have stayed longer with us," Gyp worried. "But I know you wanted to get back to your own house. I'll pick you up tomorrow morning for the drive to Tech."

In her bedroom at home, Connie summoned up the courage to look at her damaged body in the full-length mirror. A woman with drooping shoulders and dull eyes, scarcely recognizable as herself, stared back. Her hair hung limply, its normally bright color now dull. One side of her face was still a fiery red from the impact with the road. On her face and arms, clotted, reddish-brown blood lined the cuts inflicted from shards of glass. Her shoulder and arm hung in a baby blue and white sling. The dainty colors only emphasized the contraption. The image in the mirror bore purple and green bruises from neck to ankle. The final indignity was the swollen foot with which she had humiliated Wampler at Rooney's.

As Connie gazed at her reflection, the fear of that night came back. Unwilling to remember the ordeal, but because she couldn't help it, she thought about what would have happened had Stephens decided not to take a drive that night.

I'll never be able to drive past that place on the road without remembering what Wampler did to me, she thought.

After a few harrowing moments, she managed to turn her thoughts to the first problem of next morning's trip. Normally she would wear a dark suit on a business trip. Giving in to reality, she laid out her huge old cardigan sweater and sweatpants. I'll *look like such a mess,* she thought. *Poor Dr. Marmion doesn't know what he's in for.*

She limped to the computer to prepare notes for her interview with Dr. Marmion, grateful that she could finger the keyboard fairly well, although with the sling off, her whole arm ached with the effort. She paused a moment to admire the get-well flowers and plants she'd arranged on the coffee table. The card in the pink begonia included only a hastily scrawled message: *Connie, I'm so sorry. I heard what happened. I'll call you this week to find out how you are. Love, Jase.*

At Roanoke, with thirty-eight miles to cover before they reached Blacksburg and Virginia Tech, Gyp insisted they stop at a restaurant.

"Connie, you're exhausted. We have plenty of time before your appointment with Dr. Marmion," she said, overriding her friend's protest.

Connie gave in and gritting her teeth, slid into a booth. *So far, so good,* she thought. She tried to ignore the jabs of pain from her shoulder. She'd not taken any pain medication because she wanted to remain clear-headed for the conference. As she sipped hot tea, she reviewed again the information she would set before Dr. Marmion.

She became aware that Gyp was sitting across from her with questioning eyebrows, and said, "I'm not ignoring you, Gyp. I was thinking about what I would say to the man at Tech." She wished she could tell Gyp about the murders, but Cary had stressed secrecy. "Tell me more about your cousins who live in Blacksburg."

When they arrived at the campus, Connie waited in the car while Gypsy went to the Visitor Information Center and signed them in. Gyp then took Duck Pond Drive to the Tech site of the Virginia-Maryland Regional College of Veterinary

Medicine, and dropped Connie off in front of the building, saying she'd be back when Connie called her.

"Sure you don't me to help you in, Connie?"

"No, Gyp. Your cousins will be waiting for you. I'll call you later. And thanks again. I never could have made it here without you." She waved as Gyp drove off.

In the reception area, a colorful VMRCVM banner hung behind the desk. A pleasant woman took Connie's name, made a telephone call, and said Dr. Marmion would meet with her as soon as he could. There had been an emergency. He and his colleagues were working with a seriously compromised horse whose frantic owner had brought her to the Large Animal Hospital earlier.

Connie walked slowly to the waiting area and picked up some descriptive material on a table. Cary had discussed the VMRCVM with her in broad terms, explaining that its facilities at Tech and the University of Maryland offered comprehensive services for companion and agricultural animals and horses.

The college granted the Doctor of Veterinary Medicine degree and other advanced degrees. It provided clinical services, engaged in research, and supplied educational programs for specialized groups. Now Connie's eyes widened as she read what doctors here could do to help an ailing horse, using state-of-the-art diagnostic tools. CT scanning combined the x-ray and the computer to observe internal structures. Echocardiography used ultrasound to see the structure and functioning of the heart. Electro-encephalography recorded brain waves. Connie was fascinated with the doctors' use of electromyography to assess muscle damage by using an instrument that converted the electrical activity in muscles into a visual picture and sound.

Dr. Marmion and the other surgeons performed miracles. Through arthroscopic surgery, they repaired joint injuries. And using cryosurgery, they were able to freeze and destroy malignant tissue before cancer surgery, decreasing the likelihood of recurrence and seeding. They could reconstruct hoofs, solve problems in the abdomen and the respiratory tract, repair faulty reproductive structures, and even stabilize the bones in the neck.

"Ms. Holt, Dr. Marmion just called." The receptionist's voice brought her back to reality. "He's almost through. He'll meet you in the Vet Med Café. It's just down that hall."

Connie sat down in the restaurant and looked around. In the kitchen, someone had a radio station tuned to rockabilly. The room hummed with conversation, as students, faculty members, and staff sipped hot drinks and nibbled on snacks. Connie noticed that the students chattering all around her represented a diversity of cultures.

Resuming her reading, she learned that getting into this school was very competitive. Only fifty Virginia and thirty Maryland residents were accepted. The students would face three years of class, clinic, and lab work, and then in the fourth year, a series of clinical rotations. They would major in one of five different areas, including government and business. Some would opt to do post DVM work. One of only twenty-seven colleges of veterinary medicine in the United States, this school had educated over one thousand vets and granted many MS and PhD degrees. Connie let her mind drift for a moment, wishing she had chosen veterinary medicine instead of teaching. *Bet I could have gotten through the classes*, she thought. But her wistful mood was broken when a young lady at the next table said happily, "It puked all over us." Connie grinned to herself and selected a brochure about the Pet Loss Support Hotline.

A few minutes later, a voice said, "I'm Jim Marmion, Ms. Holt. Sorry you had to wait."

She looked up as a man with thinning white hair and kind brown eyes behind wire-rimmed glasses put his tray on the table and sat down.

"How do you do, Dr. Marmion," she said, and shook his hand.

"Please call me Jim," he said. "Have you been here before?"

"I haven't had the pleasure. And I'm Connie."

He took a sip of his coffee and said, "I know you're here on serious business, Connie. You and Cary must be very worried, anxious to get to the bottom of this mess. I hope I can help.

"But would you like to walk through the horse facilities before we go to my office and talk?

"Incidentally, sorry I was late. A horse with torsion. Ate the wrong food, got obstructed. Had to have surgery. The last time we passed water down her, it stayed down, so I think she's out of the woods."

Connie had told Gyp on the way down that she hoped she might get a chance to see the equine part of the facility. Fearing an imposition on Jim's time, she hadn't wanted to ask for a tour.

As they walked through the facility, Jim slowing down for Connie's limping progress, he pointed out a research lab. "There are more than seventy here," he said. They passed the Student Center, the library, and the classrooms.

At the equine receiving area, Connie noticed that everything was very clean. She had seen too many dirty barns and ill-housed horses in her work. They saw a horse who had just arrived for a checkup. A fractious stallion in the meadow where both were grazing had kicked him in the shoulder, injuring his nerves. A doctor, a group of technicians, several students, and a faculty member surrounded the animal, while his anxious owner stood by, hoping that the horse's muscles hadn't atrophied. A technician petted the nervous horse as the doctor inserted electrodes in the damaged shoulder. The noises from the machine and the pattern of electrical impulses displayed on the monitor would tell the group whether the horse had deteriorated since the last visit. "Electromyography," said Jim.

The Surgery Service Barn held horses either waiting for or recovering from surgery. Connie noticed a pony with ugly exposed tissue at the top of one leg. Jim explained: "That horse developed a lipoma, a tumor of the fatty tissue. One of my colleagues cut away as much of the necrotic tissue as possible and then did skin grafts."

A teacher and students were observing a Quarter Horse's gait. "That old fellow has navicular disease," Jim explained. "It centers in the navicular bone at the back of the hoof. See those small forefeet with the short, upright pasterns? When a horse has that kind of feet, his weight falls directly on the navicular bone. This predisposes him to the disease. This horse was always ridden and jumped hard. His owner noticed that one foot was bothering him. We used a hoof tester and found pain in the navicular area. We tried different shoeing and trimming, but those didn't work, so one of the students—with the teacher's help, of course—is going to try to reduce the horse's pain by cutting the appropriate nerves leading to the foot. That's called 'nerving.'"

In the Large Animal Prep Room, they saw a block and tackle moving a frightened mare to the anesthesia location. "Persistent abscess of her uterus," said Jim. "Her owner decided on a hysterectomy." Later the apparatus would take her to a comfortable padded recovery area.

The last stop of the tour was the necropsy room. Through the window in the door, Jim and Connie watched for a moment as a group of students dressed in regulation blue coveralls huddled around the body of a horse on the table and listened attentively to the instructor. She was wearing the official maroon shirt and khaki pants.

"Let's go to my office, now," said Jim. On the way, he talked about the high level of equine care at the facility. "Advanced technology, as you've seen, and powerful pharmaceuticals. We're even experimenting with acupuncture."

When they reached his cubicle, he took a pile of books, papers, journals, and computer printouts off the visitor's chair. "Sit right down," he said. "Would you like something to drink?"

"Oh, yes," Connie said. She was feeling depleted and now that she was actually going to talk about the murders, anxious. "Would you have any tea? Black is fine."

"Sure." He dashed out for a moment and returned with a steaming cup. Connie smiled her thanks, and pulled her notes and a pen from her attaché case. She handed a copy of her notes to Jim so he could refer to them as she explained the murders.

"Now, tell me what this is all about," Jim said, settling into his chair.

* * *

Deep in Nelson County, a nineteenth-century stone farmhouse with a tin roof stood at the junction of two back-country roads. On this cold January morning, a light shone in an upstairs window. Earlene Collins had risen at four as usual to feed and minister to her horses. As she pulled on her shabby watch cap, she heard Molly in the kitchen, flinging cupboard doors open and slamming dishes down on the old oak table. A wide grin of anticipation split her weathered face, as she smelled the imported coffee. How lucky she was that Molly had decided to come and live with her.

Most people who met Earlene had the wrong idea about her age. "She's seen a lot of summers," someone once said at the feed store, when Earlene's name came up. A rawboned woman, her skin was scorched and scored by the burning sun. She pulled her thick, straight gray hair back in a tidy pony tail but didn't care about her looks, never had. Despite popular belief, she was only fifty-two.

Earlene was never seen in anything but threadbare jeans, transformed by rigorous washings until they were pale imitations of themselves. She wore tee shirts and sweaters she picked up at consignment shops. She once caused much merriment when she appeared in an extra-large black shirt that advertised a popular brand of motorcycle. It bore its message in glittery red letters: "I'm a Hog and Proud of It!" When one of the regulars at the feed store kidded her about it, she laughed. "I didn't even notice."

A few old-timers remembered that Earlene had graduated from Lynchburg College thirty years ago. She became a high school English teacher in Lynchburg and was a success with the students from the beginning. They liked her because she was honest and fair, refused to tolerate insolence or laziness, and taught her classes with exuberance and love. Her present-day customers would find it hard to believe that she owned many books, including a large collection of poetry anthologies. Only Molly knew that she had published some poems, using a pseudonym. She still liked to write poetry in the evening, a large whiskey by her side.

Chapter Seventeen

As a young teacher with an independent streak she had preferred to live in Lynchburg during the week, but she had looked forward to the weekends when she would go back to Nelson County and visit her folks and her brother Howard and his wife Amy, who all lived together in the old stone house.

Her father, Earl Collins, had taken his son into the family horse breeding business when Howard was eighteen. A few years older than Earlene, Howard was patient and kind, and taught everything he learned about the business to his eager sister.

But over the years, the Collins family gradually dissolved, visited by sickness and death.

First Amy and her baby died in childbirth, leaving Howard alone. He never did find another wife. Then Earlene's folks passed away. Earl had willed the family home and farm to Howard, trusting that he would help his sister if she needed it. Her father thought that Earlene could always support herself by teaching.

Both the home and farm proved to be more than Howard could manage, so Earlene gave up her job and went to live with her brother. At thirty-five, Howard Collins was diagnosed with multiple sclerosis. As he became increasingly ill, Earlene took over more and more of his duties.

By the time of his death, she was managing the whole operation.

She had never met anyone she wanted to marry.

The honesty and fairness with which Earlene had treated her students were now hallmarks in her business and community relationships. Earlene did what she could when her Nelson County neighbors were in trouble, and they reciprocated when she needed help. You can depend on Earlene, everyone said.

Earlene accepted her lot. It was up to her to make the life she had into something good.

I have many blessings, she often told herself. One was Molly Suitor, who lived down the road with her husband Chuck. Another was the little Baptist church farther down the road that helped her keep her bearings.

But she was lonely when Howard died, so Molly's decision to come and live in the old house with her after Chuck's fatal coronary was heaven-sent. Molly sold her place and added her income to Earlene's so that her friend could expand her business.

Like other horse breeders, Earlene searched for the Holy Grail of horse breeding, the perfect stud. And now she was sure she had found him. With Molly chipping in, she had managed to buy Ali Ben Bahir from his owner in Kentucky. Ever since she had transported him to his new home, she was still surprised and thrilled every morning when she found the magnificent creature in his stall.

That she could make a lot of money by using him as a stud wasn't as important to Earlene as the opportunity to teach the chestnut horse everything she knew and watch the results. Ali was the most promising horse she'd ever owned, and she looked forward to the golden hours she would spend training him.

She fed him expensive, scientifically planned food, cleaned his stall several times a day, and telephoned Jase to come by and check him every time the colt behaved in an atypical way. Jase liked to kid her when she'd tell him the latest story about the horse's great intelligence: "Has he started reading yet, Earlene?" So far, Ali was in perfect health. On the basis of the horse's papers and potential, Cary had insured him for $125,000.

Chapter Seventeen

Now Earlene hurried down the stairs, through the kitchen, and out the back door. She paused on the porch steps. Looking across the broad yard, she saw that the light over the barn doors was out. She sighed. She'd put in a new bulb two days ago. In the darkness, she could see only the massive outlines of the old horse barn, its timbers and stones black and crusty with age. She made her way to the doors of the barn, which were normally barred, and she found them standing open. She thought for a moment. Had she been careless the night before? She'd been very tired. But no, she had barred the doors. She ran down the dimly lit central aisle in the long barn to Ali's stall. She had put the Arabian at the other end of the building to spare him the blast of cold air that hit the front stalls every time the doors were opened. She realized that the horses in the stalls on both sides of the passageway were acting disturbed, but she didn't stop.

As she ran, she called to the colt. But this time, there was no answering nicker. She reached his stall and looked in. He was lying on the floor. He was still. No part of the once dynamic body moved.

Heart pounding, she opened the stall door and entered, knelt down by the horse. She knew, even before performing some perfunctory experiments, that he was dead. And from what she could see, his body was unmarked. Nor was there anything in the straw to indicate that he'd been sick in the night.

And then it occurred to her to check the other horses. She looked in every stall. It was clear they were agitated but unharmed.

Unsteady on her feet, she made it back to the house and went directly to the telephone on the kitchen wall.

"Hello, Cary? Cary." Earlene paused. "Ali is…" She swallowed. "Ali is not moving. Would you send Connie out? Oh." She had to stop again. "I'll call Jase. Thanks, Cary." She telephoned Jase, told him about Ali, and hung up. Her face was grim as she looked at her friend.

"You heard, Mol. Ali is dead," she said. "Cary is coming out himself because Connie is out of town. And Jase will be here soon."

Then she sat down, resting her arms on the scarred, stained wooden table, face in her hands, eyes closed, saying nothing more.

Molly said, "Earlene, don't you want a good strong cup of coffee?" In the tragedy of Ali's death, coffee was the only practical comfort she could provide. Earlene only shook her head.

In the barn later, Jase murmured, "Sorry, Earlene," and started his examination. When it was over, he said, "I don't know why he died. Was he out yesterday, running hard?" At Earlene's nod, he went on. "Maybe his heart gave out on him. Or perhaps he had some other problem we didn't know about. The post should show something." Then he blurted out, "I'll…I'll send someone to get Ali later." At these words, Earlene's face was so full of despair that Jase could not stand it. He hurried as fast as he could back down the aisle and out into the cold. Where had he seen that look before? Oh, yes. On the face of Rod Payson, when Woolwine died.

* * *

When Cary arrived, he took his friend's hand and said, "I know what this is doing to you, Earlene. Why don't you go back to the house? I'll come in when I'm through."

He took almost an hour to examine the body and stall, but found, as he expected, nothing amiss. Over coffee in the kitchen, Earlene finally wept.

"He was so wonderful, Cary. Good-tempered, full of high jinks, smart. Such promise. What could have happened? What on earth could have happened?"

Cary could only keep repeating, "I'm so sorry, Earlene." Finally he left, saying he'd call her when he knew something. As he drove back to the office, he knew Ali had been murdered. Once at home, he took off his damp, smelly clothes and changed into a heavy sweater and slacks, careful not to wake Pam. He went through the kitchen into his office and got out the files for Woolwine, Finn, and Pete, reading them again, looking for any details he had missed. Several times, he got up to consult some reference books.

Around seven thirty he made breakfast in the kitchen and took a tray back to his office. After three cups of coffee, he had jotted down a few preliminary ideas as to the next steps in the investigation.

* * *

In Dr. Marmion's office, Connie's cell phone rang. Jim reread Connie's documentation of the horses' deaths while she answered the call. It was Cary, who told her about Ali's mysterious death and the unbarred doors.

At her low "Oh, no, Cary," Jim looked up.

"Jase's report won't be ready right away, of course, but I'm convinced that Ali was murdered," said Cary. "Can we get together first thing tomorrow morning, about eight? You can tell me what Jim said. Then we'll decide what to do next."

"See you tomorrow," said Connie and hung up.

"Another one, Jim," she said. He shook his head. They went back to their discussion—now adding Ali to the equation.

By the time Gyp dropped her at home, Connie was beyond tired.

A card stuck in the front door told her that someone had tried to deliver flowers earlier.

Once inside, Connie called the florist, who said that the truck was still out and he'd send it back to her home.

While munching a sandwich, Connie read her rough notes from the meeting at Tech. She was just going to her computer to arrange them in better order when the doorbell rang. The delivery man handed her a large florist's box. Connie stared in awe at the contents. Wrapped in green tissue paper were at least six dozen roses in various shades of red and pink. The enclosed card read, *Will you have dinner with me tomorrow night? Tony Stephens.*

* * *

While Connie was reading the message with dismay, Tony was cursing himself for having sent the flowers. He stalked through the barns on his nightly inspection tour with unseeing eyes. He made his way down to the lake, loathing himself for being such a fool. *Just because I came along when she needed someone is no reason she'd go out with me*, he told himself. So many times, the women he'd taken to four-star restaurants were all too transparent about their interest in his wealth. Desiring a woman like Connie was a new experience for him. He'd learned that she was smart and brave and honest. *It probably killed her to get in good with me by having to feed me that stuff about how great the farm is.* He'd made it a point to find out what had happened between Connie and Wampler in the restaurant, and was filled with admiration. *That took guts.* He was reminded of the letter she had written, thanking him for rescuing her from Wampler and taking her to Lynchburg General. She'd even offered to pay him back for the hospital costs. He had sent a restrained note saying it wouldn't be necessary.

Gazing at a fallen tree limb festooned with lake detritus, he made up his mind to call her after dinner. He'd try to receive her turndown with some measure of grace, even though the brief call would be a major ordeal.

* * *

When the telephone rang, Connie expected that it would be Stephens. She had thought about what she would say when he called.

"This is Tony Stephens," he said formally.

"Hi," said Connie. "The roses came. They were so beautiful. I've put them in every room of the house."

"How are you feeling?"

"Not very well yet. I've gone back to work—no field work, just the office. I'm tired by the end of the day."

"Sounds like dinner is out."

"Yes, I'm sorry. But I wouldn't be good company for you."

"I see."

Connie was relieved that he didn't sound angry, only resigned.

After an awkward moment, she said, "Thanks again for the flowers."

He paused, and then said in an unfamiliar voice, "I'll think of you, Connie." She heard the tenderness in his words. After a moment, he hung up.

Connie sat motionless. His last words had betrayed the way he felt about her, spoken with the voice of a Tony Stephens she'd never known. Now she remembered him helping her dress by the side of the road, and the way he'd cradled her in his arms when he carried her to his car. With a sigh, she went back to her notes.

Chapter Eighteen

The weather had moderated overnight, and Cary's office was flooded with unusually bright January sun. He noticed with pleasure that his brass ship's clock on the wall was glowing with reflected warmth.

Cary had called Connie earlier to say he would provide breakfast. The conference table held scrambled eggs, Danish pastries, juice, coffee, tea.

"Thank Pam for me," Connie said, smiling. She took a bite of Pam's famous scrambled eggs made with cream cheese and chives.

"How did you get here this morning?" Cary asked. "Gyp told me you wouldn't let her drive you."

"Took off the sling and drove. And I don't want to talk about it."

Cary laughed. "Wouldn't think of it."

"By the way, Cary, my friend Eula Jones from the Virginia State Police called me. Jack Wampler has been placed on paid leave. He's been charged with, to quote Eula, 'alleged offenses connected with an unidentified female.' She said that he'll have to appear in Lynchburg General District Court. I know, of course, I'll be called to testify. But I don't look forward to it."

"Would you like me to go with you that day?"

"I certainly would. Thanks, Cary." *I could have done it alone but with Cary there, it will be much easier*, she thought. *I need his moral support.*

He smiled. "Sure. Now, to business."

"Tell me more about Earlene's horse," she said, pouring orange juice into her glass.

Cary told her about Ali's death, adding that Jase had called him with the post mortem results late last night. He'd found a leaky heart valve.

"Maybe we have one less murder to worry about," said Connie.

Cary looked noncommittal and said, "Let's talk about what we know, try to arrive at some conclusions. And in case you're wondering, I'm not going to bring the police in on this until we find out who's doing it and can give the police solid evidence."

Connie nodded, understanding his decision.

"Tell me what Jim said yesterday."

Connie glanced at her notes. "He thinks the horses must have been killed by injection.

"I had already decided that myself," she added. "It was the only method that fit. But I didn't know what kind of injection."

"I thought so too," Cary admitted. "That's one of the reasons I sent you to see Jim. Was he able to isolate the specific type?"

"He narrowed it down to two that might interest us. One is a massive insulin injection that causes a horse's blood sugar to drop. Eventually, the horse dies. I read about that in my file, but discarded it because a post mortem can pick it up, and Jase's and Carter's reports said nothing about a suspected insulin injection.

"The other injection Jim talked about sounds more like our cases. Very hard to detect afterward unless the pathologist is looking for it.

"Potassium chloride is injected into a horse's jugular vein. It's toxic to the heart. The horse drops, lies in the stall for an hour or two, and then dies. But it's also possible, Jim said, that an animal might struggle after the injection and at some point, ram into a wall, and then slide down it. Whoever found the dead horse might see his head tilted up."

"Like Woolwine," said Cary. "But there was a hole in the wall in that case."

"Jim thought that with Woolwine's high-strung disposition, he might have been afraid of the intruder or of what was happening to him, and kicked that hole. Later, he rammed into the wall and slid down it.

"Remember, Cary, that Finn was just lying on the floor of the stall with no apparent marks of any kind on his body. Apparently, he didn't react to the injection as Woolwine did. But he was a more tractable horse. Perhaps he wasn't as sensitive to the murderer being in his stall."

"Is there any way to find the exact spot where the potassium chloride was injected?"

"Jim said there might be a hematoma at the jugular vein. It would look like nothing more than a bruise. A vet doing the post might see this but discount it. I know I didn't see anything like that on either Woolwine or Finn."

"Nor did I when I examined Ali," said Cary.

"I thought Jase said Ali had a leaky heart valve."

"He did. But just for the sake of argument, let's consider Ali along with the other horses. Let's talk about everything. How does the potassium work?"

"The potassium," continued Connie, "leaks into the bloodstream and is hard to find. If the vet suspects this method, there are ways to prove it. But the cause of death might well be diagnosed wrong to start with.

"It seems to me this method fits the deaths we've seen."

Cary weighed this for a moment, and then asked, "What did Jim say about the vets' reports explaining the cause of death?"

"He said that a diagnosis of a heart problem without substantiation could mean anything. When he said this, he looked straight at me and raised his eyebrows."

"Jase's report said that Woolwine died of a 'presumable heart attack,' and Carter wrote that Finn's heart 'just gave out.' And now, Ali dies of a 'leaky heart valve.'"

"But Jase said he found that faulty valve in his post," Connie protested again.

Cary's face was impassive as he sipped his coffee.

"Let's keep going. We haven't mentioned Bud Hurdle's horse yet, Connie. I agree with you that the murderer went to Hurdle's farm to kill Pete and then left without finishing the job."

"I'll bet we might have found Hurdle's horse Pete dead in either of the two positions in the stall if the murderer had succeeded. By the way, I've been thinking about that night, Cary. I believe I know why Pete wasn't killed like the rest. The murderer saw that there was a good chance Pete might die from colic, and thought his work was done for him. Took off in a hurry in that dark car I told you about. If Pete hadn't been sick, he would have gotten a fatal injection too."

"Makes sense," said Cary.

"Jim went on to say that the murderer must have had a tough time giving the injection: getting it into the right place in the neck, operating in a stall with little or no light, knowing he or she might be trampled to death, trying to hurry and finish the job to avoid discovery. He thinks the murderer must be someone skilled in giving injections. Maybe an owner who has worked with horses a long time, even a vet."

"Did he say anything about a professional killer?"

"Yes. But he said that they are often crude in killing horses. Burning, electrocution."

"Nevertheless, we can't rule out a professional for now, Connie.

"I wonder about the theory of a skilled owner as the murderer. The Lathams don't have the know-how to do it themselves."

"Yes," said Connie. "And one of Hurdle's neighbors told me he has problems just worming his animals."

Cary grinned for a second, shook his head. "Bless his heart."

Then he was serious again. "Both Rod and Earlene could handle an injection."

"I'm having a tough time thinking of all these people as suspects, Cary."

But Cary insisted. "For the sake of argument, they all have to be considered. They could have hired someone to do it.

"And the vets are also under suspicion. Carter, and his assistant, Mary Evans. And Jase."

Connie's mouth tightened at Jase's name. She opened her mouth to speak, but Cary hurried on. "Let's assume, then, that all the horses died the same way. Now, the other basic facts: time, location."

"Right," said Connie. "The horses were killed in the early hours of the morning. They all lived here in Central Virginia, in rural areas where the farms were set back from the main roads. And the time span was short: November to December. Unless," she added, "the murderer is going to kill again."

"All the more reason to find him or her as soon as possible.

"How about access to the barns?"

"Rod's barn has a lock but he was depressed over his wife's death and admits he could have left the doors open. The Lathams and Earlene both have old barns. Easy to get into. They thought their horses were perfectly safe, since they live in isolated places. Didn't need to have locks put on their doors. Hurdle is a careless man. His barn did have a lock, but he could have left the barn unlocked because he was checking his sick horse from time to time or just out of sheer laziness.

"There was such a lack of security with all the doors that it was easy for the murderer to slip in and give the injections."

"That strengthens the case for the murderer as a resident of Central Virginia," said Cary. "Someone who knew things about the people involved—Rod's depression that led him to be careless, Hurdle's slipshod ways. The security situation on the farms. It seems logical that the killer has to be a local owner with the expertise to execute the murders, or a vet with the same skill. A professional killer would probably not have the necessary information, although come to think of it, someone who did know these things could have hired a pro and told him."

"Back to an owner being the murderer, Cary: Why would one of the owners kill three horses and make an attempt on a fourth? One owner might kill or have his horse killed for the insurance money. But what would be the motive for multiple killings? Blood lust? Jealousy?"

Cary considered, took a sip of juice, and shook his head. "Unlikely."

Connie nodded.

"No, I'd sooner think that one person killed the horses, using potassium chloride each time. I'm leaning toward a vet as the murderer," he admitted.

They were quiet for a few minutes. *I'm afraid of where this is going,* thought Connie.

Cary broke the silence.

"Let me sum up what we've said. Then we'll move on to what we can do. The horses were killed by injection, probably potassium chloride. The murderer is someone knowledgeable about giving injections.

"We've talked about the difficulties with the theory of an owner killing the three horses. But let's keep it in the back of our minds that Rod and Earlene are good enough to have given the injections. By the way, Connie. Would Beau Taylor know enough to pull it off? Rod considers him a genius with horses. He might have done it in a misguided move to help Rod. He's quiet and deep, I never know what he's thinking."

"No. Rod always handles the tough things himself. Beau is better at gentling horses, and helping Rod with procedures."

"Well, at least we can eliminate him as a suspect. What else have we decided?"

Connie said in a tired voice, "You think the murderer is more likely to be a vet." She rushed on, unable to bear the strain any more. "But I can't believe Jase could do such a thing, knowing him as I do. The idea of killing a horse would be against everything he believes about keeping horses alive.

"Now, Pres Carter has no principles."

Cary shook his head in disgust. He'd known about Carter's vices for a long time.

Connie continued, "He always needs money to finish the 'ancient Carter homestead,' as he refers to it. I'm sorry to say it, but I can easily see him as a murderer. I don't know much about Mary Evans."

"She's new in Central Virginia," said Cary. "Why would Carter take on a woman as his assistant? From what I've seen through the years, he hates most women, thinks they're no match for men. Like Tony Stephens, he's a real cave-dweller type. You'd think he'd insist on a man in that job."

"No mystery there. I've seen her, she's young and beautiful. A possible conquest."

Cary grimaced and went on. "Of course, it's no secret that Jase is in hock up to his neck for that white elephant house he and his wife are restoring. And Les has a string of horses that must cost a lot to maintain. I know he has to work very hard to meet his debts."

"That's all true," admitted Connie.

"I have to think the murderer is one of the vets who worked with the horses, or at least, had the vital information he or she needed to gain access to them. Think about it. A vet would have the opportunity, the knowledge and the skill."

Just then, Gyp knocked on the office door. Cary excused himself for a few minutes to deal with a disagreeable new client who was demanding to see the boss.

"Next, we plan a strategy," he said, as he left the office.

Connie had been so intent on what they were saying that she'd eaten very little. Nor did she want anything now. She had a terrible sense of foreboding. Feeling the desire to do something, anything, she pulled away from the table and walked to one of the windows behind Cary's desk. She hardly saw the snowcapped Peaks of Otter. *He's right*, she thought, *a vet probably is the murderer. I thought of a vet days ago but I blocked out the thought of Jase as a suspect. Now I've got to accept the premise, at least, until we find the truth, but I still can't believe in my heart that Jase did those terrible things.*

"That is one foul-tempered guy!" Cary said, as he came back in. "He had second thoughts about the insurance rate I quoted him and wanted to argue.

"But enough of him. I have a plan I want to run by you, Connie.

"While we've come a long way this morning, I think we need more information. I'd like you to go back to the owners and question them. Go over the details of the deaths again, ask if they've hired anyone new to take care of their horses or seen a stranger hanging around. Find out everything you can."

"Hurdle ought to be included, Cary, even though his horse didn't die."

"Right."

"But won't they all know we suspect murder? My questioning might give a heads-up to the killer."

"I don't see how we can avoid it. It's necessary that you talk to them again. I'll leave it to you to work out the way to approach them. Meanwhile, I'll look into the finances of the owners and the three vets. The motive has to be financial gain."

Connie knew that Cary had a long list of confidential contacts he consulted when he needed help. By the time they met again, he would have a complete picture of the suspects' finances.

"Any other ideas as to how we can proceed?" he asked. "I can't think of anything else to do right now."

"I can't either," she admitted. "Any extra information we can put together will put us that much closer to finding the murderer. But Cary, whatever we do has to be fast. The murderer might kill again."

He nodded, his face grim.

Connie said goodbye and left the office.

There's still a chance it isn't Jase, she told herself.

Chapter Nineteen

"Come in, come in," said Dick Latham. Laura appeared behind his shoulder, smiling a welcome.

Connie's taste buds sprang to attention, and she hoped whatever Laura had been baking was for her visit.

At the office that morning, she'd reread the Latham, Hurdle, Collins, and Payson files, made appointments, and decided what questions she would ask. The Lathams had said that after lunch would be fine. She'd eaten a bacon cheeseburger on the way, smothering her guilt by deciding to watch her diet next week.

In the parlor, the three sat down at the drop leaf table, unfolded their napkins, and talked about little things, observing the graceful ritual of hospitality that Connie had found so attractive when she moved to the South. Laura poured the tea and offered almond cookies.

When the small talk gradually wound down, Connie said, "I'm here to ask you a few more questions about Finn."

Dick hesitated, then said, "We filled out the document Cary sent as completely as we could."

"I'm sorry I have to ask you to talk about Finn again," said Connie, "but we just want to be sure we have the whole picture. Would you tell me once more what happened on that night?" She took another cookie.

The couple repeated the story of how they had found the horse dead, each one jumping in when the other forgot a detail. "And," concluded Laura, "you know what Pres said about Finn's heart."

There was a brief silence. But before Connie could go to her next question, Laura began to talk about the dead horse who had been so promising. She described the difficulty in curing Finn of his mange—"We thought it would never clear up"—and the wonderful discovery of Finn's sweet temper. "He was responding so well. Midge Larkin, our trainer, never had a chance to develop his full potential."

Dick listened, nodded his head, then asked, "Laurie, do you remember that day Midge came in the house, so happy that Finn had let her ride him with a saddle for the first time?"

The couple's faces were masks of sadness. Connie realized that their sorrow had hardly abated.

At the first pause, she asked, "Did you hire anyone new to take care of Finn? Did you see any outsiders on your property around the time he died?"

Both Dick and Laura stared at Connie.

"You don't mean that you suspect…?" Laura exclaimed.

"We're just covering all bases."

"In answer to your first question, no," said Dick. "We did have a high school boy who came in to help, but he was trustworthy. Goes to our church. We did everything else for Finn, except, of course, what only Pres Carter could do.

"Our horse turned out to be worth a lot of money," he continued. "But that wasn't important. We loved him for who he was, and he loved us in return. That was Finn's real value.

"I suppose a lot of horse owners would laugh at us for feeling that way."

Connie smiled, thinking of Cary's devotion to Proud Mary. "You'd be surprised at the number of people who would never confess to loving their horses, but they do."

"You know," Dick mused, "if he had lived, I don't think we could have brought ourselves to sell him."

"And my second question: did any strangers come here around that time?" asked Connie.

"As a matter of fact, a man did come to the door a few weeks before Finn's death."

"Who was it, Dick? Do you remember his name?"

"He sort of mumbled it," said Dick. "And I didn't care enough to ask him to repeat it. Remember anything, Laurie?"

"It was something like 'Noble'," she said.

"Tell me about it," Connie said.

"Well, in early November, a man came here, saying he wanted to see Finn. He'd heard about him, heard he had great possibilities. Since he was polite, Laurie and I saw nothing wrong in taking him out to the barn. He complimented Finn a lot, said he wanted to buy him. He'd pay top dollar, "10,000, as I recall. My wife and I were firm about turning him down. He took it pretty well, just asked us to call him if we changed our minds, and gave us a business card with only a telephone number scratched on it in pencil. A Roanoke number, I remember."

"What did he look like?" asked Connie.

"Small man, about five feet, six inches. Couldn't have been more than forty years old. His hair was blonde, streaked with gray, and he had a little blond mustache. I remember it because he kept touching it while he talked. He wore a suit."

"Did he know horses?"

"Oh, yes," said Laura. "He was very knowledgeable. Acted as though he had experience with mange, too."

"Do you think he was from around here?"

Laura thought for a moment. "I would say so." Dick nodded.

"Do you still have that business card?"

"No," said Dick. "We threw it away. We thought we'd never need the number."

Connie's heart sank.

"What about his vehicle?"

Dick said, "He was driving a light-colored car, probably one with a Japanese name. I'm sorry. I didn't pay any attention to it."

"Oh, Connie," said Laura, "we made a big mistake in showing him Finn, didn't we? Do you think that man had something to do with Finn's death?"

Connie evaded the question and said, "You didn't do anything wrong by taking him into the barn. I know what it is to be proud of a horse and want to talk about him. I suspect that Cary sometimes puts out a road block on US 221 with a detour leading directly to his barn. That way, he always has plenty of people to see his horses!"

She was glad when they smiled.

Connie rose. "I'd better get along now. Thanks for answering my questions."

Laura went into the kitchen to fill a box with almond cookies for her, while Dick retrieved her coat.

"If you think of anything else about this man," she said on the front step, "please call me. And I'll have to ask you both not to discuss what we've said with anyone. Our investigation is still ongoing."

They nodded. Laura hurried to say, "One thing more, Connie. Dick and I can only imagine what you went through with your…accident, and we hope you're better now."

Connie nodded and smiled, but said nothing. She couldn't bring herself to talk about the Wampler attack, but she appreciated the couple's genuine concern for her.

As she drove away, she looked back. Laura and Dick were still on the front step, waving, and she honked her horn in response.

She hoped she hadn't made their burden worse, but she feared she had. Now they would worry that they had caused Finn to die by admitting a stranger to their barn.

The frosty look on Bud Hurdle's face as he admitted Connie to his double-wide told her he was not happy to see her. *So much for Southern hospitality*, she thought. But Cary's firm insured Bud's horses, and there was no way he could refuse to talk to her. The door opened directly into the kitchen.

"Hi, Mrs. Hurdle," she said to the woman sitting at the table, stubbing out a cigarette in an overflowing ash tray. Janey Hurdle nodded, without friendliness. Her sun-marred skin and dry hair made her look much older than she was. That and the hard life she led with Bud.

"Come on in my office," said Hurdle. He indicated an unused bedroom. Once inside the cluttered room with its battered desk piled high with papers and horse equipment, he motioned toward the chair Connie should sit in. The covering of the plaid recliner was dirty, the stick to adjust the chair splintery.

"Now what do you want to talk about?" Hurdle asked without interest, as he settled into his own chair, a decrepit old monster that had been an upholstered wing chair in another life. "I gotta go somewhere."

"I'll make this as quick as I can," promised Connie. "Do you remember that night I came out, when Pete was so sick?" she started.

"Course I do," Hurdle said, annoyed. "Janey is always on me for forgetting. It ain't as if I'm dumb or something."

"I don't think that, Bud," said Connie. "Now I told you that night about a car that almost ran me down. And we noticed that the barn doors were open."

"Yeah. I filled out that sheet you sent me."

"Yes. We got it. I told Cary about the car, Bud, and he asked me to come out here. We heard there might be someone coming on to people's land." Connie had decided that she wouldn't try to explain too much to Hurdle. Better that way.

"Okay."

"Can you tell me if there were any strangers on your property back before Pete got sick?"

"Yeah," he said right away. "There was a guy from Ernie's to look at my busted truck."

"You'd never seen him before?"

"Sure I seen him. At Ernie's."

"You ever talk to him at Ernie's?"

"Sure. Lots. He's an old guy who works there."

"Well, then, he's not a stranger, is he?"

"No," Hurdle admitted.

"I meant a person you never saw before, maybe sneaking around in the woods."

"Nah. If I did, I'd sure take care of them," he said, gesturing toward the shotgun standing in the corner.

"How about someone ringing your doorbell, wanting to talk to you about Pete?"

"Nah." He shifted in his chair and stared at the battered alarm clock on his desk.

"Would your wife remember, do you think?"

"Maybe."

He called his wife in who said, "Sure. There was that fella who came to the door and wanted to buy Pete."

"Oh, yeah," said Hurdle.

Connie took a quick breath. Another mysterious buyer.

"What can you tell me about him?" she asked.

Hurdle looked at his wife. She responded with enthusiasm, pleased to be center stage for once.

"He was a big guy, bigger n' Bud here. Only a little hair on his head. His face was funny looking, kinda red."

"What did he have on?"

Hurdle looked up at the dirty ceiling and yawned. Connie could almost hear what he was thinking. What did any of this matter?

"Heavy coat, looked like a lumberjack's. Jeans. Boots," Mrs. Hurdle replied.

"How old?"

"Had to be at least fifty," came the answer.

"What kind of vehicle was he driving?"

Hurdle chimed in. "One of them Chevy trucks, black, probably a '93." I can remember plenty about trucks," he said with pride.

"That's really helpful, Bud. What did he say?"

Bud looked to his wife.

"Just could he see Pete," said Mrs. Hurdle. "And then after Bud showed him, he offered to buy him for a lot of money. I think it was $7,000. Bud said no. Bud wants to wait to sell until Pete is older and trained, you see."

"Did he give you his name?"

"No. Just said he was interested. Did give us a telephone number, though. On a little card."

"Do you still have it?"

Janey Hurdle frowned. "Maybe," she said.

She went back to the kitchen, Bud and Connie following, rummaged in a drawer, and came up with a bent card. She handed it to Connie with a triumphal flourish. But it had been stained with something greasy, and only a partial number remained.

"I guess it got in the way of my cookin'," said Janey.

"That's all right," Connie said. "Would you mind if I take it with me?"

Both shook their heads.

Connie paused a moment to see if either remembered anything more and then thanked them.

"Please don't tell anyone about our talk today," she said. "We're still looking into…things." She could only hope that the Hurdles would keep their mouths shut.

As she walked to the door, she said, "By the way, Bud, how is Pete? Did he get over his colic?"

"Sure," Hurdle said. "He's great."

Until the next time, Connie thought.

She went down the front steps, averting her eyes from the rusty water heater on the porch and the junked car with no wheels in the yard.

As she drove slowly down the gravel driveway, she looked in the rear view mirror and saw Hurdle jump into his truck. He followed her for a while but she saw him turn off at a cement block building with beer signs hanging in its windows. The parking lot held a few trucks, one sporting a Confederate flag. *So that's where Bud was so anxious to go*, she thought.

Chapter Twenty

The next day, Connie had two appointments, one at ten in the morning with Earlene Collins and the other at one o'clock with Rod Payson.

On the way to the Collins farm in Nelson County, she stopped at the office to open her mail, get her phone messages from Lonnie Flemmings, check her e-mail, and check in with Gyp.

"Cary's acting very mysterious, Connie. He's shut himself up in his office and says he can't be disturbed for any reason. Must be something important. He doesn't do that very often."

"Oh?" She knew Cary was contacting his sources to get the financial information they needed. On her way out, Connie waved to Joe Mattox in his office.

"Lookin' pretty good now, Connie," he smiled.

"Thanks, Joe," she said with a grin. She did feel better, having discarded the pesky sling altogether. Although her shoulder ached now and then, the rise in her spirits made up for the pain. She would start physical therapy soon.

When she reached Earlene's old house at the intersection of the two country roads, she paused for a moment to look at it before she got out of the truck. The gray stone house had character with its dark green shutters and window boxes. Then she noticed that the doors of the barn had shiny new locks on them. She thought of the old proverb about locking the door and horses. If only Ali had been stolen. He might have been recovered.

As she approached the tall, narrow front door, it opened, and there was Earlene.

"Now don't say no," she said, "but Molly has baked up some biscuits, and we want you to sit right down and have some with strawberry jam she put up last summer. And you know, she's got that fancy coffee ready, too."

Earlene led the way back to the kitchen, and they sat down at the weathered table. Molly took the biscuits from the oven and then joined the others. While Earlene poured Connie a cup of coffee, Molly pushed a green glass dish of jam toward her. "Spread em' while they're hot!"

The conversation was comfortable. Connie was glad they could relax for a while before she had to start the questioning. Earlene had heard a funny story about a notorious horse who flipped everyone off his back and was sold and returned fourteen times until the original owner gave up and kept the animal. Molly told her own tale of a new device she'd seen in a catalog that would really keep deer from destroying her garden.

"How many things like that have we got in the back room, Mol?" asked Earlene, with a fond smile. "She's always sending away for stuff like that, and none of it works!"

When they finished eating, Earlene said, "Would you like to go into the parlor, Connie?"

"No, this is fine, if you don't mind. I'm comfortable at this nice old table.

"Cary has asked me to go over the details of Ali's death with you once more, Earlene. I'm sorry I have to ask you."

"That's all right," the other woman replied. "But I did fill out that form Cary sent."

"I'll be asking different questions in a little while," replied Connie, "but first, could you tell me what happened when you went out to the barn that morning?"

With a sigh, Earlene told how she had found Ali in his stall. She insisted she'd seen nothing wrong with him before his death, describing in detail how active and strong he'd been in the pasture the day before he died. Tears filled her eyes as she said, "I miss him every day."

"Did you see anyone trespassing on your property before Ali's death?"

Earlene was quick to understand. "You think Ali was killed by someone."

"We don't know at this point."

"Not many strangers come this way. We're pretty secluded back in here. But I'll tell you something odd. A man came to the door in December, after Christmas some time, wanted to see Ali. I said, why do you want to see him? He said he'd heard that I had a great horse. Maybe he could buy him if Ali was as promising as people said he was. Well, I ran him right out of here. I didn't take him into the barn, just told him straight out I wasn't interested. Practically slammed the door in his face. Did he have a hissy fit!"

"This is important, Earlene. Can you remember what he looked like?"

"As a matter of fact, I do. I don't like mustaches on men, and he had one. A little blond one. Grayish-blond hair. Small man. Had on a suit. I remember thinking how funny it was to see a man in a suit during the week. The only time anybody around here dresses up like that is on Sunday."

"Age?"

"Oh, I'd say around forty, forty-five."

"Did his voice sound as if he was from around here?"

"Oh, yes."

"Did he give you his name?"

"Said his name was 'Nagle.'"

"Are you sure it was 'Nagle?'"

"Yes. I once had a friend at Lynchburg College named Nagle. I asked him if he was any kin but he said no. I was relieved he wasn't related to my friend. He was a slick article. I didn't trust him."

"How about a telephone number?"

"Well," chuckled Earlene, "as I was slamming the door in his face, he was trying to give me a card. I assume the number was on it."

"And you never saw him before?"

"Never. I watched through the window until I was sure he got in his car and drove away. I thought he might try to sneak in the barn to get a look at Ali, and if he'd done that, I would have taken Dad's shotgun and scared him plenty.

"But he didn't look as if he'd be able to kill a fly, Connie. He was so small and frail-looking. I was surprised he had anything to do with horses."

He looked frail, thought Connie. The Lathams didn't say that.

"What kind of vehicle did he have?"

"A small sedan, light-colored, white, maybe."

"Can either of you remember anything else about Nagle?"

The two women said no, and after asking them to call her if they remembered anything, Connie prepared to leave.

Chapter Twenty

Earlene took her heavy barn coat and watch cap from a battered oak clothes tree by the front door. "Got a lot to do before lunch," she said. "I'll walk you to your truck, Connie."

Once there, the big woman waited until Connie unlocked her door. "You've been tactful about the reason you came here today, but I know what you and Cary are thinking: Ali was murdered. And I agree.

"I don't think for a minute that horse had something wrong with his heart. I've worked with too many horses, seen too many of them with heart problems to believe a story like that. I don't understand why Jase's report said that was the cause. Now, I'm going to keep quiet about this and let you and Cary do your work. I respect you both." Connie knew Earlene wouldn't talk about it if she said she wouldn't.

Earlene looked at Connie with shrewd eyes. "Are you all right now?"

Connie knew this was Earlene's way of expressing her sympathy for what she had gone through with Wampler.

"I'm fine," she said, and started the truck. As much as she liked Earlene, she couldn't talk to her about it.

Earlene nodded with satisfaction and strode toward the barn.

Connie looked at the dashboard clock and decided she had time to go to the office and work on her interview notes before she went to see Rod Payson.

As she drove up the long winding hill to Rod's farm, Connie remembered Woolwine lying in his stall. The first death. It seemed so long ago, but it had happened the day after Thanksgiving.

Less than two months had gone by.

So much had occurred since Woolwine died. Wampler's attack and her injury. Two more horses dead and another almost killed. The bleak meeting with Jase in Charlottesville.

Jase. She allowed herself to think about him. After a few minutes, she was surprised to find that the anguish she felt about loving Jase was less intense. At once, she felt lighter, as if the weight of her hopeless love for Jase had been dragging her body down.

When she parked in front of the show barn and walked down the path toward the fieldstone house, it was with the hope that Rod had been able to shake the depression brought about by Donna's death, that he was somehow engaged in life again. She'd been encouraged by his appearance at Cary's party, but now she warned herself not to expect too much.

Rod opened the door before she could ring the bell.

"Hey, Connie," he said.

She was glad to see him smiling.

"Come right in."

The Labs came running to meet her, and she petted their smooth black heads. "Good boys," she said.

She was relieved to see that the parlor seemed to have been cleaned. The bookshelves were tidy, and the colors in the Oriental rug glowed once more. A middle-aged woman was just putting on her coat to leave, and Rod introduced her as Julia, "who helps me keep this place together."

Julia smiled and left after saying that the Brunswick Stew he had asked for was done. "It's keeping warm on the stove."

Rod said, "How about it, Connie? Will you eat lunch with me? I asked Julia to make her specialty, the stew. There's a green salad and Julia's rolls. And I picked out the ice cream."

"Chocolate," he added hopefully.

"Of course," she said, laughing.

Rod led her to the dining room. Connie remembered when Donna had found the antique mahogany table and chairs in Charlottesville.

Rod was looking much better. The black circles under his eyes were gone, and his face was rested. Even the scarred side didn't look as bad as it had in the cold stall in November. He wore a crisp white shirt tucked into jeans and a bright red pullover. His hair had been trimmed. He still liked to wear it long, she noticed, and it waved back over his ears.

At first, the two friends made small talk, but eventually Rod brought the conversation around to his depression.

"I wouldn't tell anybody but you about this, Connie, but you're a friend, and I know you'll understand.

"I don't know how I fell into that state, Connie. I wanted to live, wanted desperately to live, but something kept saying to me that it was no use. With Donna gone, I couldn't muster up enthusiasm for anything, not even my farm. I let everything go, laid off most of the help, just stayed inside the house and let the few people who remained take care of the farm. And of course, without me to see that everything ran just so, it all just fell apart. A lot my customers took their horses to Stephens. Can't blame them. Even when Woolwine died, it didn't seem to matter, although I did realize I had to have that money from the settlement.

"Cary's party was a turning point of some kind, even though he told me in his office that he was still working on Woolwine's case and couldn't send me a check right away. After that, I started to feel better again—I can't explain the change—and threw away the pills the doc had prescribed.

"Now I'm trying to put the farm back together. I hope I'll be able to rehire some of the people I let go in the spring. Remember old Buck? He had to go to work for Stephens. I wish I could get him back." Connie told Rod how she had met Buck at Fayence and about his fear of Stephens. She was sure he'd be happy to return. Rod nodded.

"I bought another horse, a broodmare this time," said Rod. "I'm planning to breed her, get my business to where it was before."

"Won't you need a lot of money, Rod?"

"Things are going to be tight, but what the hell, I was strapped when Donna and I started this place up. It just means a lot of hard work, but that's the best thing for me right now."

"Will you show me the mare before I go home, Rod?"

"Sure will," he said, pleased at her interest.

"By the way, I have some good news about Beau. He's decided, on his own, well, not entirely on his own, I helped him make the decision, to finish high school. He's going to night classes this term. He quit in his senior year, you know, broke his parents' hearts. When he graduates, he's thinking about going to Blue Ridge Community College in Weyers Cave. The Veterinary Technology program there would train him to be a vet assistant. I sent away for a catalog, and when he read about the courses he'd take, he was excited. His face was…I don't know, hopeful, I guess."

Connie thought of the shy, insecure young man by the paddock, who out of loyalty for Rod wouldn't tell her anything.

"It's no life for him," Rod continued, "just taking care of my horses. He's capable of doing a lot more. He finally realizes that his dyslexia isn't his fault. He can go to school and learn. It will just take him longer, but the college will make allowances for the problem.

"You know, Beau and I have a great deal in common. We both had miserable high school experiences. But he's going to succeed now, I know it."

After a careful pause, he said, "Are you doing all right? If only I'd been—myself—I'd have helped you. Do you want to talk about it?"

Connie found she did want to confide in him, perhaps because Rod had enough trust in their friendship to tell her about himself. At any rate, she thought, they had both gone through terrible ordeals.

It took a while—with many starts and stops—to tell him about the night stalking by Jack Wampler. As she brought out the story, Rod nodded in encouragement, so that it became easier to tell him everything.

When she related the details of the attempted rape, he drew in his breath sharply. "Oh, if I had only been there!"

"It was lucky for me Tony Stephens decided to go out for a drive that night."

"Maybe he's not as bad as I thought," said Rod. "I'm so glad that's all over for you now."

"Me too," she said, taking a bite of ice cream.

They were quiet for a while but it was a companionable silence.

Then Connie said, "Let's get the questions about Woolwine over with, and then we can go out and see the mare."

Rod helped himself to more ice cream and repeated the details of finding Woolwine in the stall. He admitted he probably had not locked the doors because of his miserable, sleep-deprived state.

"But I put all that in the form that Cary sent," he said.

"I know, Rod. Now I have only a few extra questions."

When she asked about strangers, he said in a quiet voice, "Someone murdered Wooley, you think."

Without waiting for an answer, he told her yes, a man had come before Thanksgiving to see his prize horse. Rod apologized for being unable to remember many details about the visit.

"I was on that blasted anti-depression stuff, Connie. Walking around in a daze." But the stranger's appearance had made an impression. Rod said he had a curious red face and not much hair, and was dressed roughly in a lumberjack coat and jeans.

"I didn't allow the man to see Woolwine, but he quoted the price he'd pay, sight unseen. I thought that was strange, and asked him to leave. I made sure he was gone before I went back in the house. And then I forgot about the whole thing."

No, he didn't remember what kind of vehicle the man was driving or whether he was local. "I wasn't paying much attention. And I'm sorry, Connie, that I don't know his name.

"I remember he wanted to give me a telephone number in case I changed my mind but I brushed him off. I just wanted him to leave."

The same man who had visited Bud Hurdle, thought Connie.

"I can't remember anything more," Rod said.

"Don't give it another thought. I'll tell Cary all this and we'll go on with the investigation. You've helped a lot, only you just don't realize it. I'll have to remind you not to talk about the case to anyone, Rod."

"Of course I won't."

"Now let's go out and see that mare. How old is she? Where'd you get her? Can I see her papers? Is she sweet-tempered? And what's her name?"

Rod laughed at her flood of questions and they went to the barn. After Connie had admired the large mare munching away at her feed, she looked at her watch. She hadn't realized she'd been there so long.

She apologized, knowing that Rod had work to do. But he put his hand up in protest, and said, "I'm so glad you came."

Then he added, "Would you like to start riding again when the weather gets warm? I managed to hang on to Jasmine, the horse you always liked. She's in the far barn."

Connie laughed and shook her head. "Good old Jasmine. It took me a while to show her who was the boss, remember?"

"Sure do. I had in mind to give her an attitude adjustment, but you wanted to teach her all by yourself."

"I'd love to come back, Rod. I've missed this place so much."

Driving away, she felt a sensation that might have been called happiness. *Rod is better. And he's given me something to look forward to.*

But on the way to her office, her thoughts returned to the investigation.

The interviews had only deepened her belief that the Lathams, Earlene, Rod, and even Hurdle could not have been responsible for the murdered horses.

Chapter Twenty-One

"And so," said Connie to Cary, "we have two strangers. One is small and frail-looking, with blondish-gray hair and mustache, driving a Japanese car of some make, maybe white. The other man is large, red-faced, bald, driving a black Chevy truck. Both men offered to buy the horses, in Earlene's and Rod's cases, sight unseen. The small man's name seems to be 'Nagle.' The big man didn't give his name to the Hurdles, and Rod doesn't remember a name. The short man wore a suit, the other man a lumberjack coat. The only telephone number I have is for the little man, but it's obscured by whatever brand of cooking oil Janey Hurdle uses. I can't read the whole number. The other owners either didn't take the telephone number offered to them or they threw it away.

"I wonder who those men were."

Cary looked up from his desk where he was putting cream in his coffee, and said, "Oh, I know who they are."

At that moment, Connie thought she must look like a cartoon character: eyes popping, mouth agape, exclamation points over her head.

"How do you know them?"

Cary shrugged. "I've dealt with them before. Their physical descriptions are a dead giveaway. Of course 'Nagle' isn't the real name."

"Tell me more."

"The two often act as agents for people who don't want it known they're after certain horses. But the men also broker horses on their own. They work out of a nasty office in Roanoke. The last time I was there, the place reeked of cigarettes and beer. I noticed hairy green food in the wastebasket. It's a tiny office, but they don't need more in their line of work."

"Do they really know horses well?"

"Quite knowledgeable. They have to be."

"What are their real names?"

"I'm not going to tell you. Better you don't know."

"What were you doing at their office, Cary?"

"I've been there twice in the last five years on business for two longtime clients, a man and a woman. Both asked if I could do anything about their problems with the brokers. I said I'd try. In one case, my naïve client sold his horse to the brokers on a handshake, but as you might expect, didn't get the full price agreed on. The woman refused to sell her horse and just managed to keep a mysterious fire from burning down her barn.

"Of course, the two brokers couldn't be taken to court. No solid evidence."

"Have they ever been prosecuted?"

"Not to my knowledge. They skate along the thin edge of the law, always escaping prosecution."

"What happened in your clients' cases?"

Cary said, grinning, "The brokers paid the balance of the money due on the horse and for the damage done to the barn."

"How did you get them to do that?"

"I managed."

Connie knew she shouldn't inquire further, so she asked, "Now what do we do?"

"Let me make a telephone call, Connie. Do you want to check your mail or something?"

"Sure," she said, leaving his office and strolling into Gyp's, shutting the door behind her. He was going to call the brokers, she was sure.

Gyp and Connie were talking about a quick dinner after work and then a visit to a new bookstore in Lynchburg when Cary came bustling out of his office, rubbing his hands together.

"Can you go to Roanoke with me right now, Connie?" he asked.

"Certainly," she said. *He's looking forward to this*, she thought, amused. Gulping the rest of her tea, she pulled on her coat and warm hat.

To Gyp, he said, "Will you cancel any appointments I had and reschedule them for next week? If I remember correctly, I don't have anything earth-shaking right now. I don't know when I'll get back today. And will you call Pam and tell her? Come on, Connie, we'll take my car."

Gyp nodded, showing no surprise.

The drive from Bedford County to the city of Roanoke would take about forty minutes. Connie settled back in Cary's silver Jag and managed to relax a little as Cary told her more about the two men's unscrupulous practices.

"We have to find out if they were acting on their own," he said, "or if they were agents for someone."

"And they might be the murderers," said Connie. "Or if they were working for someone, that person might have killed the horses, or had them killed when the brokers couldn't buy them."

"Knowing them, I don't think they did the killings. They're trash, but smart trash when it comes to self-incrimination. That's how they've escaped the law so long. They wouldn't dare do anything as blatant as murdering animals themselves. They might hire a murderer, though. I wouldn't put it past them. Maybe the person who hired them to buy the horses also asked them to find a killer when the owners wouldn't sell."

As they entered Roanoke, Connie began to wonder if Cary had used good judgment in making an appointment with the men. They sounded dangerous.

It was no good worrying about it now, she decided, as the car pulled up in front of a tiny one-story concrete block building on a shabby downtown street. There was no identifying sign on it.

She squared her shoulders and followed Cary through a metal door into the building. It was businesslike inside. A secretary was tapping at a computer and drinking from a mug balanced on the monitor. There was no nameplate on her desk.

The woman acknowledged them with a nod and jerked her thumb toward one of two offices, then returned to her computer.

When Connie and Cary entered the office, she saw two men, a large, red-faced bald man sitting behind a desk, and a small, thin man with a blond mustache standing at the window. She recognized them by their descriptions immediately.

The men stared at their visitors. Red Face gestured toward two chairs in front of the desk.

They took their seats, Cary not introducing Connie. Red Face said, "What do you want, McCutcheon?"

His voice was clear and smooth, belying his rough appearance.

"We've had three horses murdered up our way and an attempt on a fourth. Both of you approached the owners and offered to buy those horses. We want to know your part in the murders."

In an attempt at bravado, Blond Mustache said in a shrill voice, "Why should we talk to you at all? What we do is none of your business."

But for all his bluster, his face was strained. His hand moved back and forth, back and forth over his sparse blond mustache. It was obvious he knew something.

Red Face was inscrutable. He kept his eyes on Cary, who waited, saying nothing.

The standoff was broken when the big man said, "What do we get out of it if we tell you what we know?"

"Don't tell him anything," the little man piped.

"Shut up," said the big man. "Well, McCutcheon?"

"You tell us the truth, I don't inform the law."

"There's nothing to tie us to the murders," the little man yelped.

Red Face turned in his chair and glared at his partner.

"I thought I told you to shut up," he said. There was menace in his voice and face. "Get over there and sit down. And shut up!" He gestured toward a chair in the corner.

The little man subsided and did as he was told.

"He's a fool," the big man said, "but he does have a point."

"We have enough to link you to the murders as accomplices, even if you didn't do the actual killings. Don't you think it's a coincidence that you both tried to buy four horses and were turned down, and three died later, with an attempt on the fourth? The law could make a lot of that. We've…negotiated twice before. You know me, so you know I keep my word. I won't tell the police anything about you. But we need to have this information."

Red Face inclined his head and raised his hand to stop any more dialogue.

"I want to think about this for a minute." He swung his chair around toward the window, which looked out on a dumpster, and was quiet.

Connie glanced at Cary. He sat upright in his chair, his handsome patrician face composed but uncompromising. He looked over at her without smiling and turned his head back toward the desk.

She willed herself to be patient and waited.

After a few minutes, the big man swung around, his mind made up.

"I'll tell you about it. I'm going to trust you, McCutcheon. I'm going to trust you," he repeated. "If I find myself or my partner implicated in any way, I'll pay you back. You understand?"

Cary nodded. "We'll use what you tell us to find out who murdered those horses and why, and then we'll bring the police in on it. But your names won't be mentioned."

"All right. First, we didn't kill the horses or hire anyone to kill them. We only acted as agents for someone.

"A man called me late last fall. He wanted us to look at four horses with great potential, the best horses around, he said. If we liked what we saw, we were authorized to pay a lot of money for them. If for some reason, an owner wouldn't let us see a horse, we should still try to buy the horse. He must have wanted them bad.

"Then he asked what we would charge. I told him. Two days later, we received half the amount in an envelope. No check. So we did the job.

"You probably know we only got to see two horses. The other two owners wouldn't let us into their barns. I reported back to the man at a number he'd given me. Told him none of the owners wanted to sell. Two days later, we got another envelope of cash for the balance. And that was that. We never heard from him again. By the way, the envelopes had Roanoke postmarks. Word-processed, by the look of them. No return address."

"And that was the extent of your involvement?"

"Yes."

"You don't have any idea who he was?"

"No. He didn't talk a lot. Only gave me the addresses of the horse owners and explained what he wanted us to do."

Connie had an idea. "The best horses," Red Face had said.

"Can you describe his voice?"

"Sure. It was…low, flat. He sounded tough. Let's put it this way. I don't ever want to meet him."

"Was it the voice of someone from around here?"

"Nah. Northerner, I think."

"Anything else you can tell us?" said Cary.

"That's it. That's all I have."

"All right."

Red Face relaxed in his chair.

"Now," said Cary, "give us the number."

Red Face sat up as if to resist, then slumped in defeat. He called his secretary, asked her to bring a numbered file. He opened it, took out a page from a desk calendar, the kind that has holed pages that slide over a wire hoop. He copied the number on a piece of paper.

"The date, too," said Cary.

The man complied and handed over the paper.

"It won't do you any good to call that number," he said. "It's a restaurant in Lynchburg. They just took calls for the guy."

Cary stood up.

"We'll be going now. Thanks for your cooperation," he said, with a slight twitch of his lips.

The big man recognized the irony and grimaced.

Blonde Mustache just looked sullen.

Once they reached the Jag and got in, Connie exhaled with relief. The tension had been palpable. Cary threw himself over the steering wheel and burst into laughter.

Connie stared at him.

Finally he stopped. "Those two bozos," he spluttered, and then chortled again. "I wouldn't be able to make a good legal case against them. I was faking them out.

"Now I'll call the number their employer gave them."

He punched in the numbers on his cell phone and listened to the response, a grin spreading across his face. "How about an early lunch?" he suggested.

* * *

Back in the office, Red Face was confronting his partner. "I've put up with you for a long time. But I'm finally fed up. I told you over and over sometimes you have to deal with a guy, not lose your temper. But I see now you'll never learn. Look at the way you acted with McCutcheon. He could have gotten us in real trouble if he got mad at you."

With a dismissive gesture toward the door, he said, "Time I found myself someone else to work the racket. Get out."

* * *

An hour later, Connie and Cary were sitting in a modest restaurant in the heart of Lynchburg. The booths were upholstered in red—some of the seats mended with duct tape—and the counter was covered with red vinyl. Tall cylinders of glass contained shelves holding slices of cake and pie. The restaurant was filled with the smells and sounds of hamburgers frying and French fries spluttering

A beaming waitress put two glasses of water on their table and paused.

Cary asked, "Would you see if Iva can spare me a few minutes?"

"Sure, honey. Order later?"

Cary smiled and said they would.

An attractive woman came out of a back room and approached their table. She had well-cut gray hair and wore a conservative suit. She'd obviously been working because wire-frame glasses were pushed up on her head. Connie guessed she was about sixty years old.

"It's been a long time, Cary," she exclaimed. "How are you?"

"Sit down with us for a minute, if you will, Iva. I need to talk to you. This is Connie Holt, my associate."

She nodded to Connie, sat down next to her, and looked across the table at Cary, raising her eyebrows.

He gave her an affectionate smile.

Connie thought, *How does he know this woman?*

"Business okay?" he asked. She told him it was booming. This restaurant was due for a renovation soon. From what she said, Connie learned that Iva owned three restaurants in Lynchburg, Rustburg, and Buena Vista. The places charged low prices for their food and catered to people who didn't have much money but wanted a good meal. The restaurants stayed open twenty-four hours daily.

After Cary congratulated her, he got down to business, saying, "Iva, without telling you the details, it's serious. I only need to know one thing from you, and you won't be implicated. But it's essential information, and I have to have it."

Iva nodded. "Of course."

"I've been told that a man got some telephone calls here, would have been last fall before Thanksgiving."

"Yes," said Iva. "He only got a few."

"How did you know him?"

"He came in here once in a while to eat. My 11 to 7 girls told me he usually appeared in the middle of the night, but I saw him here several times in the daytime before he spoke to me."

"What did he ask you to do?"

"He told me he wanted to give this telephone number to a company he was doing business with, assured me it wasn't drugs. It would only be for a short time and then no more calls. He offered to pay well, and I didn't see anything wrong with it."

"Nevertheless, I wouldn't do that again, Iva."

Iva nodded. "I won't. I realize now I was taking a chance."

"Tell us what else you noticed about him."

"He was very quiet, didn't talk to anyone, tipped big. Always polite to my girls. Ate fast, then walked out."

Chapter Twenty-One

"How was he dressed?"

"Very well. His clothes were expensive. I noticed because my restaurants cater to poorer folks. He didn't look as if he belonged here."

Connie's head started to throb as she listened to Cary's questions and Iva's answers. Would Iva be able to give them the man's name?

"What did he look like, Iva?

Turning to Connie, he said, "Her memory is exceptional."

Iva flushed with pleasure.

Again Connie wondered about the relationship between the two.

"He was handsome, in a sort of…heavy way. Dark complexion, very dark eyes. His hair was black with some gray in it, and it was wavy and curly. Perfectly cut." She hesitated, then went on. "He could frighten many people, I think, but he was polite and gentle with me."

Tony Stephens, thought Connie, and immediately felt sorry he was involved.

Cary pulled several pictures from his attaché case, spread them before Iva. "Do you see him here?"

She took her time.

"Yes," she said. "There he is."

Connie didn't need to see the man Iva picked out.

Cary said, "Thank you, Iva. Let me know if there's anything you need. Now I think we'd better order. My associate here is hungry, aren't you, Connie?"

Iva got up and put her hand for a moment on Cary's shoulder. "You know, Cary, that I will always be grateful to you—"

Cary interrupted her. "Not another word, Iva."

Iva smiled and signaled to the waitress that Cary and his companion were ready to order. Then she went back to her office.

Connie thought about Iva's identification as they waited for their food.

"Let's not talk here about what we heard," said Cary in a soft voice.

"All right. I'm wondering about something. Can you tell me how you know Iva?"

"There's nothing scandalous about Iva and me. Did you think there was?"

To avoid the question, Connie drank her water.

He teased her by not answering right away. Then he said, "Iva used to be my cook. She wanted to open a restaurant and I bankrolled the first one, this one, as a matter of fact. She has long since paid me back. I thought it was a good investment. She's been very successful. She could have opened up a restaurant for people who appreciate her skills for haute cuisine. When I remember her desserts…well, anyway, she had firm ideas about what kind of place she wanted."

The waitress brought their food then, and told them it was on the house.

Cary accepted the favor, and after homemade lemon meringue pie, they left.

In the car, Connie said, "Do you mind if we don't talk about it until we get back, Cary? I want to sort things out in my head."

Cary slid a CD into the player, and the rational, orderly sounds of Mozart filled the car.

As they drove into Bedford County, Connie thought, with sinking heart, *I see most of it now.*

Chapter Twenty-Two

When they got to the office, Gyp told them Tyler Fox had called. Fox had looked at a Morgan and wanted to talk about insurance for the animal. With a sigh, Cary said, "Connie, let's meet here tomorrow morning. I should call Ty right away and after that, I want to do some research on Stephens."

"Explain something, Cary?"

"Maybe," he said with a grin.

"Why did you have that picture in your briefcase today? We didn't even mention Tony when we were talking about the murders."

"My picture file of owners, breeders, other people in the horse business—it's huge now—has been useful more than once. Some time I'll tell you about the Clauson case and how a picture helped me catch a rascal who gave a buyer false papers. The description of the mystery man we got from that thug in Roanoke sounded like Stephens. On a hunch, I showed the picture to Iva. You suspected Stephens too, didn't you? That's why you asked about the voice."

Connie nodded. "The mystery man said 'the best horses' on the phone. In the newspaper article about Stephens, he was quoted as saying he wanted to breed only 'the best horses.' That wouldn't have been enough to go on. But there was the description of the voice. Then Iva's physical description clinched it."

Late that evening, Connie was still wide awake. Soaking in a hot bath, she thought about Tony Stephens's connection with the case. She wondered about the depth of his involvement and hoped he had nothing to do with the murders. Maybe he only wanted to buy the horses. But if that were true, why hire thugs as go-betweens, when he could have sent a legitimate representative?

She had learned there was more to Stephens than anyone realized. Contrary to his frozen persona in public, he was capable of kindness and warmth. She had feared him. Now fear had turned to pity. But he was still a locked box for which she had no key.

When the doorbell rang, she was pouring a glass of Merlot. The clock in the kitchen said 11:20. She went to the front door and peered through one of its small windows.

Jase stood on the doorstep.

* * *

Late that afternoon, a sudden pain had shot through Jase's head as he stood at the operating table working on a cat with a crushed foot. *Oh no*, he thought. *Don't let me be sick. There's too much to do.* Later, when the phone summoned him to a farm in Bedford to look at a colt, he had to go. Now he was feeling worse by the minute. In the frigid stall, alternating waves of heat and cold racked his body. By the time he injected the horse with an antibiotic, he was dizzy and the hot dog he had for lunch felt like a chunk of lead in his stomach.

He managed to get into his truck and start for Monroe. What he needed was comfort and help, but he knew he wouldn't get it from Les. He also knew that she would be gone when he reached home. She had given up the pretense of lying about where she went so many nights, merely shrugging when he asked her about it. Jase suspected she must be having an affair, but he didn't want to know who her partner was. At this point, he could bear no more.

Driving north, he thought, *I've got to talk to Les about a divorce.* He made up his mind that no matter how sick he was or how urgent his professional calls, he would broach the subject this weekend. For some reason, she could be counted on to be home on Saturdays and Sundays. Probably her lover was married.

Knowing Les now for what she really was, he expected her to try for the biggest settlement she could get, but he didn't care. He could always work harder after the divorce to get back in the black.

He'd long ago given up trying to figure out why he married Les. It was important to save himself now. After it was all over, he could make a fresh start.

Now he was near the side road that led to Connie's cottage. On an impulse born from pure misery, he decided to go see her. She'd make coffee, and then maybe he could keep driving home. *It's late*, he thought. *She's asleep.* But he shuddered as another chill rippled over his body, and he turned down the narrow road. He saw with relief that there was a light in the kitchen. When he got out of the truck, his knees were weak.

* * *

Connie opened the door.

Shocked by his appearance, she said, "Jase, what's the matter?"

"Con. I'm on the way home, but I got sick this afternoon. Could you give me a cup of coffee? Maybe I can make it the rest of the way."

Once inside, he said, "I'm sorry to impose on you." His legs gave way, and he caught hold of a bookcase near the door.

She helped him to the couch. His face shone with sweat, and he couldn't stop shivering.

"You're too sick to drive, Jase," she said. "You can stay here tonight and then go home in the morning if you feel better."

He nodded, knowing now he couldn't even get back to his truck in the driveway.

"Have you been looking at a horse? Are your clothes damp?"

"Yes."

"Take them off and put that over you." Connie pointed to the bright quilt on the end of the sofa. "I'm going to get the old bathrobe that I use when I'm sick. It was Mike's, the only valuable thing I got when we divorced!"

Jase tried to smile. By the time Connie returned to the parlor with the robe, he'd wrapped himself in the quilt.

"I'll be right back," she promised. Then she left him alone, taking his discarded clothes with her. He was just tying the robe when Connie returned with a mug of whiskey and two aspirin.

Obediently he put the pills in his mouth and washed them down. Holding the cup with two hands, he took another sip and said, "I feel bad about what you went through with that state cop. He might have killed you. Might have killed you." Then his head drooped and his eyes closed.

"Come on, Jase, I'm going to put you to bed. Stand up now." With Jase clinging to her, they made their way to her bedroom, the only place for guests to sleep in the small cottage.

"I can't do this, Con, I'll take the couch," Jase mumbled.

"I'll be all right."

Too exhausted to protest any further, Jase sank into Connie's clean sheets and fell asleep.

Connie turned off the light and left the room.

Uneasy now, she thought it best to keep busy. Going through Jase's coat before she put it in the washer, she was startled to find a horseshoe nail, a pair of pliers, and a dollar bill in the same pocket with three fuzz-covered cherry cough drops. She noticed that his worn, knitted gloves had holes in four of the fingers and cursed Les. She started the machine.

Then she made up the couch, lay down, and surrendered to her feelings.

From the time she'd seen Jase at the door, white, drawn, and swaying with fatigue, she knew she couldn't turn him away. But for her own sake, she wished he weren't here. His presence was disturbing. And he was in her bed, no less.

She wasn't surprised that with the excitement of the long day and now with Jase here, she couldn't sleep. Finally she fell into a fitful doze. She woke when Jase cried out from the bedroom. She found him half-conscious, tossing and turning, his body drenched with sweat.

"What is it, Jase?" she asked. He tried to talk to her, but most of the words were too garbled for her to understand. She thought she heard him mutter, "Might have killed you."

She sponged his face, saying, "It's all right, Jase, it's all right," which seemed to calm him, and he went back to sleep. One arm was lying on top of the comforter, the hand covered with calluses, cuts, and bruises—marks of his trade. The sight of the ruined hand undid her defenses, and she got into bed beside him. She couldn't sleep anyway, and he needed her.

For a moment, she let herself recognize the black humor of finally being in bed with Jase—who was oblivious to her presence. She took the stone-cold hand in hers. *I can at least be here to help him if he wakes up again,* she thought. Finally her eyes closed and she went to sleep, still holding his hand.

Somewhere around three, she woke with a start.

Jase's arms were around her, his lips against hers.

* * *

At Fayence, Tony Stephens was sleepless as usual. He was sitting on a high stool at the granite counter in the kitchen, a mug of coffee before him. His cherry-red silk robe and pajamas provided the only spot of color in the institutional black, white and gray room.

It had been a bad day. For one thing, his four-hour session in the morning with his accountant had been disastrous. The man had said, "Mr. Stephens, you have a problem. You're spending too much."

Tony had looked at the meticulous report of his finances carefully, and holding himself in check, asked many questions.

By the time the accountant left, Tony was boiling with self-directed rage. He had to admit to himself that for the first time in his life, he'd spent freely, even profligately, convinced that the chances he was taking would win an international reputation for Fayence.

After lunch, he had gone to his office to study the accountant's report further. Pat Morris, the breeding manager, knocked on the open door. Tony, intent on a detail, didn't look up but growled, "Come in."

Pat hesitated, stepped across the threshold.

Chapter Twenty-Two

Tony looked up and saw Pat's face. "This is about that horse, isn't it? The second day."

"Doggie is still sick."

Morris's answer was too quick, showing Tony that it had been rehearsed. He knew Pat was afraid of what his reaction would be. He forced himself to be cold and calm. Blowing up would achieve nothing. *Maybe I'm getting smart at last*, he told himself.

"Do you know what's wrong with her?" he asked.

"It's respiratory, but I'm no vet. I tried to get Tyree but he had to go to Bedford on a case. No one at the clinic knows when he'll be back."

Stephens considered, made up his mind. "Get Carter here, now!"

"Yes, sir."

"Let me know when he comes."

Left alone, he tried to analyze the chaos in his mind and thought, *This is what failure feels like.*

* * *

As soon as he got the summons to go to Fayence, Carter told Mary Evans to take over some tricky surgery he had to do on an old horse.

She protested. "I haven't done this before. I don't know if I can do it."

He didn't bother to respond as he exited his office with indecent haste. The burden of his ongoing remodeling expenses would be lightened by what he would charge Stephens for this call. He only hoped that whatever was wrong would be simple, and he could cure the horse and spend happy hours with Les Tyree, planning how to spend the money. Their relationship had broadened. He was now using Les as a consultant for his ongoing renovation of the old Carter house when he wasn't using her in bed.

At Fayence, Pat Morris took him to Doggie's stall. When Carter saw the little horse, his heart fell. She looked miserable, with discharges from nose and eyes, and a dry cough. Carter told Pat he would need to do an internal examination to find out the condition of the fetus and placenta. He found evidence of inflammation, and looked at Morris.

"It's rhinopneumonitis, isn't it?" asked Pat.

"Maybe. I'll get some tissue samples. That'll nail it down."

He took the specimens and started to leave for his office.

"Hold up, Carter," said Pat sharply. "If Doggie does have the infection, she'll abort her fetus, won't she? And all the other pregnant mares will be at risk."

Carter only nodded. "I'll be back later."

That night, Carter drove back to report to Stephens and Morris. The master of Fayence was sitting behind his desk in his office. He didn't ask Carter to sit down.

"Well?" he said.

Carter shifted his position on the Oriental rug and cleared his throat. "The horse has an infection: rhinopneumonitis."

"Explain."

"It's a respiratory infection in horses caused by a virus." He paused.

"Go on, go on," snarled Stephens.

"In young horses, the infection is often mild. But in pregnant mares, it's deadly. The virus enters the bloodstream and attacks both placenta and fetus. It causes the placenta to separate prematurely and the fetus is suffocated. The fetus will abort. If a mare does succeed in giving birth, the foal will die shortly after it is born."

"How do you know the horse has this infection?"

"I looked at tissue samples and found EHV-1 viral bodies in the liver and other tissues. There can be no doubt."

Stephens turned to Morris. "Wasn't the horse inoculated against this infection?"

"Yes, of course. But the inoculations don't always succeed with pregnant mares."

There was a short silence. Then Stephens said, "Is that all?"

Carter swallowed and brought out, "No. The infection is contagious. There may be other pregnant mares in the stables who abort."

Tony stared at him. He couldn't grasp the fact that he might lose many other foals. He tried to stay calm.

"What can we do?" he asked.

Carter said, "We'll have to examine every pregnant mare on the place, take tissue samples, and find out if any more mares have the infection. Then go from there."

"Do it," ordered Tony. "You'll stay at Fayence for as long as it takes. You'll sleep here tonight and start at first light."

"I'll need help," said Carter. "Can I send for one of my people?"

Tony nodded. "And Carter," he added in a menacing tone, "tell no one but your assistant. I don't want this to get out. When you're through, tell me what you've found, day or night." Then he dismissed both men with a wave of his hand.

Carter felt crushed by the weight of the problem. How many pregnant mares did Stephens have, anyway? How long would it take to do the examinations and gather all the tissue samples?

* * *

Now, sitting in his bleak kitchen, Stephens wondered what he should do. If many of the pregnant mares were infected, he was lost. He accepted now that he might have overreached himself, and wondered if he ought to devise a plan to escape this labyrinthine financial structure he himself had built.

* * *

Jase was clasping Connie so tightly against his feverish body that she felt every bone. For a minute she was frightened and disoriented. Then she thought, *It's only Jase. My friend, Jase.*

"Connie," he said in a low voice. Tears ran from his eyes, making her face wet too. She listened to his murmured words, understood a few. She thought she heard him say "Les" and "no good" and "fool." And then he said clearly, "Might have killed you." His arms tightened around her. Dazed by the piercing-sweet pleasure of Jase's body against hers, she couldn't think, let alone respond to his disjointed words.

Jase buried his burning face in her neck. "Please, Connie," he whispered.

He pulled her nightgown up clumsily and put his hand between her legs. He took a ragged breath and caressed her. The longing to abandon herself to him grew, her body aching with exquisite pain.

Fiercely, she fought it.

In that curious, suspended, protracted moment in time, something within her reasserted itself, and she knew she did not want to wake beside Jase when daylight came, with the taste of ashes in her mouth.

It took all her strength to pull away from him and get out of bed. She was grateful when the cold air in the bedroom buffeted her. It helped bring reality.

Jase groaned as he felt the deprivation of her body.

She covered him up and whispered, "Go back to sleep."

He sighed and then was still.

Connie knew she wouldn't be able to rest for what remained of the night. She put Jase's clean clothes into the dryer. Then she made a big pot of strong tea to ease the painful lump in her throat, taking slow sips while the clothes leaped and tumbled themselves dry. *Don't cry*, she commanded herself.

She could still feel the pressure of Jase's glowing body on hers. At one point she half rose from her chair to go back to him. Who would care? Who would know? Jase would receive her with joy. *But he doesn't love me*, she told herself with brutal truth. *He's just sick and in need of comfort. We are only friends.*

She would have nothing for which to reproach herself, but it was not much of a consolation.

Connie was in the kitchen making breakfast at about six o'clock when Jase came in and sat down at the table. He had put on the clean clothes laid at the end of the bed.

He couldn't look at her.

"Thanks for doing my stuff, Con," he said, head down.

"Are you feeling better, Jase?" Connie asked. His mortification amused her.

"Much better. Must have been a twenty-four hour thing."

In the middle of eating bacon and eggs, he put down his knife and fork, cleared his throat, looked straight at her, and blurted out, "Connie, I apologize for what I did in the middle of the night. You don't deserve such treatment. You're my dear friend, and then I do something like that. I'll never understand what got into me, I'll never forgive myself, but I hope you can forgive me." He paused and swallowed. "If you don't ever want anything to do with me again, I'll know why."

Connie poured him a second cup of coffee and stumbled into the lame explanation she had thought of while the clothes were drying.

"Don't think of it any more, Jase. I know what happened. You needed comfort, and I was there. I lay down with you because I thought I could help if you woke up again. I was so tense—I had a bad day yesterday—that I thought I couldn't sleep, but then I did. You see, it's partly my fault. Propinquity. You didn't expect to find a woman in bed with you. And I certainly didn't expect you to wake up and want to make love. So we were both to blame."

They laughed self-consciously. Connie changed the subject and they finished breakfast.

When Jase left, his smile was broad. "What did I ever do to deserve a friend like you?"

She dressed and drove to the office. Today Cary would have the financial reports ready about their suspects. It was entirely possible that they might be able to figure out who had killed the horses and why.

She hoped the murderer wasn't the man, the friend, who had just left.

Chapter Twenty-Three

"The first thing we'll do is look at the financial picture of the people we've identified as suspects," said Cary. "And again today, we're looking at everyone as suspects, and not letting friendship get in our way." Connie understood perfectly. They were going to consider Jase as the murderer. Cary was saying that it would be easier to do if they both could remain objective.

I doubt that is possible, she thought. *How can we both forget what a close friend Jase has been? The respect we both have for him as a vet?* She sighed inwardly.

"Last time, we pretty much decided the owners weren't the killers. Do you still think that's true?"

"I've thought about it a lot, and I don't think Rod, the Lathams, or Earlene killed—or hired someone to kill—their horses. If anything, I was even more convinced by the visits I made to them. None of them are murderers or instigators of murder. It stands to reason that Bud Hurdle can't be the murderer either. He wouldn't be capable of thinking up a plan like this one, or injecting the horses himself, or even hiring it done." Her face was pale and there were blue smudges under her eyes.

Cary paused. "You look tired, Connie. Have one of these. You'll feel better." He pushed a plate of plump muffins toward her.

Obediently, she cut a blueberry muffin into quarters and took a bite of one.

"I'm all right, Cary. Let's go on."

"I agree that we can eliminate the owners. That leaves the three vets—Mary Evans, Pres Carter, and Jase Tyree—and, of course, we have to fit Stephens into the picture.

"Mary Evans first. She's been with Carter for only a few months. In my view, she doesn't have the information necessary for the killer to act: knowledge about the horse owners, their homes and barns, the condition of those barns, and so on. Matter of fact, she hardly knows anyone here and from what I was told, she does her work and then goes home exhausted. Gets to bed early. By the way, she's already unhappy at Carter's place and has started looking around for another job. No, I don't think she's the murderer."

"What's Carter's story?"

"His practice is doing well, but he's spending too much money on that wreck he calls his 'ancestral home.'" Cary laughed. "People I talked to doubt whether that house can ever be restored to its original elegance. Most of the wood inside and out is rotted. He'll have to rebuild almost everything.

"Of course, he has three children in college as well. However, there is something that probably disqualifies him as the killer. He has a trust fund he can tap into. His great-grandfather made a lot of money in questionable ventures. His grandfather and father inherited from the old pirate and both invested their inheritances wisely. Pres's father set up a lifetime trust account for his son. While he's been dipping into that account since he was twenty-one, there's still a lot in it. And his bank accounts are in order, no unusual sums deposited, as there would be if he were being paid to kill the horses. I know he's repulsive but I don't think he's the murderer."

Connie hesitated and then asked, "And Jase?"

"It's bad," he warned.

She swallowed hard. "Tell me everything you know, Cary."

"His bills have been steadily mounting ever since he married Les. From what I could gather, she's a compulsive spender. They could manage fine if her only passion were horses. But her clothing bills are huge—she flies out of town to Boston and Washington to shop. It was she, I understand, who insisted on their having three vehicles. But that house in Lynchburg is what's leading them to bankruptcy. It isn't in as bad shape as Carter's, but the renovation costs are just as pricey."

Connie told Cary what Jase had said in Charlottesville. "Les says she wants it done by Christmas! Jase has had to expand his practice to small animals just to make ends meet. Her salary at the museum isn't enough to cover the bills she's running up. The whole burden of her spending has been on his shoulders."

Cary shook his head. "Les needs counseling."

"Fat chance," scoffed Connie. "She's eaten up with pride. No way would she ever admit she's in the wrong."

"The pressure on Jase must be enormous. You know, he looks worse every time I see him. I remember the years before he was married. He was always in the best of health. Now he's lost a shocking amount of weight. He's all bones and nerves. And at the Christmas party, I'll swear he was unsteady on his feet."

"That's from the exhaustion of trying to satisfy Les's every financial demand," said Connie.

"You know him better than I do. Why doesn't he get a divorce?"

"I suppose he thinks if he supplies Les with enough money to pay for everything she wants, she'll love him back. And besides that, like his wife, he's proud. By staying with her, he doesn't have to admit to himself and the world that the marriage has failed. He doesn't want people around here to see him as the stereotypical foolish older man led astray by a younger, sexy woman."

"And Connie, there's something else. Too many people have told me Les is having an affair, which must drive Jase half-crazy if he knows about it."

"Who's the man?"

"Carter."

"It figures. They're both selfish, contemptible monsters," burst out Connie. "They're drawn together by their pretentious renovation of their houses, but more, I suspect, by their lust. She bedazzled Jase sexually—I know, I watched him succumb to her—and Carter's had other affairs through the years. That's common knowledge. I can only imagine what Mame Carter has gone through with that man."

It was a couple of minutes before she said, "I thought of something on the way to the office. Did your sources tell you what kind of cars Jase and his wife have?"

"Let me look. Yes. A white Escort and a black Lincoln."

"Remember that run-in I had with the big black car at Hurdle's farm? That could have been a Lincoln. And another thing. Last night Jase came to my house. Very sick with a virus. He was in bad shape, sweating, chills, weakness in his legs, feverish, not thinking right. He told me before I showed him the bedroom that he was sorry about the Wampler mess. He said twice that Wampler 'might have killed you.' Then in the middle of the night, he woke up crying and repeated those words. 'Might have killed you.' Suppose he was referring to the Hurdle incident?"

"My God."

"And Cary, now that we're putting all this together, I think Jase's physical and emotional problems are too severe to be caused by his awful marriage alone. Little by little, he's coming apart. There's something else that could explain his condition, his guilt over having murdered the horses."

Cary said, "I would have thought the idea of killing horses would be so evil to Jase that he could hardly stand to talk about it, much less do it himself."

"I know, I'm *sure* that he considered himself a defender of horses against any man or woman who would hurt them. If he has been killing horses, he must be in an agony of guilt."

"But he did have the means and opportunity," said Cary. "He would have known what injection to use. He knew all the owners. He was Rod and Earlene's vet. He saw for himself Rod's poor emotional condition, which might make him careless with barn security, and Earlene's primitive barn. Although he didn't work for Dick and Laura Latham, he's known them for years, visited up there often and was familiar with their accessible barn. And even though he wasn't Bud's vet, he was well aware of Bud's carelessness. Hell, he'd talked about it to me."

"And of course, we know his motivation," Connie said in a dull voice.

Cary abruptly got to his feet and went to the kitchen door. "I'm going to get a fresh pot of coffee."

Left alone, Connie thought, *Cary and his objectivity. He can't stand the thought of Jase murdering the horses and being responsible for Job Hoskins's death any more than I can. I can't do this any longer. Maybe Cary will give me a few days off while he finishes the investigation by himself.* Her throat hurt as she struggled to keep from crying.

But she knew she was fooling herself. She had to see it through.

When Cary came back, she made herself ask, "Are there any large payments deposited in Jase's accounts about the time of the three murders?"

"Following each of the killings, Jase put $30,000 in his checking account—in cash."

Connie thought a minute and said, "Fill me in on Tony Stephens's financial picture. Since he failed to buy the horses, he's the logical one who paid to have them killed."

"This was the hardest information to get, for obvious reasons. That man is smart and powerful. I had to call in all my favors from my source. But finally he told me what he knew. Stephens has overshot himself with that fancy estate in Albemarle County. He was so flush when he came here that he could spend a huge amount of money on that place and not feel it. The finest horses. The most advanced facilities. The best breeding methods. But he's spent too much, and he's at a crossroads right now. Either he'll survive or he'll fail. He's got to recoup his investment, and that means his business has to show a profit. His clients have to believe he's capable of breeding their animals successfully. He has a number of pregnant mares at Fayence right now, and if they produce fine foals, he's home free. Fayence will be known all over the world."

Connie said, "Jase told me that Stephens seemed to favor him over the other vets. As far as Stephens's motive, I believe he wanted to eliminate the competition. In the business world—and breeding is a business—the strongest corporation either takes over other companies that pose a threat or destroys them.

"Tony would be willing to do anything to get what he wants. The murder of horses would mean nothing because horses are just animals to him. When I was at Fayence checking Pride of the Yankees, he cared whether the animal was well or not, but refused to go into the stall. Buck told me he doesn't have anything to do with horses at all, won't even touch them. They are only a means to an end."

Cary nodded. "Money, power, and prestige in the breeding world."

"Did you find out anything about his past?"

"My source suspects he was involved in criminal activity."

"To give Tony his due, he does have a code of values—of a sort. He saved me from Wampler when he could have driven by and ignored what was happening."

"I'm grateful to him for doing that. But I want to see that he gets everything that's coming to him for inciting the murders—if he did indeed do that."

He looked at his watch, and getting to his feet, said, "Come out to the stable with me."

They donned warm coats and went through the French doors. In the heated stable, the McCutcheon horses were docile, searching the straw in their stalls for bits of food they might have missed. Pam was grooming Max, a well-behaved horse who had helped her win many ribbons. She smiled as she worked on Max's tangled mane. Her husband and Connie waved, exchanged pleasantries, and moved on.

Pausing in front of a stall holding a pregnant mare, the two stood watching the horse. "You remember my old Proud Mary, Connie."

Then Cary ran his hand through his hair and took a deep breath, let it out. "You know, I can't be objective any more. I thought when we discovered who the murderer is, I would want to beat him senseless—and I probably would have tried. But if it's Jase, I can't do that. He's been such a good friend to horses all these years. I remember countless times when he pulled a horse through that everyone thought was a goner. There isn't a person in the horse community who doesn't admire him.

"Yes, he did an evil thing if he killed those horses. But if he's guilty, my heart will be with him when his crime is exposed and he suffers his punishment. His life will be ruined.

"Now I'm going to suggest something. If you don't agree, I'll just drop it. We could do the easy thing right now. Give our information to the police and let them handle it. But at this point, we're just speculating. We don't know whether Jase murdered the horses for the money he would make from Stephens. And we don't know that Stephens is behind the murders."

"You want me to talk to Jase, hope that he confesses to me."

"Yes. We need confirmation of our theory, but beyond that, we owe it to Jase to give him any break we can. I believe he'd feel better if he told his story to someone who cares a lot about him. If he tells you the truth first, then it will be easier for him to talk to the police."

"I would have suggested it myself, Cary, if you hadn't. I can't throw Jase to the wolves without doing everything I can to help him. I think he'll talk to me. If he does confess, I'll offer to go with him to the police if Les refuses."

"Tell him I will too."

"I can't stand to put this off, though. I'll go late this afternoon when his clinic hours are over."

The quiet little mare snorted.

The two were again silent, looking at Proud Mary but not really seeing her.

Chapter Twenty-Four

"Dr. Tyree, seems like we'll never be through today."

Nancy from the front desk had come back to his office where Jase was taking a quick break to say that an injured dog—probably hit by a car—had to be seen right away. A Good Samaritan had brought him in. He went quickly to an examining room and set the dog's leg. Tomorrow his staff would trace the dog from the tag on his collar and call the owner.

He was still weak, but what seemed like a never-ending stream of animals and their owners needed his attention and he couldn't go home. A cat had gotten wedged in a culvert and suffered a broken leg when his owner pulled him out by that leg. She was aghast over what she'd done to her pet, and Jase had to take the time to comfort her. A terrier came in with an abscess on her back, and the anxious owner, who was clumsy at physically caring for the animal, had to be taught several times how to apply the salve. A farmer brought in an ailing chicken, but Jase remembered almost nothing about poultry from his student days. He told the farmer to take it to Virginia Tech.

When a brief respite came, Jase sat down at his desk and put his head in his hands. He couldn't stop thinking about the mess he'd made of his life. If he were going to start divorce proceedings and move away, he'd have to close his clinic. It would be a relief to be away from Les, and above all, from Stephens. If he stayed here, he would have to hire another vet, for he could no longer keep up with the workload. *I just don't know what to do,* he thought. *I've fouled everything up.* He drained the remnants of his tea and tried to focus on the work. He knew he wasn't dealing well with the animals today, thinking about his diagnoses too long and then not being sure he was right. *I can't think clearly any more about anything.* "All right, I'm ready," he told his vet assistant.

***

By six, the clinic was empty.

He was trying to pull himself together to drive home when he heard the waiting room door open and close. He went to the door of his office.

It was Connie, her face somber.

"Hi, Con. What are you doing here? There isn't anything wrong, is there? If it's what happened last night, I'm so sorry. I'm still ashamed of what I did."

Connie stared at Jase, assessing him now in the light of what she suspected he had done. He looked, she thought, like a man lacerated by guilt. His eyes seemed too large for the gaunt face. His white coat, symbol of his profession, only emphasized the pallor of his skin.

On the way to Monroe, she had tried to prepare for the confrontation, but she was numb with sorrow. About all she could do, she decided, was tell him he was a suspect in the murders, and hope that he would confess and implicate whoever paid him. Connie would have to rely on their mutual regard to elicit the confession. She had no doubt that Jase was aching to confide in someone. *How lonely he must have been all this time,* she thought. There would be no need to tell him that what he'd done was immoral, that he'd betrayed his profession and himself; he knew that well enough. She would make it clear that because of their long friendship, Cary and she would help him do the right thing, but both felt there could be no excuse for his crime.

Maybe Cary and I figured it wrong, she told herself. *Maybe Jase is innocent.* But she had no real hope.

"Jase, I have to talk to you," she said.

Silently, he stepped aside while she walked into his cluttered office. She looked for the framed quotation on the wall:

> "Think when we talk of horses that you see them
> Printing their proud hoofs i' the receiving earth."

Images of Woolwine and Finn lying dead in their stalls flooded her mind.

Jase pulled two chairs together and they sat down in front of his desk. Connie felt disoriented, as if this man with the kind, familiar face were a doppelganger of Jase Tyree, one who could find it within himself to kill innocent animals, one she couldn't begin to fathom. She folded her hands in her lap and tried to concentrate.

"Have you had anything to eat?"

"No," he admitted. "But there's that hamburger joint next door. They'll deliver if I call."

Connie hesitated, nodded. Anything to ease things between them.

After Jase called, he said, "What can I do for you?"

"Cary and I have been investigating the killings of three horses and an attempt on a fourth. We think we know how and why the horses were killed and who murdered them."

Her gaze was unflinching. When he didn't respond, she went on. She summarized the investigation, step by step. When he heard about Dr. Marmion's involvement, Jase took a sharp breath.

Now I've got to say it, she thought.

"Jase, you're a suspect in the murders of Woolwine, Finn, and Ali. We think Stephens paid you to do it. We're hoping you're innocent, but we have to know the truth."

When she was finished, she waited.

The doorbell rang. Connie saw Jase wince. *His nerves are raw,* she thought.

"I'll get it," he said in a tight voice.

When he came back, he sat down and gulped his hot coffee while Connie bit into her sandwich. But she couldn't keep up the charade of two old friends enjoying a meal. She was desperate to know the truth. Abandoning her food, she waited.

Jase stared at the wall behind Connie for a while.

"I want you, more than anyone else, to understand, Con," he said.

"I'll try. Just tell me."

"When I married Les, I was—overcome by her. I don't want to make excuses. But I had never met anyone like her. If truth be told, I couldn't stand the Southern Belle type. But I thought she was different. She was so beautiful, so talented with her horses, so interested in my practice and me. I overlooked her flirting with others and thought I could put up with it because she said she wanted only me—or so she said.

"When we'd been married about a year, I found out the truth about Les. She had been bored with her life at home and decided to see if she liked marriage any better. I don't know why she picked me to experiment with. She could have had any number of other fools. In spite of that, I was still in love with her and hoped I could make her love me back.

"She talked me into buying that house, and then started to restore it even though I told her we'd have to go slow. Spent more money we didn't have on clothes, her horses, antiques, anything she wanted. She never asked my advice. Our bank account kept getting lower. You know I enlarged my practice, took other jobs, did anything I could to earn extra money.

"Stephens liked my work up at Fayence, hired me more than anyone else. One day, he took me into his office, gave me the third degree about my finances. I think now the cold bastard knew about my problems with Les and used them to get what he wanted, but that day, I hoped he might offer me a full-time appointment as his vet. I even imagined there might be a rent-free cottage on the estate for Les and me. The prestige of living there would have excited Les. So I was ready to agree if Stephens offered me a contract. You can imagine what I felt when he wanted me to kill horses for him. He was like ice as he said 'kill.' I couldn't believe he said it, refused to believe it. I was stunned."

"What else did Stephens say?" asked Connie.

"That he had tried to buy certain horses and failed. Now they had to be killed. He asked me if horses ever just 'died.' I said yes, from weak hearts or some other natural cause. He asked if I knew any way to kill them that would appear to be natural. Not thinking, I said I did. He then told me I'd be paid

$30,000 for each horse I killed, and estimated that there were about five that he wanted done away with. The deaths were all to look natural. I was to falsify my post mortem reports to the insurance company as to cause of death."

So there was to be another one, thought Connie. She wondered for a moment which horse it was.

"My mind was racing," Jase continued. "One moment I was so appalled by what he was asking me to do that I felt sick. I was a vet. I took an oath. But the next moment I was multiplying five times $30,000 and mentally picturing what that money would do for my marriage.

"I told him I'd have to think it over. When I drove home that night, Les told me about some things she wanted to do with the house. She looked so beautiful and I—I wanted her so much—that I told her I'd get the money some way. We went to bed and…well, anyway, the next day I went back up to Fayence and agreed to do it."

Connie couldn't keep the horror from her face—and Jase saw it. He had to look away for a minute.

But she only said, with tightened lips, "Go on."

"There isn't much more to tell. I knew everyone involved, knew their farms, their barns. It was easy to slip in at night. I used potassium chloride. Wooley was always spooky and he was terrified when I entered the stall. I figure the injection scared him so much he kicked that hole in the wall and then slid down it. That's why his head was up. You know, he nearly killed me that night. Since then, I've often wished it had been me who died instead of old Job Hoskins. There would have been a kind of justice in it." He stopped to sip the coffee.

"Job. I used to talk to him, listen to his old-time remedies for sick horses."

Tears running down his face, he said, "I killed that man, I'm responsible."

Connie waited until he could speak again.

"The other horses I killed didn't react as strongly as Woolwine did because they weren't as high strung. I talked myself into thinking that I was executing them mercifully and the owners could get large insurance settlements. The money Stephens paid me was a godsend. Les started renovating the ballroom with that money.

"Then Stephens told me to kill Pete, Bud Hurdle's horse. I took Les's black Lincoln, as I had all the other times because the car was heavier and safer on the ice, I thought, than my Escort. When I got to Hurdle's farm and went into the barn, I saw that Pete looked really sick. I thought he might die that night, and felt a great relief that I wouldn't have to kill another horse. I got back in the car and pulled down the driveway. You were entering the drive in your truck. I just managed to keep from knocking your truck into the ditch. You'll never know how I felt, driving home that night. I might have killed you. That's been preying on my mind too."

I was right, thought Connie. Jase's words in bed had been about the incident at Hurdle's farm, not Wampler's attack.

"But that wasn't the end of my sins. There came a time when Stephens told me Earlene's horse Ali was next. By then, I had finally realized the destruction I was causing. I tried to explain how killing horses was killing me, but Stephens didn't understand. To him, eliminating the competition was just good business. I weakened and said I would kill Ali but that was the last one. He said we'd talk about it later. I decided I'd "grow a backbone" by the time he asked me to do it again." He grinned without humor.

He got up, wandered restlessly around the office, picked up things and put them down.

"I know you must be sickened, Con. I despise myself for what I did to Rod, Dick and Laura, and Earlene. Woolwine was Rod's prized stud and would have allowed him to compete with Stephens when Rod got on his feet again. Finn was the whole world to the Lathams. And just when Earlene got a chance to breed a high dollar horse, I killed him. And their horses weren't just valuable as investments. All of those people loved and admired their horses.

"I'll never be able to explain to you the self-loathing I felt every time I sneaked into those barns at night, entered the stalls, and injected the horses. I tried to be gentle with them, to calm them as I got the needle out, and when I pushed the plunger, I always said "goodbye" to them. What hurts me the most—and has tormented me night and day since I killed Woolwine—is that I put an end to the life of an old man and three innocent animals for no good reason. Just Les's greed and my stupid infatuation with a worthless woman. And by the way, about six months after we married, she started running around on me. She has someone now but I don't want to know who it is. I'm afraid of what I'd do to both of them.

"If you'd asked me years ago, Con, whether I'd be capable of doing such a thing, I would have been insulted that you asked. I've had to put down horses because they were sick or injured, and it's always hurt me to do it because I couldn't cure them. How did I ever get to this point?"

He brushed his arm across his eyes.

Connie only said, "Listen, Jase. You know that you have to go to the police and tell the whole story, including Stephens's part in all this."

He nodded and said, "I'm ready, it will be a relief to confess. I thought I could keep the secret and start over, a divorce, a new place to work…" His voice trailed off.

After a few minutes, he said, "I'll need time to find someone to fill in here. And I've got to make some arrangements about…other things. What if I come to Cary's office about nine o'clock in the morning?"

"Cary and I will go with you to the police if Les doesn't want to."

His smile was dreary. "Oh, I think she'll be too busy."

Then his eyes again misted. "If only it had been you and me—" he started.

She stood up abruptly and put her hand across his mouth.

"See you tomorrow morning."

She left him then, sitting in the chair, head down.

In her truck, she called Cary on his cell phone. He had told her he'd be dining in downtown Lynchburg with old friends of thirty years who would be in the city for that evening only. He didn't want to go but it was too late to back down now.

"Call me any time," he'd said. "I'll be only fifteen minutes away from Jase's clinic."

* * *

When Connie hung up, Cary turned to Pam at the dinner table, kissed her, and said he had to go to Monroe. "I'll call you as soon as I know when I'll be home." He arranged with their friends to take Pam home. Then he opened the door of his Jag, took off his elegant overcoat, jacket, and tie and tossed them into the back seat. Then he put on the down jacket he always kept in the car and drove over the bridge to Monroe. He floored the accelerator, praying the Lynchburg police wouldn't stop him.

* * *

At Fayence, Stephens was dining alone. Carter and his assistant were still testing the pregnant mares and were therefore on the premises, but Tony found them boring and himself his own best company. Usually he appreciated his chef's offerings, but tonight, the unfortunate man had served something made with tuna fish, of all things, and Tony was disgusted. He would have to make do with salad and freshly made bread. He sipped his Dom Perignon and spread out the whole problem in his mind.

First, he faced the fact that he had overextended himself, in spite of his careful examination of the accounts on a regular basis. He had thought he had a sufficient knowledge of the horse breeding business to allow for everything he wanted to do. He took a second to curse himself for his lack of foresight and went on to the next fact. Doggie's infection. The little gray horse with the ridiculous name had become the instrument by which Fayence might fall.

Maybe he could placate Doggie's owner by saying the infection could happen to any pregnant horse, and he'd get Tyree—who was good with old ladies—to back him up. If the rest of the mares were not affected, he could survive. But if they were infected, he was done for.

The owners would blame the aborted fetuses on unsanitary conditions or sloppy handling, and go elsewhere. He knew he would lose the clients he needed to keep his farm going. His fortunes depended on the regular production of top-rate foals produced by mating mares and stallions with impeccable backgrounds.

Then he thought about another vexing problem—Jase Tyree. The man had become squeamish after the last killing and refused to do any more. *They're just animals, a means to an*

242

end, Tony thought. Whether they lived or died was central to the objective he'd had in mind when he started his business, to achieve status in a community he'd always thought enviable.

Therefore, he had to manipulate horses' lives to his advantage. *Just animals,* he thought again.

There had been a keen pleasure at his success in infiltrating the horse set. Granted, many were afraid of him. But that was nothing new. It had been the same in Denver, New York, Chicago.

He forced his mind back to the problem of Tyree. If the business survived, he'd hire Jase as his live-in vet. He liked Jase's work and the money would soothe Tyree's painful feelings about the killings. He decided he wouldn't ask him to do away with any more horses, either. He had seen that it wasn't paying off, anyway. And Tony intended to ask Jase and his wife to live in a cottage on the grounds. His decorator had made it pleasant and attractive. It would probably satisfy that no-good woman Tyree was married to.

He looked at his watch. Carter had told him that he couldn't expect any news until the next afternoon. But he needed some insurance. He dialed a number on his cell phone and talked briefly.

He'd take his usual walk to the lake after he finished his dinner—such as it was.

Chapter Twenty-Five

In the parking lot at Jase's clinic, Connie waited for Cary.

She'd told him she was afraid Jase might take his own life. When she saw that look on his face when he said he needed time for "other things," she knew he couldn't be left alone.

Cary's Jag tore into the lot, and he jumped out, strode to her truck. Trying to control her voice, Connie said, "I think there's a good chance he'll do something to himself, Cary. He's in worse shape than we thought."

"Let's go in."

Hunched over his desk, Jase didn't seem surprised to see Connie back and Cary with her.

When no one spoke, he said, "Yes, I've been thinking of Lover's Leap—or some place like it."

Cary and Connie looked at one another. It was too easy to climb over the overlook rail on the Blue Ridge Parkway and jump to one's death.

Cary put his hand on Jase's shoulder. In a firm voice, he said, "We have to go forward, Jase, figure out what to do. Now the first thing is to find people to fill in for you here until…another arrangement can be made. Have any ideas?"

"I don't know, I just can't think."

"Come on, Jase, you have to try. The animals need care."

He looked shamefaced, and said, "Of course they do. I guess I'd need two people. This practice is so large."

Cary said, "Mary Evans is unhappy at Carter's, needs a change. She could work part-time here."

Jase swallowed some cold coffee. The two watched him try to concentrate and think. "I…I…talked to her at a state meeting and was impressed. She seems like a good choice. As for another person"—he rummaged in the papers on his desk—"there's a resume here somewhere from a young man who lives in Charlottesville, a Tech graduate."

Cary looked at his watch. "It isn't nine yet. Let's call them and see if they'd be willing to handle the practice until, let's say, the end of the week. They can each take a shift and be responsible for field calls."

"My receptionist and vet assistant can fill them in on what to do," said Jase. Then he thought of something else. "What am I going to tell my staff?"

"You don't have to give them details," said Connie, "only that you won't be here for the rest of the week and your plans are indefinite."

"They'll find out, everybody will find out," said Jase somberly.

"Yes," said Cary in a matter-of-fact voice, "they will. We can face that later. Now, about getting those vets. Do you have a backup?"

"There's old Ruggles in Nelson County. He's retired but he'd come in an emergency. He thinks a lot of me." Jase's voice broke.

Cary said, "Fine. Now call the substitute vets and your office staff. We'll step into the waiting room." Jase nodded, started to jot down telephone numbers from his rolodex.

Once in the other room, Cary said, "You know what's coming next."

"Yes, he has to call Les, tell her he's coming home and wants to talk to her."

"Can you get him to do it?"

"I think so."

"I'll call Pam from the car, tell her Jase will be staying with us tonight. I'll call Harrison as well." Harrison Walker was a friend of Cary's, a prominent defense lawyer.

"He certainly won't be able to stay at his own house. Not after Les finds out."

Connie went back into the office. It took quite a while before Jase completed his calls. The three vets had to be given a quick rundown on pending serious cases. He told everyone that something had come up and he had to be out of the office for a week. When he hung up, his face was a little less tense.

Connie let him relax for a few minutes, and then said, "Cary will be right back. Now Jase, let's go on to the next part."

"Les. I know I have to talk to her tonight. And I'm ready. Funny, since I told you about what I did and since the calls, I'm a little stronger. I've been carrying the guilt around so long that I felt helpless. All I wanted was to go to sleep somewhere and never have to cope with anything again. But of course I couldn't, had to keep going on and on."

"I think you ought to get this over with as soon as possible. And to be fair to Les, she has to know so she can make plans."

"I'll call and ask her to wait up for me. Say I have to talk to her about something serious."

"I'll be in the other room."

When she came back, Jase looked grim. "She was going somewhere, but I mentioned the word 'money' and she agreed to stay home."

They sat in silence now.

When Cary came back in, Connie said, "Jase has decided to talk it over with Les tonight."

"Good. Jase, do you trust your lawyer to help with this problem?"

"He's really not equipped for something like this. I only use him for the usual things like real estate and taxes."

"That's what I thought, so I've asked my attorney to help you with your financial problems and your defense. He'll also be available when you go to the police—tomorrow."

At the last word, Jase stiffened, but managed to say, "You don't have to do this, Cary. I'll go on alone."

In a rough voice, Cary said, "You know what Connie and I both think about horse killers, Jase. We'll never understand how you could become a murderer. You'll have to account for those murders and Job Hoskins's death as well.

"But you've been our friend for a long time. What kind of people would we be if we deserted you now?"

"I can do it alone from this point," Jase argued. "I know how disgusting I must seem to you both. You don't have to go home with me. I'll see Les, then go to the police."

Connie touched his arm and said, "Jase, you need our help."

Jase thought a minute and then gave in. "I'll be glad if you stick with me as long as you think you can stand it. Given what I did, well, bail out any time you want to and I'll understand."

Cary said, "Let's go see Les, Jase. And after that, we'll go to Otter Hill."

Jase put on his down jacket and they went out into the cold night. Jase drove away, the others following.

Chapter Twenty-Five

In their preoccupation, no one noticed a car lagging a long way behind them.

After a few minutes, Jase pulled into the long drive of his isolated log home. The road stretched far back in the woods. In the clearing, the house was barely visible, overwhelmed by the old trees that embraced it.

"Watch your step," Jase cautioned as they went up the wide steps of the porch. "I should have replaced that porch light, but I've had other…" His words died away as Les opened the door.

The car that followed them waited a few minutes on the main road and then, with headlights off, slowly made its way up the drive. Once in the clearing, the car backed part way down a logging path in the woods and stopped, its engine idling softly.

Les was clearly surprised to see Cary and Connie with Jase, and immediately assumed her hostess role until Jase interrupted her, saying, "This isn't social." The smile left her face.

"I'm going to tell you a story you won't like," said her husband.

Puzzled, she sat down and prepared to listen. To Cary and Connie, who stood awkwardly, Jase said, "If you want to stay, I'll be glad to have you. Or you can go in my office, through that door." Both sat down.

As Jase unfolded the details of what he had done and why, Les's pretty face hardened in contempt. At one point, she hissed, "You moron." When he finished, all she said was, "What's going to happen to me?"

Jase looked at Connie and Cary wordlessly. Cary shook his head. Then, turning back to his wife, he said, "You'll have to find a lawyer to help you get a divorce."

"My parents will know someone. I'm sorry I ever married you."

"No more than I," Jase burst out. "I'll spend the rest of my life regretting what I did. I hate myself for betraying the horses, my friends, myself. But you played a part with your greed and social climbing.

"You always wanted more and more. If I hadn't loved you so much, I wouldn't have turned into a murderer."

She only stared at him.

Then Jase looked at his wife for the last time.

"No, Les," he went on quietly, "I was wrong about what I just said. It isn't fair to blame you for what I did. You've been a poor wife with your spending, your affairs…oh, yes," he said to her surprised face, "I knew about them. But your…failures as a wife shouldn't have driven me to murder."

He paused, and said to no one in particular, "I never dreamed I was capable of something so evil."

"Better get a few things, Jase," said Connie quickly. He nodded and left the room. Moving restlessly, Cary got up and looked at the pictures on the wall. Just as tense, Connie opened her purse for something to do, found a shopping list, and read it. Les's body was rigid, her face a mask of rage.

A few minutes later, Jase came back with a suitcase, and without looking at Les, muttered, "Let's go now."

Jase, Connie, and Cary stepped onto the front porch and started down the dark stairs, Jase in the lead.

There was the crack of a rifle.

Jase fell down the rest of the steps and lay sprawled at the bottom.

The shooter's car shot out of the woods into the clearing and down the drive.

Chapter Twenty-Six

Connie was the first to recover. She pounded on the front door with both fists until Les opened it.

"Call 911! Jase has been shot!"

Les, unable to take it all in, just stood in the doorway until Connie shoved her aside and ran in. "Where's the phone?" she demanded. Les pointed to a wall phone in the kitchen. Connie punched in 911, identified herself, told police where they were and that a man had been shot.

"It's very bad, hurry, hurry," she screamed.

When she ran back outside, Cary was down on his knees beside Jase.

By now, the front of Jase's coat was drenched with blood, his life slowly ebbing away. His face was paper-white. He was barely breathing.

At the door, Les looked on with gaping mouth.

Connie took Jase's cold hand, hoping he would know somehow he was not alone.

An Amherst County Sheriff's Office car with an ambulance following pulled into the clearing minutes later. When the paramedics examined Jase, their faces were grave. One said, "He's still breathing. Let's get him in, fast." They placed Jase on a stretcher, closed the back doors, and sped away.

"What happened here?" asked one of the deputies.

"Our friend, Dr. Tyree, was shot as we were leaving his house. He's a vet. I'm Cary McCutcheon, I have an equine insurance company in Bedford County. Connie Holt here is my colleague. We've been investigating the deaths of three horses, and earlier tonight, Dr. Tyree confessed to killing them. As we were coming down the steps, someone shot from those woods and wounded him. He fell to the bottom of the steps. That's Mrs. Tyree at the door."

Another deputy let out a soundless whistle, whipped out his cell phone, and walked away from the others.

"Yeah, the man is still alive. Someone shot him in the chest. Name's Dr. Tyree, a vet. He looks bad, though. The ambulance is gone. We've got two witnesses here with quite a story. Seems Tyree confessed to killing some horses before someone shot him. We'll need an investigator. Who's on tonight? Okay."

The other deputy took down their names, addresses, telephone numbers and other essential information.

"You'll have to repeat your stories to an investigator," he told them. He shivered. "I've got to get a few facts from Mrs. Tyree. When I'm through, come in the house and wait. I'm sure she won't mind. It's bitterly cold in these woods." A few minutes later, he signaled Cary and Connie to come in. "The detective's on his way. Should be here soon," he said to Connie, Cary, and Les. He went back outside.

"May I use the phone, Les?" said Cary. She didn't answer but gestured toward the kitchen.

He called Pam, told her about the shooting, and said he didn't know when he'd be home, then went back to the living room. Huddled on the couch, Les was crying. Connie nodded to Cary to say something. She knew Les would respond better to a man.

In a kind voice, Cary said, "Don't you want me to call your parents, Les?" Sniffling, she finally agreed. When he told her Mr. and Mrs. Wingfield would come right away, her face lost some of its tightness.

Then Cary said briskly, "Do you think we could have some coffee, Les? I'll help you make it."

When the coffee was ready, Les said, "I'll just sit out here in the kitchen." She had quieted down and had a little more color.

"Will you be all right?" asked Cary. She nodded. "I'd like to be alone for a while."

Sipping coffee, Cary and Connie sat on the couch in the wood-paneled living room without talking. Connie's eyes focused on a copy of a nineteenth century engraving of the Civil War prison camp at Andersonville that was hanging on a wall, but she wasn't seeing it. Some of the shock of the shooting had worn off, and she was thinking hard. She thought she knew who shot Jase, and had just turned to Cary to talk about it, when the investigator knocked at the front door and walked in. He was terse, hard-bitten, and all business.

Responding to his questions, they recounted the steps of their investigation into the murders of the three horses and the death of Job Hoskins. When Connie said that Jase had confessed the killings to her and implicated Tony Stephens, the policeman's eyes widened.

Then he said, "I don't understand why you didn't come to us earlier."

"We had our reasons," replied Cary. "For one thing, we had no proof and couldn't accuse anyone. We had to...well, deduce...who the murderer was, and who hired him, and then we still didn't have airtight proof. Connie is a close friend of Jase, and we reasoned that if he would confess to anyone, it would be to her. We planned to go with Jase to headquarters." He didn't mention that he had intended to let Jase get a few hours sleep at Otter Hill first.

"You'd help a murderer? Why, he just as much killed that old man up at Payson's."

"He's our friend," said Connie. "We hate what he did, but we feel we owe it to him to give him any help we can. He doesn't have anyone else."

The policeman shrugged. "What about the wife?" he asked, motioning with his head toward the kitchen.

Cary shook his head.

The questions resumed.

"Now, do you have any idea who would try to kill Tyree? Would Stephens have a motive?"

"I don't think so," said Cary. "There's no way for Stephens to know Jase confessed, so there's no reason to kill him."

"Does Tyree have any enemies?"

"Everyone likes and admires him," put in Connie. The investigator raised skeptical eyebrows. He was having a hard time trying to understand the dual portrait of Jase—benefactor of horses, killer of horses—that Connie was drawing.

"He's a fine vet, helped out a lot of people around here."

Then she put up her hand to forestall another question, and surprised, the investigator let her go on.

"I've been thinking. Suppose Jase wasn't the intended victim. Suppose it was Cary."

The men stared at her.

"Remember, they're both tall, both were wearing similar, light-colored down coats. And in the dark, the shooter might not have been able to tell the difference. I think the shooter might have been stalking Cary, followed us from Jase's clinic to the house here, backed his car into the woods, and waited until we came out. He shot at the man he thought was Cary. It wasn't only the coat. Jase was the first one down the steps. Normally a guest—Cary—would be first. He shot quickly and drove out of here fast, so in the shock of the moment, we couldn't identify the car or him."

"But who could that be?" said Cary. "I don't have any enemies I know of."

"I've been worried ever since we saw those two men in Roanoke. The younger man, the one with the blond mustache, was so angry he could hardly keep it in. I thought...well, I thought he might be unstable."

Cary looked uncertain and said, "Oh, I don't think they'd do anything. The older guy is smart, knows they wouldn't get away with killing me. And there's no reason, anyway. He gave me some information I needed in exchange for not talking to the police about his shady deals."

When he heard "not talking to the police," the investigator opened his mouth to say something.

Cary hurried on. "I conned him. There wouldn't be anything solid for you to go on, even if I did report him.

"Getting back to the shooter, I don't see how it could be the younger man. He's stupid and easily controlled by his partner, does as he's told. And I didn't do anything to him."

"But maybe something happened after we left, or maybe the younger man wanted to kill you to get in good with his partner, or…there are other possibilities."

The investigator was interested. "Who are these people in Roanoke?"

Cary gave him the names of the two and the location of their office.

"Is there anything else you can tell me?"

When they shook their heads, he got up, went into the hall, pulled out his cellphone, and talked in a low voice for a few minutes.

When he came back in, he said softly, so that the woman in the kitchen couldn't hear, "Tyree didn't make it. He died on the way to the hospital. It's now a case of murder."

Cary said, "I didn't have much hope for him." Connie's eyes filled with tears.

The investigator went to the kitchen, and in a quiet voice, told Les that Jase was dead. She didn't say anything. Then he said, "Do you feel up to a few questions?" She nodded.

He went over the facts of Jase's confession, trying to find out if she knew anything about the crimes he'd committed or Stephens's role, but she only said, "I didn't know anything about those things until my husband told me tonight." When he had gotten what little information she knew, he told her that a deputy would wait until her parents came.

Then he said that Cary and Connie could go home.

"This is just the beginning," warned the investigator. "We'll need you again." Giving them his business card, he said, "If you think of anything else, call me."

When they hesitated, he said quickly, "We'll interview all the people you mentioned, try to get to the bottom of this."

Outside, Cary told her he would follow her truck all the way to her Bedford cottage. At her door, he said, "Don't worry about the office. I'm going to sleep as long as I can. You do that too."

He took her hand and squeezed it, she touched his sleeve. She shook her head, new tears in her eyes. He nodded in understanding, got back in his car, and drove away.

She prepared for bed like an automaton, all the while trying to grasp the idea that Jase was dead. Dead. In bed she lay rigidly, her eyes scratchy with tears and regret.

* * *

Later that day, the red-faced man was sitting in his office in Roanoke, mulling over several important questions. Who was he going to hire to help him in his business? While unquestionably stupid, the little man who'd been with him over five years had obeyed him without question, although not without a lot of irritating whining. He also had the habit of bursting out with infuriating regularity when the boss was dealing with customers.

The last straw had been when McCutcheon was here. Suddenly, he'd been unable to stand his partner any more. He had no regrets about firing him, but he did have a problem now. He needed someone. He had a couple of jobs on the burner. Maybe he'd get a woman this time. He'd met one in a bar, lived in Campbell County. After she told him she worked for a horse trainer, he only had to buy her six beers before she loosened up and said she hated the trainer and was ready for a change.

The secretary opened the door and announced visitors—two investigators from the Amherst County Sheriff's Department. One was the hard-bitten man who had questioned Cary and Connie. They showed their credentials and sat down, looking at him steadily. The hard-bitten man said, "Your name Joseph Lacy?"

"Yeah."

"You have a man working for you, Aaron Moss?"

"Correction: I did. I let him go a couple days ago."

"Why?"

"I got sick of him. He was mouthy and dumb, and I just got sick of him. Why are you asking about him?"

"About ten o'clock last night, a vet named Jase Tyree was shot and killed. Two witnesses saw the murder and we questioned them. We think the murderer might have mistaken Tyree for a man named Cary McCutcheon. They were dressed the same and it was dark. We know McCutcheon and his colleague visited you here."

Oh, yeah, Lacy thought. *The witnesses must have been McCutcheon and that good-looking redhead.*

"Do you know anything about that murder?"

"Me? No.

"But you do know McCutcheon."

"Sure. We had...business dealings."

"Was there ever a time when you got mad enough at McCutcheon to feel like killing him or have someone else do it?"

"Nah. We got along okay."

"What about this Moss guy? Did he ever say he hated McCutcheon?"

"Nah. He didn't have nothing to do with customers, I did. He just took orders from me."

"And you didn't put out an order to kill McCutcheon?"

"Of course not! I'm smarter than that."

"Are you sure Moss might not take it into his head to kill McCutcheon?"

Chapter Twenty-Six

"I don't know why he would. His firing had nothing to do with McCutcheon."

"Do you know where he is now?"

"No. But I can give you his address in Roanoke. I don't know nothing else."

"Look, Lacy, you got a record. Sure, you've skated along all these years without being arrested. You've always escaped prosecution, paid a few fines here and there for shady stuff. You're escaping this time, too, but if we find you had anything to do with this murder, you don't have a prayer."

Lacy shrugged. "I don't know nothing about this Tyree's murder," he repeated. He rose, opened the office door, and told his secretary, "Give these men Aaron's address and telephone number."

The detectives took the information and left.

Lacy thought about what Aaron had done. Got things all mixed up in his mind, had to get revenge on someone for his firing. Lacy had no doubt that Moss had killed Tyree by mistake. Couldn't even get that right.

Well, this changed all his plans. He'd have to close this office down, get out of Virginia, go somewhere else, maybe Tennessee or Kentucky, anywhere there were a lot of horses. Horses were his bread and butter. He'd saved a little, enough to travel for a while and get the lay of the land elsewhere. He'd find another partner and go into business again.

He twisted around in his chair to look out the window at the dumpster.

"What a klutz," he said aloud.

* * *

The two policemen found Moss at the address they'd been given. They weren't surprised to find that the little man lived in a shabby rooming house in one of the worst neighborhoods in the city.

They pounded on the apartment door until Moss opened it, swaying as he stood there. Moss was fuzzy with much drink and no sleep, and smelled to high heaven.

"Whadda wan?"

"Are you Aaron Moss?"

"Yeah. Whadda wan?"

"A man was shot and killed this morning in Monroe."

"Who was it?"

"Name of Jase Tyree."

"Well, I didn't shoot nobody named…that name."

"Did you shoot anybody?"

He leered with drunken craft. "Maybe."

The detectives relaxed. They were going to get a confession.

"Who did you shoot, Moss?"

"Mc…Cutcheon. Guy from Bedford County, got me fired from the only good job I ever had. Now, I got no job. What am I goin' to do?"

He started to sob. He was so busy crying and cursing Cary that he barely heard the detective reading him his rights as they handcuffed him, and they had to repeat his rights twice more before he said he understood.

Chapter Twenty-Seven

At seven thirty that morning, Preston Carter had come to Tony's office from the lab in the stables. By not taking any time to sleep, he'd been able to complete his work earlier than he had estimated. He'd tested Doggie again, and then all the other pregnant mares. Now he was here to report.

Tony sat hugely at his desk and nodded his head for Carter to start. *The little weasel looks terrified*, he thought. *Must be bad.*

The vet had worked himself into a state of terror for nothing. Tony was the ultimate realist. That is why he'd called his lawyer in Denver. Without any greeting, he'd simply ordered the man to come to Fayence as soon as he could. If he got good news from Carter, he could justify the attorney's trip by asking his advice about a plan he had for expanding Fayence. But if Carter's results were bad, Tony's lawyer would be a key figure in the grand plan to enable him to leave the state and pursue a new life elsewhere.

Carter hurried to say, "My testing showed that all the mares are infected. There's no doubt."

Tony's expression was unchanged. "All right, you've done your job. Be sure your reports on each horse are complete and on my desk by tomorrow morning."

"What—what are you going to do?" he ventured.

Tony glared. "My accountant will send you a check for your services. It should be enough to include your assistant." Tony saw the expression on Carter's face change from fear to greed. *I bet he'll take most of the money. Weasel.*

"Anything else?" said Tony.

Carter shook his head.

"Get out, then!" snarled Tony. Carter wobbled from the room.

Tony then phoned the Denver lawyer, Jay Ervins, in the bedroom upstairs where he was sleeping after arriving in the firm's plane in the middle of the night.

"Jay, will you come down to the first floor office? There's enough breakfast here for two. Hurry, will you?"

Tony could hear Ervins groan as he hung up the phone, but he knew the lawyer would quickly be on his way down.

Ervins soon arrived in Tony's office. He helped himself to the sumptuous breakfast the chef had prepared, and sat down at the conference table where Tony was already seated. Tony closed the financial report he'd been studying and said, "I want you to stay for a while and help me tear down this whole operation."

Tony saw his lawyer purse his lips so tightly they were white. From past experience, he knew that Ervins was probably screaming inside. Tony realized that putting his breeding business together had been an ordeal for Ervins and his firm. And now he was asking him to tear it down. He would pay him more this time. He owed it to him for his loyalty.

"I want to leave here as soon as possible," Tony explained. "My local accountant—he's good—will work with us."

The lawyer relaxed and focused on the problem. With smooth assurance he said, "All right, I can do that. It will involve, of course, consulting many others: horse people, insurance people, real estate agents…"

Tony waved a hand. "Whatever you think. Again, I want it to be over as soon as possible. I'll set up an office for you down here."

The two men went to work immediately to tear down the empire Stephens had built. Throughout the morning, they made decisions about what had to be done and who to contact to help them. They took a quick break for lunch and resumed their planning. Ervins refused wine, confessing, "I'm having a hard time concentrating, Tony. Unlike you, I have to sleep every night, all night. I'll just have coffee." Tony grunted, and drew his attention to the next hurdle. He didn't mind Ervins's reference to his insomnia; they'd been together a long time.

During dinner, a servant interrupted their work to say that two police officers were asking for Tony. Tony looked mystified and asked Ervins to step out to the foyer with him. "I can't imagine what this is all about," he told his lawyer.

The male deputy said, "Mr. Stephens, you've been implicated in some crimes. We're here to talk to you about it."

What crimes? Tony thought. *I haven't done anything.* Aloud, he said, "We'll talk in my office."

The female officer started the discussion.

"Earlier today, a man named Jase Tyree was shot and killed outside his home in Monroe. A witness to the murder testified that Tyree had confessed to her earlier. He'd killed three horses. He said that you were the one who hired him to do it. A second witness backed her up."

Tony said nothing, but thought, *If I wasn't finished here already, that confession would have ruined my business.* The officer had said "her." The first witness must have been Connie. She was so close to Tyree, he probably would have told her. Tony was sorry. He'd hoped she'd never find out about his complicity in the killings. *I could hardly look worse in her eyes.*

He turned his attention to the officer, who was saying, "We want you to talk to an investigator at headquarters about your alleged involvement in these crimes."

"I'd like to confer with my lawyer."

The police agreed, and Tony took Ervins into an anteroom. As soon as the door closed, Ervins said testily, "Killed three horses?"

"Yes," said Tony. "I got Tyree to kill some horses for me. They were good ones, ones I tried to buy and couldn't. They were competing with my horses."

At Ervins's appalled stare, he continued, "They were only animals, Jay."

For a moment, Ervins didn't say anything, just closed his eyes. Then he recovered his poise, became a lawyer again, and said, "Well, you should be completely cooperative. Go now and make the statement. I'll go with you."

"What do you think the penalty is?"

"I don't know. I'll have to research Virginia law. There might be another charge here, come to think of it—defrauding an insurance company. They can get you big time for that."

"I only wanted to get rid of the competition."

"I'll have to see what they charge you with. Listen, Tony. I know you. Don't lose your temper. The procedure will be much longer than you like. The police will ask a lot of questions."

"I know," said Tony.

"When they ask the questions, you confer with me. I don't care if it takes all night. We'll do this very carefully. Above all," he warned again, "cooperate!"

"Of course," agreed Tony. "But Jay, I trust you to get me through this."

They went back to the office and told the police Tony would be glad to give a statement. They'd follow the officers to headquarters.

The investigator wasn't fazed by Tony's notoriety, and questioned him relentlessly. But Tony dug in and would only admit he'd hired Jase.

Back at Fayence, Ervins said he would appear for Tony in court and answer the charges, pleading "no contest." He would try to keep him out of jail. Tony's black eyebrows rose at this.

"Well, I just don't know, Tony," said the lawyer. "If they charge you with fraud, that's a felony. And that might mean jail. Now can I finally go to sleep?"

Tony nodded. He went into the kitchen, poured a glass of wine, thought over the situation. He envied Ervins being able to sleep. Suddenly he remembered he'd tried a popular sleep remedy months ago. It had given him an extra couple of hours even though it had produced a hangover the next morning. He'd hated the aftereffects, regretting his loss of mental acuity. But tonight he took two pills.

In bed, he decided he wasn't too worried about the situation. Jay was good, and with the help of a lot of people, whom he'd pay well, he'd scrap this operation and leave. *I probably would have moved on soon, anyway,* he thought.

He'd disliked the farm life with its sights and smells, and found the horse community accepting of his money but not of him. *I should have never hoped I'd fit in.* The minute he thought that, the problem of his isolation and alienation reared its head again. Through sheer strength of will, he forced himself to suppress that obsessive line of thought. *I only wanted to do something different, establish the business, live among another kind of people for a while.*

He turned on his side, pleasantly surprised that he was starting to feel drowsy.

His mind reverted to the failure of his breeding business. He'd found it unprofitable through the years to worry about wrong business moves. He'd made a few of them, recovered quickly. Now he'd find something else to do; what it would be didn't much worry him. His reputation was sound among a certain kind of people who'd be happy to get him and pay a lot of money. He'd turned down many offers when he decided to do this crazy thing—moving to Virginia. *I'll make some calls when I set up another base, see what they have in mind, choose the best offer.*

He regretted only one thing: Connie Holt.

He slipped into sleep, longing for her.

* * *

Connie woke to the sound of birds in the woods behind her cottage. She wondered how they could sing their intricate trills so well in the bleak January cold.

The pale light filtering through the blinds in the kitchen befitted the day when Jase would be laid to rest.

As she ate breakfast, she thought about the investigation that began with Woolwine's death in November and was now almost at an end. Shot and killed by an unstable man who'd mistaken him for Cary, Jase had escaped the punishments he would have surely received: large fines, loss of his right to practice veterinary medicine in Virginia, and a prison term.

Soon Tony's lawyer would appear in court to plead for his client. She wondered what punishment Tony—the man she considered the perpetrator of Jase's crimes—would get.

The elements of the mystery had been like shards of colored glass, their odd shapes jagged and sharp with pain: the death of Job Hoskins, three dead horses, friends and clients under suspicion. She'd struggled to piece the shards together to form a mosaic that would reveal the truth. The completed mosaic, she thought, was as intriguing and complex as the Italian floor in a Gilded Age mansion she'd seen in Newport.

For a moment, she allowed herself a small burst of professional pride at her part in the investigation.

But she'd made mistakes. She'd been unforgivably naïve. While her file of graphic news stories established beyond doubt that killing horses for profit existed, she'd never expected she'd have to investigate that crime in her own safe, familiar community. And even worse, the murderer was Jase, someone she thought she knew as well as her own hand. But she hadn't known the whole man, only the one she'd imagined in a sweet dream.

She'd made another mistake when she assumed that the reason for the killings was merely financial profit from insurance settlements. It was Tony Stephens's desire to succeed in business and win prestige that resulted in the chain of killings. She'd underestimated the depth of Tony's obsession and what could result from it.

To make matters more complicated, Tony, like Jase, was not what he seemed. If Jase had proved not to be the hero she so fondly imagined, Tony was not the complete villain she'd thought he was.

In barely two months, she'd learned a painful lesson. She would never again make easy assumptions about human motivation and behavior.

The small burst of pride vanished. *You're some hotshot investigator,* she thought, as she went into the bedroom to put on the new black dress.

The funeral was held in a small country church in Nelson County. Les Tyree hadn't wanted to be bothered with planning Jase's funeral, and wasn't even expected to attend. So it fell to Cary, Pam, and Connie to plan the service. Luckily, Connie remembered Jase talking about the minister of a small mountain church whose horse he'd treated. He'd visited the minister whenever he was in the mountains, and had even gone to a few Sunday services. "He's a truly good man, Con, one of the very few I've ever met," Jase had said.

The funeral had not been advertised for fear curiosity seekers would come. The McCutcheons and Connie called people in the community who might like to say goodbye to Jase. After much debate with herself and a conversation with Cary, Connie finally included those whose horses Jase had killed.

Connie was afraid the news of the funeral would leak out and people who only knew Jase as a murderer might be sitting in the pews. But when she went up the stairs from the basement, where she'd been helping Pam set out the refreshments, and entered the church, she recognized the quiet mourners as people Jase had helped, including, she saw with a tightening of the throat, Rod Payson, Earlene Collins and her friend Molly Suitor, and Dick and Laura Latham. Some people she'd expected to see weren't there, torn, she supposed, between the Jase they knew and the man who committed the crimes. She sat quietly beside the McCutcheons, her eyes on the closed coffin in front of the altar. She thought that their decision to ask the mourners to contribute to a charity rather than buy flowers had been appropriate.

The service was short and simple. After a prayer asking for understanding and forgiveness and two stanzas of "The Old Rugged Cross," the minister said, "We are gathered here to pay homage to Jase Tyree. I'll ask each of you to tell your favorite story about Jase, the one you will always try to remember when you hear his name. I ask today a very hard thing of you all, that you forget the Jase who out of desperation committed crimes. Keep in mind what the Bible teaches us: 'Let he who is without sin cast the first stone.' Remember, instead, the Jase who was such an important part of this community and whom you called friend."

The stories came haltingly, evoking laughter and tears. Many told how hard Jase had worked to save very sick horses. Several mentioned his reluctance to charge a high fee when he knew farmers were in debt. One time, someone laughed, Jase had even accepted a huge pumpkin for his payment.

After the recollections came the final stanzas of "The Old Rugged Cross" and a prayer of dismissal. The minister then announced that there were refreshments in the basement. The mourners went down the linoleum-covered stairs and stood in small groups, holding plates of cookies and sandwiches and cups of fruit punch. The talk was quiet.

Then it was time to go to the old graveyard adjoining the church, where Jase would be buried. It was very cold, and many mourners left for home instead. Only a small group stood at the grave as two frozen-faced men from the local funeral home stood ready to lower the coffin. Reverend Everett asked God to forgive Jase his sins and grant him eternal rest.

Afterwards, Cary said, "Thank you, Reverend Everett. Jase would have been happy." Pam smiled and shook his hand. Connie added, "I'm glad he knew you and we could have the funeral here, where he was so comfortable."

Cary handed an envelope with a generous check to the minister and the three walked to the parking lot. Connie pulled out slowly, taking a last look at Jase's grave.

Several weeks later, Cary accompanied Connie to the Lynchburg General District Court to testify against Wampler. She had planned to tell her story quietly without crying, but to her intense self-disgust, found herself weeping when she told the details of the near-rape. After one look at Wampler, she averted her eyes. She was shocked by how old and shrunken he looked, and confused somehow, as if he couldn't understand what was happening to him. She noticed Emily Wampler and her family, too. Dressed in their best clothes, they sat with white, staring faces as they listened to the testimony. Connie thought they, too, were confused, unable to take in what Jack had done.

At last she was able to take her seat in the courtroom again, and watched as Tony Stephens was called to testify. He sealed Wampler's fate when he recited the graphic facts about what he'd seen in the cruiser's headlights on Christmas night. His impassive voice only intensified the terror of the assault on Connie. Wampler's public defender did the best he could in the face of the evidence, but could only plead the trooper's unspotted service record be taken into account. Wampler was found guilty of malicious wounding and attempted rape. The sentencing would take place later in January. Connie decided she would not go.

Toward the last of the month, Connie and Cary were told what happened at the sentencing by Harrison Walker, Cary's lawyer. Cary had asked him to attend.

"The judge was enraged over Wampler's dereliction of duty, Cary, and sentenced him to fifteen years in prison on both charges with five years suspended. He'll be locked up for ten years, and on supervised probation for five. He has to pay Connie $10,000 in restitution and was ordered to stay one hundred miles away from her for the rest of his life. That's a zone of protection so he can't harm her again."

"Hell," said Cary. "That punishment wasn't enough for what he did to Connie."

"It's all right," said Connie. "He'll have another punishment. He'll never escape the disgrace."

At lunch with Eula Jones several days later, Eula pointed out that Jack would be imprisoned with many of the criminals he'd help put away.

"He'll be lucky to get out alive," she said. Connie saw her smile with satisfaction.

Early in March, Connie was entering a report on a horse from Campbell County that was injured in a transportation accident. She was trying to concentrate on getting the facts right, but finally gave up in disgust and reached into her mini-refrigerator for a soda. Cary was waiting in his office for a report from Harrison Walker, who was sitting in court this morning to see how the Commonwealth decided Tony Stephens's case.

Connie's phone rang. "Come to my office, okay?" said Cary.

As she walked through the door to Cary's office suite, Connie stopped for a minute to ask Gypsy to eat lunch with her. She'd been under a strict code of silence since the beginning of the investigation, unable to discuss it with anyone but Cary. She missed confiding in Gypsy and with what seemed like the last loose end to tie up, Stephens's punishment for his part in the crimes, she felt sure she could now tell her friend the whole story.

When she entered Cary's office and sat down, he was frowning with disgust.

"Stephens was convicted on only a misdemeanor. Jay Ervins, his lawyer from Denver, appeared for him and pleaded 'No contest.' Ervins admitted right away that Stephens had been wrong to instigate the murders and said his client wanted the court to know that he was apologizing to everyone in the Central Virginia horse community," Cary snorted.

"Then Ervins argued in a beautiful courtroom voice—Harrison is frankly envious, says Ervins sounds like Orson Welles—that Stephens hadn't killed the horses himself. He said that a sentence of a year in jail (which Stephens could well have received), would be an 'inappropriate' punishment in this case. He said he was prepared to immediately pay any fine the court proposed. The judge agreed, named a very large figure, Ervins produced his checkbook, and that was that."

"Not fair or just," said Connie.

"No. But there is one bright side. The whole awful thing is over."

Connie said nothing more, shaking her head as she left the office.

Chapter Twenty-Eight

After the investigation had officially come to an end, and a glum March was shambling toward spring, Connie found herself in an unsettled frame of mind. She'd thought it would be easy to resume work at the office, free of the constant anxiety and dread of what she would find out about the murders that had hung over her the last three months. Things would return to their natural state. But she realized one day, sitting idly at her desk with several unfinished reports, that along with a residual sadness and fatigue, she felt no sense of finality about the case. She needed to bring the matter to a close in her mind.

Something is still wrong, she thought. The murders were solved, and the clients had accepted the inevitable, coping with their losses as best they could. And, Jase was gone.

Stephens. That was it. The last piece of unfinished business. She was still angry that he had only paid a fine and was free to start over somewhere else. She wanted to see Tony, make him realize what he'd done to Jase, Rod, Dick and Laura Latham, and Earlene.

She scolded herself. *Just let it go. If you did get a chance to talk to him, he wouldn't understand. Anyway, he's probably in another state by now.*

But she couldn't just drop the matter. She finally sat down to write to Tony. If it was impossible to tell him her feelings in a one-on-one meeting, she'd at least set them down on paper.

In an hour, she'd finished the letter, although she had trouble setting the tone. Remembering that he'd rescued her from Wampler and that he had liked, perhaps even loved her, she softened the harsh words that first came to her mind about the destruction he had caused. As she put the letter in the outgoing mail, she thought, *if he's really gone and has changed his mailing address, the post office will forward it. But even if he never gets it, I won't be angry any more. Maybe I can finally close this case in my mind.*

The next morning, she was preparing a report on a retired race horse that had died. She had stopped typing for a minute to consider a change in phrase when Lonnie, the receptionist, came in and said, "Sorry to disturb you, Connie, but this came for you." She handed Connie a thick manila envelope with the address of a prominent auction company in Charlottesville in the upper corner.

Connie opened the package and took out a thick catalogue. On the cover was a picture of Fayence in color, photographed in the fullness of a Virginia autumn.

Contemplating the impressive building surrounded by stately old trees with red and yellow foliage, Connie remembered the first time she'd driven to Fayence. She'd stopped the truck for a few moments to stare at the house and wonder what was inside. Later, Stephens had told her never to come back to his farm.

The catalogue itemized the riches to be auctioned Saturday and Sunday two weekends away. The book was thick because it included everything inside the house that could possibly be sold, from splendid eggshell satin draperies to kitchen china in stark black and white to antique furniture from all over the world. There were long and detailed descriptions of the provenance of the antiques, paintings, and art objects, accompanied by small color photographs of some of the rarer items.

Connie took some cranberry juice from her office refrigerator and started to read the listing of items to be sold. Her body stiffened when she came to page 66 and she read the description carefully. Then she went to the next page. At last she came to the back cover, where an invitation to attend the preview to be held on the Friday before the two-day auction was attached. Then she reread page 66.

She wondered why she had received an invitation. She'd never been able to afford to bid on anything at an auction of this scope. Could Tony be responsible? He was supposed to be gone. But why else would she get the catalogue? She gave up on the little mystery and thought, *I want to go to the preview. Seeing everything he's losing might make me feel that some justice at least has been served for what he did.* Writing the letter hadn't achieved the release she'd hoped for. She hated living each day with smoldering anger.

And she admitted to herself that another reason for going was page 66 of the catalogue.

She went through the door in the back of the main office and smiling at Gyp, said, "I need a minute of Cary's time." His door was closed so she knew he was busy.

Gyp said into the intercom, "Cary, Connie would like to speak to you. She says she'll make it short."

"Sure," Cary's voice boomed from the speaker.

When she went in, he looked away from his monitor.

"What's up?"

"I received a catalogue for the auction at Fayence."

"So did I. Actually, I got two, one for the mansion and one for the farm equipment, horse tack, all the outside stuff. But I'm not going, even though Stephens is selling some good things. I'm a sore loser, still mad at him. Wouldn't give him the satisfaction of knowing I bought something."

"I only got the catalogue for the mansion."

"I'm surprised you got one at all," said Cary. "I know you don't ordinarily go to these things."

"Maybe Stephens saw to it I got one for his own reasons. But Cary, I want to go to the preview."

He frowned, hands still over the keyboard.

"Why? I know you're still angry that Stephens escaped with only a fine. And why would you want to be reminded of him by going to his home?"

"You know I love old houses. Who wouldn't want to see the inside of Fayence?" she asked, with a bright smile.

"Cary," she continued, "I'll need that Friday off."

Cary smiled and shrugged. "Okay. So be mysterious. Friday is fine. You're due for some down time."

"Thanks," she said, with a wave of her hand as she left the office.

Connie left her home in Bedford County at five thirty on the morning of the advance showing. It would take her about ninety minutes to reach Fayence, and while the doors were supposed to open at nine, she wanted to get a good parking spot. She was well-prepared to sit in her truck for as long as it took to get in, having packed a thermos of tea, two bear claws, and a book about Jefferson's construction of Monticello. She would compare Monticello with Poplar Forest.

But when Connie pulled into the long driveway, she saw that others had come early too. People in the long line of cars and trucks waited patiently, while men hired for the occasion, probably off-duty police, directed each vehicle toward a long stretch of brown, stubby grass set aside for parking. Connie pulled her truck alongside another one, in which a man was lighting a cigarette and shaking open *USA Today*.

She opened her book and started to eat her breakfast. She read steadily, never looking up, and had just started the part about Jefferson's penchant for alcove beds when there was movement all around her. People were getting out of their vehicles and queuing up in front of the mansion. Connie rummaged in her bag to find the ticket, then got out of the truck and took her place in line.

The door opened promptly at nine o'clock and everyone filed into the foyer. Four women from the auction company sat behind a reception table. Connie presented her ticket to a young woman in a dark suit who checked off her name on a list. Smiling courteously, she said, "Here's a map of the house. The rooms that are open are marked in red. Hope you find something to bid on tomorrow!"

Connie thanked her politely and went on her way, smiling to herself at the woman's assumption that she could afford to bid for one of Tony's valuables. Getting her bearings, she discovered that four bedrooms upstairs were open, as well as the parlor, dining room, library, and kitchen downstairs. She decided to start upstairs and work her way down, her usual pattern when she visited a museum. And certainly, Fayence was a museum.

She would save the pleasure of the bedroom she'd come to see, the bedroom of page 66, for last.

Reaching the top of the massive marble staircase, she went into one of the open bedrooms. The map told her this was the Red Room. Consulting her catalogue, she read about the imposing Jacobean bed with the scarlet spread and hangings that gave the room its name. She tried and failed to imagine sleeping in the bed. She stared at a massive Dutch dresser and other pieces from the same period. When she'd looked at the room enough, she left and went down the wide upper hall to the next open door.

Named after the famous French gardens, the Tuileries Room was furnished in exquisite French antiques, many pieces in white and gold. The silk wall covering was copied from an eighteenth-century wall in a palace, while several chairs had cushions supposed to have been embroidered by a friend of Marie Antoinette.

In the third bedroom, furnished in the Victorian manner, Connie felt breathless and trapped. There was so much of everything that it was claustrophobic. And to her eyes, many of the furnishings were ugly. A grotesquely carved bed of the period sat among ebony Japanese cabinets. A ponderous square table held a porcelain bowl with a writhing snake painted on it. And a huge round glass container supported on mahogany legs, sat on the floor, filled with authentic faded artificial flowers. She left the room as fast as she could.

Now, at last, she came to the room she'd come to see. Connie had read about the Shaker Room on page 66 of the catalogue with intense anticipation. When she was still married, she had made the Shakers a personal interest, and had a small collection of books about them and the things they made.

When she lived in the North, she'd enjoyed driving to the Shaker sites so lovingly preserved in New England.

The quiet beauty of the Shaker pieces far eclipsed the pretentious furniture she'd seen so far. How out-of-place this simple but elegant room looked in Fayence, with its dark, overwhelming furniture that had been constructed for princes.

Stepping closer to a chest of drawers, she looked for the joining of the boards and could barely see the lines. *Every piece for God in its perfection,* she thought, the Shaker craftsman's theology. She looked around. Humble hooks on the wall to hang clothes on or furniture when the floor was being cleaned. Patiently crafted Shaker baskets and boxes sitting on simple tables. A small, Shaker child's bed, as carefully made as furniture for the elders.

She couldn't help but notice a jarring note in the corner. The decorator knew that something more was needed for modern guests, so she had installed a large, graceless bleached wood armoire.

Connie turned her eyes away from the piece and decided she would stay in the gentle room until she had studied everything thoroughly. She stood quietly as other guests jostled her and talked loudly about what all of this must have cost, given the great demand for Shaker furniture. Finally, Connie left, eyes and spirit refreshed.

In the upper hall, Connie looked around. Several doors were posted with signs that said "No Admittance." One of them had to be Tony's bedroom, the one she'd puzzled over in the newspaper photograph. The map didn't identify the closed rooms.

Before she went downstairs, she walked around the hall slowly, looking at the art on the walls and consulting her catalogue. When there was nothing left to see, she started down the staircase. She wondered if Tony would miss living here. If he had looked at his beautiful—and dreadful—things every day with a collector's eye. If he had appreciated the Shaker furniture.

In the foyer, now packed with viewers, Connie looked at her watch. She decided to examine the paintings on the walls of the entrance hall, tour the downstairs rooms, and then leave for home.

Many of the guests at the preview were hoping to catch a glimpse of Tony Stephens—if indeed he was still in the mansion. Although the rumor persisted that he had left the state, some people swore he'd been seen dining at a four-star restaurant in Charlottesville with two well-dressed men earlier in the week. But if the master of Fayence was there, if he had emerged for a moment from one of the rooms marked "No Admittance" and was looking down from the carved balustrade, observing the excited, milling crowd below with his saturnine gaze, no one recognized him, no one saw him.

A small painting depicting the sale of a race horse caught Connie's eye. She always enjoyed that type of picture. The metal plate on the nice old wooden frame said *Buying Jupiter.* The artist had signed his work carefully in the lower right corner: James Browne. The oil had a dark background in which part of a stable yard and a bit of green foliage could be seen. But in the foreground, several figures and a horse were brightly painted. The horse dominated the center and was superbly drawn. Browne certainly knew horse anatomy, thought Connie. Two prosperous gentlemen were examining the glossy roan Thoroughbred, while a groom with a silly, pudding face held him. The owner stood away from the others, to the left of stable hand and horse. With indolent hand on hip, he showed off his brilliant red waistcoat. One buyer, in side view, stood to the right of the horse with finger on lips, his ruddy face smiling as he contemplated the horse's conformations. Only the back of the second, rather portly buyer showed as he bent down by the horse's hind leg, coattails parting to reveal elegant fawn trousers.

Lost in the painting, smiling widely, Connie was surprised to feel a touch on her arm. A small, nondescript man said with deference, "Mr. Stephens asks if you would please come with me. He wishes to have a word with you."

For a moment, she was speechless. She had convinced herself Tony was gone. The little man waited patiently. Connie made up her mind, nodded her head. After all, she did want to talk to Tony about what he had done. She followed the man—heart fluttering in her chest—up the marble staircase to one of the rooms marked "No Admittance" on the second floor.

They entered a pleasant but conventional sitting room.

The man smiled and said, "Please sit down, Ms. Holt. Mr. Stephens will be with you in a few minutes." He stepped back into the hall, pulling the door closed.

Connie took a deep breath, sat down on a sofa and looked around. Through open doors, she glimpsed an office and a bedroom.

Tony was talking to someone on the telephone. He ended with a sharp "Get back to me later," and hung up. She knew he would soon enter the sitting room. She sat up straighter, her fingers tightening on her bag.

Chapter Twenty-Nine

Tony heard his assistant's polite words and knew Connie was in the sitting room. He paused in the doorway for a moment to pull himself together before he greeted her.

Tony stared at Connie, reveling in the sight of her presence in his private rooms. *How beautiful she is, with her flaming hair and blue eyes.* Her gaze was steady, but he noticed the whitened knuckles of her hand, and thought, with shame, *she's frightened. Maybe she thinks I might hurt her.* With grim resolve, he advanced into the room, and chose the chair farthest from the sofa. He would talk to her the right way for once, telling her as much about himself as he dared. There were many details about his life he knew he couldn't reveal. They would shock her, but more important, they were dangerous for her to know. But he wanted to change—if possible—the way she thought about him. The underlying message of her letter had been clear enough—and it had devastated him.

Connie started the conversation with southern courtesy. "Your house is lovely," she said. "I couldn't resist coming. I've had such a good time looking at everything."

"Thanks for agreeing to see me," he said, unsmiling.

"How did you know I was at Fayence?" she asked. "There's a huge crowd downstairs." She paused, then said, "Oh, of course, it must have been the woman at the table."

"I had them alerted to tell me when you came. I've been working on some business and finally finished so I could ask my man to go and find you."

"You saw to it that I got an invitation, didn't you?"

"Yes."

"Did you think I would come?"

"I hoped," he said as gently as he could.

Uncomfortable, she didn't respond.

He spoke quickly. "Connie, I want to talk to you about your letter—and about other things.

"I read your letter carefully, several times," he went on. "I tried hard to understand how you feel about what happened to Tyree and the horses, and the way you think about me."

She looked up at him and suddenly Tony saw her face grow angry.

"Tony, did you stop to think of what would happen to the owners when you paid Jase to kill those horses? They loved their animals. The horses were more than just a business, as they were for you. And Jase is dead, killed by one of those thugs you hired in Roanoke. You had everything here at Fayence, you didn't have to destroy other people's lives.

"And the horses themselves. They were innocent and didn't deserve to die."

She stopped, out of breath.

Choosing his words with care, his voice level, he said, "I want to tell you about myself. You might get some answers to your questions. But it will take time. Will you listen?"

Connie nodded. Her voice was now steady again. "It's only fair I give you the opportunity to explain things. I've accused you twice, once in the letter and once just a minute ago, and I wouldn't feel right about walking out of here before you have a chance to defend yourself, if that's what you want to do. But given how I feel, how angry I am, it will be hard for me to be objective about you."

"Fair enough." He looked at the clock on the wall. "It's lunch time. I've been sitting in there all morning"—he gestured toward the office—"trying to get rid of this damn place." He smiled.

Connie stared at him with a look of amazement.

He regarded her, amused. "What are you looking at? Oh, I get it. You didn't think I could smile. Once in a while I do. There just aren't many times when I feel like it."

"It's just that you usually look...well, sullen and hostile. When you smile, your face is full of warmth, even sweetness."

He shrugged his shoulders, saying, "Sweet? Me? That's a new one." Quickly he changed the subject.

"Eat with me and we'll talk. If you don't mind, I'll have the lunch sent up here, since there are so many sightseers downstairs."

He went into the office and called his chef. "Charles, lunch for two in my sitting room, as quick as you can."

Tony came back, settled into the chair again, and for a few minutes, couldn't bring himself to start. He thought, *Now that you've got her here, talk to her the right way.* But he was about to confide things he'd never told anyone, and the fear he couldn't make her understand was making him tongue-tied. He'd tried to convince himself it didn't matter what she thought of him. Why not leave Virginia and forget her? But he couldn't. If she hadn't come to the auction preview, he would have found another way to see her.

But all he could find to talk about was the suite they were in. "There are three rooms. This sitting room, my bedroom, and a small office. I like to work in this upstairs office at night even though I have a much bigger one downstairs. When I can't sleep—and that's often—I go into the next room and work on business problems." He felt he was babbling.

Connie nodded.

The conversation again languished. She was starting a question when the door opened and two servants entered, went into the office, and spread out the meal on the work table, nodding to Tony when they were done.

Tony stood up, led the way into the office. The table held pasta primavera, fresh fruit, hot rolls, and a bottle of wine in an ice bucket.

They'd been eating for only a few minutes when Tony said, "This isn't easy for me, Connie. I don't talk to anyone about myself. As far as that goes, I prefer not to talk much at all. You've seen that." He toyed with his fork. "The only reason I'm telling you this stuff is because there are things I want you to know. Some of what I'm going to tell you about me you'll probably think is—bad. I'm not using any of it as an excuse for what I did. Just trying to explain."

"Why do you feel you owe me an explanation, Tony?"

"We'll get to that," he said.

He set his teeth, and plunged in.

"I was born in a city in the north, never mind where. I...I always felt as if I didn't belong in my family. I only had a mother and father, no other relatives. They came here from the old country, learned enough English to get by. Settled in the part of the city where others like them lived, and never left it. They were very religious, ran a bakery.

"I know they loved me, but I didn't care much for them." The shocking words were flat.

"Did they mistreat you?"

"Oh, no. They loved me. But I felt as if I…didn't belong to that family. I often asked my parents if they adopted me." He paused and said in a surprised tone, "I've never admitted that to anyone. Not even to my psychiatrist. I was too ashamed."

It was hard to believe Tony had sought professional help. He came across as a proud, imperious man, always in control of himself.

"No one liked me very much in high school and I'm not surprised. I grew very large very fast, and I didn't know how to talk to anyone. The only thing I was ever any good at in school was math. Oh, I made myself study and I graduated. But there was no way I'd go to college like you did."

"How did you know that?"

"I checked up on you when you flattered me into letting you come back to the farm. When someone puts something over on me, I like to find out more about them."

Then Tony told her about Mr. Angeli. "When I was eighteen, he gave me a job in his organization. It was in another city. I never went home again, even when my parents were dying. I called once in a while, sent money to them. They died within six months of one another. Each one died in the hospital. I made sure they had good care, but I didn't go back for their funerals. Talked to the priest, though, made sure they were buried the way they would have wanted."

He looked at her stricken face and wondered whether to continue. It was so hard to talk to her this intimate way. Maybe he should just stop, finish lunch, say goodbye.

No, he felt compelled to go on. This time, he wouldn't blurt out short, quick, sharp words that meant, "Here's the information, but I don't care what the hell you think of me," which was his usual way of communicating. This was Connie.

"Once I started working for Angeli, and learned what I had to do with numbers, I went from one organization of his to another, all in major cities."

"What did you do for him?" asked Connie.

"I suppose you could call me an 'accountant.' I won't go into detail about my jobs. You wouldn't like to hear what I did with those numbers. And it could be dangerous for you to know.

"I was so good at dealing with numbers that a lot of people in the…group Angeli belonged to asked for my services. I've lived all over the country, made a lot of money. And when Angeli died, I inherited from him. Now I was finally very rich. That's how I was able to start my breeding farm."

"Why did you go into breeding? And why here, in Virginia?"

"I wanted to start over, live in a new place, establish a new business. I'd read a lot about horses, liked to bet on them. I thought horse breeding would be interesting and I'd be part of a new group of people. I was sick of associating with the Angeli group I'd been with so long. 'New' was important to me. A completely fresh start.

"But it was the same here as everywhere else. You've probably noticed I'm a loner. I have no friends here or anywhere else, only business associates. I know I come across as crude and frightening. I noticed I scare you too. But I have to talk to the people I pay like that. If I didn't, they wouldn't respect me and do what I want them to do.

"Still can't talk to other kinds of people easily, like McCutcheon can.

"And my face doesn't help, either," Tony said equably. "Can't help that. Maybe plastic surgery?" He flashed the smile for a moment, then grew serious. He had only just realized he was keeping up a conversation.

Connie waited while he struggled again with his thoughts.

"I know you're surprised I went to a psychiatrist. I wanted to find out why I can't be at ease with others. Like McCutcheon.

"The doctor said I'm very angry inside, and that keeps me from being 'normal,' you might say."

"Why didn't you keep on with the treatment, find out more about yourself?"

"Another lifelong problem: impatience. The doctor said it might take years. I didn't want to wait. So I try to control my anger, be more patient. But it hasn't worked. People still don't like me. I'd gotten used to being alone until I met you."

Connie lowered her head, and concentrated on buttering a roll.

"But now, this is all gone," he continued. He told her about the infection that had raged through the pregnant mares and the reasons why he had to give up his business.

"I'm afraid your reasoning is right," she said. "A breeder has to have the goodwill of his clients. They have to trust that a breeder is running a place where they can be sure their horses are safe. Reputation is everything.

"What will you do now?"

"I don't know. I'm still in demand for my…talents, so I can easily go back to work. Someone in Los Angeles called me the other night, and there's a guy in Austin."

He took a sip of Bordeaux.

"Now, your letter…"

His head had begun to ache, and he realized that this conversation was costing him a lot. But Connie was really listening to him. It seemed so important, in this quiet little room, that she know him better before she left Fayence and he never saw her again. He was not the monster she thought him to be.

"For a long time, I had to make a lot of decisions. Sometimes they were illegal. But there was one rule I learned early on in Mr. Angeli's organization. All decisions—business or personal—had to benefit the company.

"When I was eighteen and new in the organization, I was stubborn at first when someone asked me to do something dishonest. My parents taught me right from wrong. Dragged me to church. But as time went on, it became easy to ignore the effects my decisions would have on the people affected by them. I was never good at understanding other people's thinking or actions anyway."

He paused, trying to frame his thoughts clearly.

"I closed my eyes when my company destroyed someone's livelihood by eliminating the competition. I looked the other way if a person was—threatened—when he wouldn't cooperate.

"And there were worse things I turned my back on," he said grimly.

He looked at Connie and saw the effects of his words. Her face was white.

"For years, I've always applied that test when making decisions. Was it good for business? When I realized here at Fayence that other people had valuable stallions that threatened the monopoly of the breeding business I was building, I wanted those for myself. I did what I've always done. Got rid of the competition. I did try to buy the horses, but the owners refused. So I decided to find someone to get rid of them."

"But you caused so much pain and unhappiness and loss," she protested.

"For what it's worth, I did think about the owners and believed Tyree's false reports might get them insurance settlements. But," he continued honestly, "they weren't my first concern.

"Here's another thing you don't like about me, Connie. I don't feel the way some of you do about horses. I was interested in them only for the challenge they provided in breeding. The day you looked at Pride of the Yankees, you noticed I didn't even want to go into the stall. The truth is, I can't even relate to a dog or cat. To me, they're all simply animals. I look only at their usefulness.

"You see," he said heavily, "I'm telling the truth about myself."

Connie said, "I'll never forgive you for the way you used Jase. You ruined him, made him do something immoral."

She put up her hand to stop his response. "Yes, I know what you're thinking. 'Immoral' to Jase and I and most of the horse people here. But not to you.

"If you could have seen those dead animals in their stalls as I did." There were tears in her eyes.

"I'm sorry for making you cry, Connie. I do understand this much: you and your friends see horses in a different way than many people do, including me. But I think I'm right in saying that even people who work with horses sometimes don't see them as anything more than a means to an end."

"We'll never agree about horses," he said, and changed the subject.

"You loved Tyree, didn't you?"

"How do you know that?"

"It's pretty obvious, isn't it? You keep coming back to him.

"Do you still love him?"

"I don't know any more, since I found out he killed those horses."

"Connie, you say I ruined him. But he did himself in." His voice grew sharp. "He took my money to kill the horses."

"But you were the one who bribed him."

"Don't you think he would have done the same thing if someone else offered him money to kill? I've never seen a man so desperate. He could have said 'No'."

"You're right," she admitted. "Jase would have done anything to get more money."

Tony scowled.

"I don't understand how he could ruin himself for that greedy wife of his. He had everything going for him. He was good at his job. He had you."

Connie sat back in her chair. "No, he didn't, Tony. He looked at me only as a friend. I don't think he ever realized I loved him. I tried never to let him know.

"And I'm sorry I said you were responsible for making Jase corrupt. You were right when you said he probably would have taken a bribe from someone else, if not you. I always looked up to him. But he wasn't the person I thought he was. There was something weak inside him I didn't even suspect."

"I was planning to set him up here as the resident vet. That would have made his wife happy and taken the pressure off him. Maybe things would have turned out better."

"What terrible irony. He told me when he confessed his crimes that he was hoping you'd offer him that job. Instead, you asked him to kill the horses."

She got up from the table, went to the window, and looked out. "The driveway is swarming with cars and trucks," she said idly. "The guards are having a hard time preventing gridlock. Everyone wants to see Fayence."

Then she turned, looked at Tony. He looked at her, unsmiling, waiting for her to speak.

"I can't lie and say I forgive you for the killings and what they did to the people involved."

"I didn't want you to forgive me—you can't, I know. I just wanted to explain a few things about myself."

"Then I'll ask you again. Why did you feel an explanation was necessary?"

"Because there's one more part of the story."

Chapter Thirty

She returned to the table, accepted the glass of wine Tony poured for her.

He went on, steeling himself for her rejection. But he had sworn to himself that he would be honest with her.

"I know," he said slowly, "you don't feel about me the way I do about you. But…but I love you." He had never said that to a woman before.

"I realized how I felt when I saw what that trooper was trying to do to you. And right here, I want to tell you I would have stopped if it had been another woman. But it was you, Connie, and I wanted to kill him for hurting you and scaring you so badly. I broke his ribs and wanted to do so much more to him, but I had to take care of you. I could hardly stand the pain of seeing you lying there bleeding, uncovered. I couldn't speak for the pain. What I really wanted to do that night was to bring you here, to Fayence, get the best doctors, take care of you. Watch over you myself. But I took you to the hospital and went away."

He closed his eyes for a minute, then went on.

"It wouldn't have done any good telling you how I felt. But later, I asked you to have dinner with me. I was going to try—I don't know. I thought better of it the minute I sent the flowers and the card. When you turned me down, I understood. Why would you even consider me?

"I've never in my life felt that way about any woman. Oh, there have been plenty of females who have climbed all over me, but it was clear why. My money. You, you…are different."

He changed position in his chair, started again.

"My treatment of you when you first came to Fayence was terrible. I never should have talked to you like I did. But I had developed a distaste for women over the years. When I found out how good you are at your job, how much you know, I tried to apologize at McCutcheon's party. But I messed it up. And I knew it. I drove home that day cursing myself."

"I'm sorry I didn't realize it was an apology, Tony. I wasn't very nice to you."

They were both silent then. There seemed to be no more to say. Connie stood up, walked toward the sitting room to get her bag and coat.

But Tony didn't want her to go just yet.

"After hearing all this, you probably want to get out of here as soon as you can. But I'd like to do something more for you to…to make up for everything. Well, I know I can't make up for everything, but…" He stopped, wordless now, hoping he could keep her here for a little while longer.

He knew Connie heard his desperation and was being kind to him when she said after several minutes, "I would love to see all the rooms behind the 'No Admittance' signs, Tony. Could you show them to me?"

His face cleared.

"Sure. I'll show you my bedroom first."

He led her out of the office and through the bedroom door. There was the strange room in the newspaper photographs. They stood in the center and looked around, Tony scrutinizing her face, trying to figure out what she thought.

"I designed the bed and chest myself," he said. "First time I ever did anything like that.

"Not so great, are they? No one would have bid on them at the auction. But I like them, so they're going with me—wherever I end up. So is the bedspread."

He was pleased when she told him she admired the bed covering.

"It has the Greek key design I remember from when I was little. Since I always try to forget those days, I don't know why I wanted something that brings them back.

"I wanted to breathe freely in here," continued Tony, "without a lot of…stuff taking up room. I've learned one important thing from this experience. I always thought Angeli's house was perfect, and I tried to duplicate it with Fayence. But I really don't want to live this way any more. Wherever I live in the future, it won't be in a place like this."

"You didn't enjoy all your belongings then? The paintings? The antiques?"

"Most of them, no. I recognize their value, though. Angeli taught me that. They'll bring a lot at auction."

"The one thing I don't understand is that painting over the bed. Tell me more about it."

"That's one of the few things I chose myself for this museum of a house. I like it. I can't tell you why. I don't know what the artist was trying to say, if anything. But I know what it means to me. I've always liked meeting challenges, and with the right amount of concentration, I can solve just about any problem—except myself, of course. Maybe I see a problem I can't figure out in the painting. But that sounds stupid, doesn't it?"

They walked to the huge windows showing the Blue Ridge Mountains in their March dress. After they'd looked at the vista for a while, Connie turned to leave. But Tony held her back with gentle hands.

Wrapping his arms around her, he held her tightly.

"I've imagined this so many times, Connie," he whispered. For a second, he rested his cheek against hers. As he expected, her skin was smooth and warm. But then he let go of the iron control over himself he felt he always to maintain, and kissed her with all the passion he felt for her. And something he never expected happened. She was kissing him back.

Tony released her reluctantly. He looked at her for a moment and thought, *I have to do this right. I feel sick with wanting her, but she must choose. It's the last thing I can do for her.* Cupping her face in his hands, he said, "Shall we stay here or go into the other rooms?"

Tony heard her rough breathing.

Finally she brought out, "The other rooms, please."

He wasn't surprised or angry, only sad as he led the way back out through the sitting room to the hall. He didn't have any real hope she would stay with him in his bedroom.

She followed him to the other rooms, keeping up a flow of "guest" chatter, to which he replied politely. Once she stumbled for no good reason, and he caught her arm to support her.

When they had finished the tour, they came to the top of the marble stairs. Here, he took her hand and said in a quiet voice, "I won't say goodbye, Connie." Then he went through the door to his suite, closing it behind him.

She stumbled down the stairs and out to the parking lot, all thoughts of the unseen downstairs rooms flown from her mind.

In the parking lot, she started up the truck mechanically, finally made it down the long winding driveway past the incoming vehicles filled with people eager to see Tony's treasures, and turned south on US 29. She had to concentrate hard all the way home because she could still feel the pressure of Tony's lips on hers.

When he had pulled her into his arms, Connie could hear his jagged breathing, smell his subtle cologne. His cheek was hot where it touched hers.

I should stop this, she had thought. She had tried to push his arms down.

But then he kissed her as if he didn't know they could never be together. As if he'd waited a long time—years maybe—to kiss her. As if he was going to die and needed the comfort of the kiss to take with him. She found herself kissing him back the same way, chaotic impulses sparking through her mind from one synapse to another. To feel the skin under his clothing. To take the few steps to his bed.

When Tony had placed his hands on her face, he smiled like a sweet angel militant. His dark eyes were full of new knowledge about her. When he asked her whether she wanted to stay with him or go to the other rooms, the implication was clear. He was giving her a choice.

As she tried to consider the question, her breathing had given her trouble. Her heart seemed to have grown huge in her chest. It had pounded alarmingly. She had clasped her hands together, ramming the fingernails of one hand into the palm of the other to bring herself under control. Finally, she had made the decision. He had behaved like a gentleman, then, escorting her through the other rooms and parting at the top of the stairs. He wouldn't say goodbye, though. Did he mean to see her again?

That night, she couldn't sleep. In the darkness, she searched her mind. She felt her face grow hot as she remembered how her body had succumbed to Tony's passionate kiss, and asked herself what on earth had caused her to respond that way.

I couldn't love him, she thought. *He never did admit he did anything wrong by having the horses killed. Besides that, he probably committed other crimes in the life he led before he came here. He admitted as much. And he's too alien. Unlike anyone I've ever known. Unlike me.*

It would have been a great mistake to tell him to call me from wherever he's going.

Then why did I want him to?

Epilogue

June.

Connie was cantering on Jasmine through a warm summer meadow at Payson Stud.

The smooth, steady, one-two-three rhythm of the Arabian's body, the smell of the well-oiled saddle, the tension of Connie's calves against the horse's barrel sides, the pressure of her toes gripping the iron stirrups: *this is pure joy*, she thought. She smelled the heavy southern air, pungent with sweet honeysuckle and bitter milkweed. Her eye caught the profusion of white Queen Anne's lace, orange Butterfly Weed, and golden Black-eyed Susans in the green, green expanse of the meadow. Even though it was early in the morning, the Virginia sun blazed down on her neck and arms, making her glad she'd worn her thinnest tee shirt. She adjusted the new Stetson to further shade her eyes.

Easing the horse to a trot and then a walk, she urged Jasmine up a hill and into the cool haven of the woods. It was time to give herself and Jasmine a rest. She had to guide her horse carefully among the trees. Despite her obedience in most places, Jasmine liked to pretend she was going to walk straight into branches and bump her rider off. Connie was amused by this peccadillo.

Every horse is an individual, she thought, one of the reasons she liked them so much.

Soon she found the spot she remembered. She'd not been here since Donna died. The cool, shady clearing was dominated by an ancient oak. Its thick, twisted roots provided a comfortable place to sit and reflect. Dismounting, she tied Jasmine to a low tree branch. The horse stood quietly, as if glad to be out of the sun. Connie sat down on one of the roots, taking a candy bar from her pocket. As she bit into the chocolate, she felt a rare surge of well-being.

In her prior visits to this refuge, she remembered her mind had most often been occupied with Jase and her hopeless love for him. She could think of him now with far less pain. He had been two people. She preferred to remember the Jase who had been a benefactor of horses and her friend.

Her mind drifted to the other people in the case of the dead horses.

Mary Evans had bought Jase's practice in Monroe, happy to get away from Pres Carter. Almost everyone liked her work. A few men were disgruntled, but like Connie, Mary was determined to work hard and win their respect.

Les Tyree had suffered since Jase's death. Her mother and father had to take her in since she had no money. She'd called Pres Carter but he didn't want to be tarred by the scandal of Jase's crimes and his murder. Their affair was over. Besides, he had his eye on a young woman who'd come to live in Lynchburg and work at the museum. Not only a beauty, she knew more about restoration than Les. People who saw Les now told Connie she was moody and abrupt, her face strained and old-looking.

Connie stretched out her legs. A wayward breeze caused a gentle susurration of the old tree's leaves.

Then she thought, *Where is Tony Stephens now?*

Fayence had been sold to a rich horse fancier who'd retired at forty-five after selling his telecommunications business. He, his wife and their six children liked to ride and compete. The ex-CEO told Cary, who insured his horses, that he and his family were delighted with the mansion except for the master bedroom.

"Marion's having fun renovating the 'peasant's bedroom,' as she calls it," he had laughed.

One day late in March, Lonnie Flemmings brought a large, thickly wrapped package to Connie's office. Inside was the minimalist painting that had hung over Tony's bed. There was no note, but Connie knew that the parting gift carried a message from the inarticulate man. She believed that it conveyed his love for her and the hope that she wouldn't forget him.

She found its famous Japanese artist on the Internet, together with a photograph, description and critical discussion of the painting.

She learned that its title, translated into English, was "Message." It suggested nothing about what the painting signified, nor was it meant to. The painting itself was small, centered in the middle of a large white canvas. It was composed of a few randomly intersecting, vertical and horizontal black lines, to which thin red and yellow diagonal slashes had been added. It looked like an ideogram, but critics said it meant nothing in Japanese. It was indecipherable. It was enigmatic. Like Tony. She still didn't know who Tony Stephens really was.

She would hang the gift at home as a reminder of the mysterious man who saved her from Wampler, loved her, and wanted her to remember him. She admitted to herself that he was also the man who stirred her to a degree of passion that commonsense told her existed only in a novel or on the screen. Jase's embrace in her bed had been nothing compared to Tony's kiss. She still thought about what had happened in Tony's bedroom at Fayence—and couldn't dismiss it. She'd never told anyone about it.

But Tony had instigated the murders of Woolwine, Finn, and Ali, and to the end, failed to understand why Connie was sickened by his "business" decision.

The owners of the dead horses, whom Tony and Jase had hurt so badly, understood why Cary could not pay them for their losses. All had expressed their sorrow over Jase's apostasy when they found out their friend had killed their animals. All had come to Jase's funeral. Earlene summed up everyone's feeling best: "I can't be bitter because I remember too much that was good about Jase. But it was all so useless. Three horses died for nothing, a good man turned bad."

Rod was working hard at building up his breeding program again. Now that Stephens had dissolved his business, and Rod himself was back in control of his farm, many of his old clients had returned. Occasionally he talked about Woolwine, always saying, "There will never be another one like him."

The Lathams had not bought a new horse to train. Finn's death had so badly scarred them that they could not conceive of starting over. Right now they were traveling in Europe.

Not long ago, Earlene Collins invited Connie for lunch, and while they were eating, announced that she was going to start looking for another horse to train. Her eyes misted as she said, "Won't be as good as Ali, though."

Driving back to the office that day, Connie had thought of a way she could help both Earlene and Bud Hurdle. Hurdle's farm had finally failed and he was going to declare bankruptcy. Maybe he'd sell Quicksilver Magical Pete to Earlene. He said he'd talk about it, and Earlene and Connie drove to Hurdle Farm. Earlene's lips tightened as she assessed the slovenly farmer's accommodation for his horses. But when she saw Pete, her face eased. When Earlene, Connie, and Bud went into the double-wide to talk about the sale, Earlene negotiated the deal of her life, three thousand dollars for a horse with Pete's papers and potential. It was all Connie could do to keep her face still during Earlene's masterful dickering.

"Now I'll need the negative Coggins for him, Mr. Hurdle." Bud nodded miserably. "And I'll send Mary Evans to look at him. Don't worry, you won't have to pay her. If everything turns out all right, I'll be out next week to get Pete."

Bud had a fair idea of what Pete was worth but he was up against the wall. He needed money fast. Connie had heard that his wife was so furious with his financial failure that she was threatening to leave him.

A couple of months later, Connie went to Nelson County to see Pete at Earlene's invitation. Connie watched as Earlene taught the sleek, well-fed animal how to move with grace and economy.

"Of course," Earlene had said fondly, "he's not Ali."

Now it was time to leave the woods and take Jasmine back to the stable. Connie was just getting ready to mount when she heard the sound of another horse making its way through the woods. Rod rode into the clearing on his large black stallion, Cody.

"Thought you'd be here," he said with a smile.

Not long after the investigation was over, Rod called Connie at the office. After a few pleasantries, he got to the point.

"When you were here for lunch, I invited you to come and ride Jasmine any time.

"But I don't want to wait to see you until it's warm enough to ride." He paused for a moment, then said in a hesitant voice, "Could you see your way to have dinner with me some time? If it's too soon after what you've been through, I'll understand."

At the other end of the line, Connie was quiet.

"Hey, Connie," said Rod. "Are you there? I finally got up the courage to call, and now you won't answer me. You're making me nervous, girl." Connie was torn. Sometimes she felt much as she had while recuperating from Wampler's attack— frail, somehow, and still pained by what had happened.

"It is too soon, Rod. But could you call me again, say, in about a month?"

"Sure," he said. "Believe me, I understand." Connie knew he was thinking about Donna.

As it got closer to the time when Rod would call again, Connie talked to Gypsy.

"I'm pretty much over Jase now, but uncomfortable about going out with Rod. He and his wife were my friends, Gyp. But Rod has changed the equation. I think he's looking at me as more than a friend."

"How do you feel about him?" asked Gypsy.

"He's a sweet, kind man who was a wonderful husband to Donna. To tell you the truth, I always envied them for their happy marriage. But what about Rod's feelings for Donna?

Would they stand in the way? Would I be a good companion or would I be stiff and tense? What if—?"

The anxious questions tumbled over themselves.

"Connie, stop." Gyp took a deliberate sip of her cappuccino and then said, "I know you admire him a lot as a person. But I have to ask because it's important. Are you attracted to him physically?"

"Did you see him at Cary's Christmas party?" was Connie's only answer.

Gyp laughed out loud. "I sure did." Peering at Connie from under her long white bangs, she said, "I think you really want to go out with him. How long is it since you've had a date?"

"Stop teasing, Gyp. You know I went out with that fat little client from Lovingston who owned the string of quarter horses. Must be about three years ago."

"Would you be less nervous about everything if Dan and I cooked dinner for you both? You could invite Rod when he calls."

"That would be great, Gyp. Thanks."

Exactly four weeks later, Rod telephoned again. To Connie's relief, he was delighted to have dinner with Gyp and Dan.

For Connie, the evening was unexpectedly easy. Her strain at the beginning hadn't lasted long. The four had laughed their way through dinner as Dan and Rod tried to top one another with the funniest stories they knew. Afterwards, she and Rod had gone to a jazz club in Lynchburg, conversing easily between sets.

Later, sitting in her driveway in his car, both found themselves silent.

Then Rod said, "Look, Connie. This is how it is. I want this to go on. I know it will be hard at times, we've both lost people we cared about. I've no doubt you really loved Jase and you know how I felt—still feel—about Donna. You're the same kind of person I am. You don't abandon someone you love because they're not with you any more. But we can keep our memories of Donna and Jase. I think we've got a chance to be good together. Do you want to try?"

She thought back over the years of being alone, of the hopeless love for Jase, of Tony, of what she knew about Rod as a man and husband.

"I think I do want to try, but can we go very slowly?"

"Of course," he said. He squeezed the hand lying in her lap and got out of the car.

Walking with her to the house, he held her arm politely. He made no effort to kiss her but only waited while she unlocked the door.

"Slowly," was the last thing he said before he went back to his car.

Since then, they had been together whenever they could. Cary and Pam were delighted with the romance and invited them often to Otter Hill. Sometimes they went with Gyp and Dan to a movie. Occasionally she made dinner for him in her small cottage. She found herself driving to the farm on Saturdays when she wasn't on call. She'd check the house or the barns, looking for him.

Not long ago, she'd come upon him in the outside ring, longeing a horse. Rod smiled as he flicked his whip lightly at the horse's heels and said "Trot!" The horse responded by circling smoothly around him. "Good boy," cried Rod with satisfaction. When he'd turned and seen Connie watching, his eyes changed. He was looking at her with an expression that she knew could only mean love.

Rod made her feel "comforted," she'd decided. It was an odd word but the only one she could think of to explain how safe and warm she felt with him.

In the coolness of the clearing, the thick tops of the trees barely admitting any sunlight, Rod and Connie sat down on one of the large roots. Smiling at him, she took off her hat and smoothed back her hair.

Rod took her hand. "You're so beautiful, Connie. Your eyes are like, well, I'm no poet, but they remind me of a dark blue sky." Then he laughed. "I know you're probably thinking that's pretty corny."

"Tell me a lot more corny stuff like that," Connie said, grinning.

"Well, if you insist. I love your hair, even when it's all snarled up like today. And you've got that small waist and long legs."

"I'm not too thin?"

"Are you kidding?"

He kissed her, and then Connie saw his face change.

"I have to talk to you, honey," he said.

"Have a problem, do you?" she said in vast amusement, for she thought she knew what the problem was. He smiled back.

Connie had been glad Rod had not asked her to deepen their relationship by sleeping together. Although he had shown in a number of little ways that he was attracted to her—putting his arm around her waist, resting his hand on her back, unexpectedly kissing her neck—he had not taken things further. If their kisses became too warm, Rod would break the spell with a little laugh and a hug. Connie had thought he was probably wrestling with himself over taking another woman to bed. It would be hard after living with Donna so long to respond to someone else sexually. Perhaps he felt like a traitor.

Connie had wondered how long it would be before their relationship changed.

Several weeks ago, she'd caressed his scarred cheek as she was saying she hoped he'd watch that stallion he was working with. "I don't like that rolling eye, Rod." He'd kissed her sweetly. But he had to exhibit more and more self-restraint recently, and Connie knew what he was going to ask her. *It's time*, she told herself as Rod took her hand. She'd given it a lot of thought in her customary way of analyzing things. But she was worried by the prospect, much as she had felt months before when she was getting ready for their dinner date.

Now Rod said, "Connie, I want to…to ratchet us up a notch." Then he roared with laughter at himself. "What a way to put it! I sure am clumsy!"

Then he grew serious again. "It's been tough trying to adjust to being with another woman after Donna. But I've thought about this a lot. I really want to be closer to you now."

He took her in his arms. "Would you like to go away next weekend? We could stay overnight somewhere and have Saturday and Sunday together. Beau will be glad to see to things here. He's always home on weekends. And you're not on call."

She didn't answer right away. He released her, smoothing back several locks of unruly red hair from her face. She smiled at him uncertainly.

"Have I embarrassed you for some reason? What's wrong, honey?"

Then he thought he might know.

"Connie, I'm such a jerk. You do know I love you, don't you? I wouldn't ask you to go away with me if I didn't. I respect you too much."

"It isn't that. I know how you feel about me. I've seen it in your eyes. But I'm…well, the truth is, I'm…scared."

He took her in his arms again and kissed her. "I am too," he admitted. "Let's just relax and try."

Relieved, she laughed. "It could be fun," she said with a mischievous grin.

They led the horses out of the clearing and mounted them in the sunlit meadow. Before they started back, he said, "Do you know a place you'd like to go?"

"Oh, yes. How about the Peaks of Otter Lodge?"

"Perfect!"

They put their horses into a canter, then, flying across the meadow side by side. From time to time, Connie looked at Rod and found him looking back. They smiled with shared pleasure. Jasmine and Cody kept pace with each other and seemed happy for the competition. *'Proud hooves' indeed*, thought Connie.

Without any warning, doubt crept into her mind.

I'm not sure I can love Rod the way he wants me to.

But then she rallied, and thought, *At least there's a chance of happiness with Rod, one worth the risk of being hurt again. And I'm going to take this chance and run with it.*

At that moment, she realized that the last remnants of her despair and pain over the terrible events of the winter were gone.

Acknowledgments

I would like to express my deep appreciation to the following:

Jeffrey S. Douglas, Director of Public Relations, Virginia Polytechnic Institute and State University.

Kenneth J. Kopp, DVM.

Randy Krantz, Commonwealth's Attorney, State of Virginia.

Dr. Craig Thatcher, Professor, Large Animal Clinical Sciences, Virginia Polytechnic Institute and State University.

Jana Rade, Director of Design, American Book Publishing.

Chris Krupinski, Designer, American Book Publishing

Allan G. Macpherson, Director of Editing Services, American Book Publishing.

Author's Bio

Born in Buffalo, New York, Marilyn Fisher moved to Central Virginia as an adult. She considers the area one of the most beautiful and fascinating places in the United States. A college English professor for most of her career, she specialized in seventeenth and nineteenth-century American literature, and read and corrected at least ninety thousand student essays and research papers—an estimate she says is conservative. Along the way, she wrote literary criticism and articles for newsletters and newspapers.

She now lives outside of Nashville, Tennessee, in Walking Horse country. Her horse colleagues, a dozen or so from a nearby breeding farm who dangle their heads over her back fence seeking attention, and two from down the road, strolling by her front windows with their riders, provide her with constant inspiration.

She still teaches English part-time, when she is not attending horse shows, collecting old American mysteries from the thirties and forties, touring historic houses, or traveling to art museums. Two of her ongoing interests are Celtic mythology and the Shakers.

She has combined her love of riding and owning horses with her admiration for the American mystery novel to write *The Case of the Three Dead Horses*.

As a full-time writer, she divides her time between the next Connie Holt novel and freelance articles about the humane treatment of animals.

Visit her online at mmfisher.com.